ONE UNDER

JL MERROW

RIPTIDE
PUBLISHING

Riptide Publishing
PO Box 1537
Burnsville, NC 28714
www.riptidepublishing.com

One Under
Copyright © 2018 by JL Merrow

Cover art: Garrett Leigh, blackjazzdesign.com
Editor: Carole-ann Galloway
Layout: L.C. Chase, lcchase.com/design.htm

ISBN: 978-1-62649-687-3

First edition
March, 2018

Also available in ebook:
ISBN: 978-1-62649-686-6

a PORTHKENNACK
CONTEMPORARY

ONE UNDER

JL MERROW

RIPTIDE
PUBLISHING

With thanks to all those who helped with this book: Pender Mackie, Kristin Matherly, Jenre. And especial thanks to Alex Beecroft for creating the wonderful world of Porthkennack for me and my fellow authors to play in, and giving it such a rich and inspiring history.

TABLE OF CONTENTS

CHAPTER ONE

The phone rang, shockingly loud in the hush of the almost-deserted naval museum. Especially seeing as the lone young man who'd been mooching around the exhibits had set his ringtone to . . . well, Jory couldn't have named the song or the artist, but it was something modern and rappy, and seemed to be largely about *Yo Momma*.

It cut off as the young man answered the call. "'Sup?"

He listened for a minute, then spoke again. "Aw, Mum, no. Not Hermione. You're sure?" The tone was completely different from the one he'd used only minutes ago when speaking to Jory— *"Two pounds? You serious? How do they even pay your wages? I mean, no offence, mate, but it ain't like you got punters queuing up down the street"*—and not in a good way.

Then, it had been light. Carefree. Gently mocking. It had seemed to imply a cheeky grin and a wink might not be out of the question. Not that Jory was in any position to judge how accurate that was, given he'd slipped into his usual habit of blushing and staring at his feet when confronted with anything vaguely resembling flirtation. He'd probably only imagined the flirtation. And now . . . Now the tone promised only troubled frowns, with a small but not insignificant possibility of tears. Jory glanced up from his desk, and a sympathetic pang shot through his chest. The man looked devastated.

There was a pause. Jory tried not to stare too overtly while still appearing alert and available should any assistance be required. It *wasn't* just because the visitor was so good-looking, although if he was entirely honest with himself, Jory might have shifted his chair around earlier to ensure a better view of those cut-off jeans and, more to the point, what was in them.

Now he felt guilt stricken for ogling the poor man in the face of his obvious distress.

"Why didn't you tell me she was ill? I could've come back. You should've told me. I could've been there for her when . . . when it happened. Ah, *shit*." The young man sagged against the wall, his free hand raking through his light-brown hair, narrowly missing *The Wreck of the Troilus*. Not that the painting would be any great loss had he knocked it clean off the wall and let the artwork go the way of its subject.

"Yeah. No. Yeah, I'm fine. Mum, I'm fine. It's just . . . it's Hermione, you know? We've been through a lot together, me and her, and now she's . . . No, I'm good. I'm fine. You'll do right by her, yeah? Proper burial? Yeah, yeah, I know. Yeah, love you too."

He hung up, shoved his phone back in his pocket, and scrubbed his face with both hands. There was a loud sniff.

Unable to carry on as a passive witness—it wasn't like there was anyone else around to offer comfort—Jory scrambled to his feet. "Are you okay? Sorry. Stupid question. I mean, is there anything I can do? I'm so sorry about . . . I couldn't help overhearing . . .Tea. I could make you some tea?" He stepped out from behind the desk, hoping to appear more approachable, and came within a whisker of bumping into the bust of Admiral Quick whose twice-broken nose jutted out a bit too far for comfort in the narrow space.

"Nah, I'm good, I . . ." The young man cast his gaze around the room. Whatever he was looking for, he didn't seem to find it in the cases of nautical antiques on display. His shoulders sagged once again. "Shit. Yeah. Cheers, mate. That'd be magic."

"Right. Come this way. Mind the admiral, he's a bit unsteady on his plinth." Jory gestured for his companion to precede him into the small office behind the reception desk, which was mostly used for writing funding applications. As Jory followed him through, he caught a whiff of the young man's aftershave, a surprisingly subtle, woodsy scent with a hint of spiced orange.

Tea. He needed to focus on the tea.

There was just enough water in the antique jug kettle for two mugs, and while it looked a bit brackish, the tea bags were cheap enough that the taste would be overpowered. Jory set it on to boil.

"Please sit down," he said, indicating the one chair in the room, and perched on the edge of the office desk so as not to loom too oppressively. A stack of papers threatened to dive, lemming-like, to the floor. Jory shoved them hastily to safety and tried not to wince at the unmistakeable sound of something falling off the other side of the desk. He coughed. "I'm Jory, by the way." People, even tourists, tended to have preconceptions attached to his surname, so he'd fallen into the habit of not giving it when he didn't have to.

"Mal."

At least, Jory was pretty sure that was what he heard, although in that South London accent it sounded more like *Mao*. He blinked. "Right. Milk?"

Mal—probably—nodded. "Two sugars if you've got 'em."

"Ah. Sorry. No."

"'S okay. Trying to give it up anyhow."

The kettle had turned itself off. Jory drowned the tea bags he'd hastily chucked into the mugs. Thank God he'd had a second one clean. Then he picked up the carton of milk, decided it would be too awkward to give it a sniff to check it hadn't turned during the day, and settled for giving it a quick slosh around. It still seemed to be liquid, so Jory glugged a reckless amount into each mug and handed one of them over to Mal, wincing inside as he realised it was the one emblazoned with *Keep Calm and Hug a Curator*. Then again, the one he'd kept for himself would be even *less* appropriate, seeing as it had a dodo on it, and dodos were notoriously dead, which might seem a bit insensitive, and, oh God, he was going to have to say something, wasn't he?

Jory cleared his throat and forced himself to look at Mal, who had both hands wrapped around his mug. "I, er, I gather you had some bad news. A . . . bereavement?"

Mal nodded. Then he sniffed. "Ah, sod it. I dunno why it's hit me so hard." He seemed to flinch. "I just wish I could've been there, you know? But she had a good life."

"She was quite old?" Jory asked hopefully.

"Nearly four."

Oh God. That was awful. Far worse than Jory had thought. Whatever the relationship, to lose a child so early— Common sense, which had been banging on the windows for a while now, finally broke through to settle, panting, in the hallway of his mind. "Hermione, yes? She was your . . .?"

"Pet rat. Had her since she was a baby."

"Oh, thank God for that." Heat rose in Jory's treacherous cheeks as he took in Mal's hurt look. "I'm so sorry. I don't mean to belittle your loss. Pets can be very . . . Would you like a biscuit?"

Mal ignored the question. "People have the wrong idea about rats. They're really intelligent. And affectionate. Clean, too."

His tone had changed from devastated to defensive, which Jory supposed could be seen as an improvement. "I'm sure they are," he lied. "I just meant . . . I thought you were talking about a person. A child."

"Oh. No. Yeah, I guess . . . Right. Nah, she'd lived out her time and then some, Hermione had. A lot of rats only make it to two." Mal stared at the wall for a moment. Jory wondered what he saw. The Sailors' Knots calendar wasn't *that* fascinating, at least not this month. Clove hitches didn't have a lot in the way of creative flare.

Mal gave himself a little shake, and pasted on a clearly fake smile. "You gotta be thinking I got you to make me this tea under false pretences, yeah?"

"No, of course not." Jory grabbed the plastic tub of biscuits and thrust it at Mal. "Please have one. They're good. I baked them."

Predictably, Mal's eyes widened. "Yeah? No offence, mate, but you don't look the sort to put on a pinny and do the old *British Bake Off* bit."

And that, right there, was why Jory never mentioned his surname. He got quite enough of people making assumptions about him based on his appearance. "What do I look the sort for?"

"Dunno. Lumberjack?"

"Cornwall isn't *particularly* noted for its forests. Not logging ones, anyway."

"Uh . . . fisherman, then? Hauling in nets and stuff? Yeah, I could see that. Fits with the theme, dunnit?" Mal waved a hand around vaguely.

"This is a naval museum. Not a fishing one."

"Same difference, innit? It's all sea stuff." Mal grinned suddenly, this one seeming genuine. "You know, you're like if Tintin and Captain Haddock had a kid together."

Jory stared. "That's possibly the most horrifying thing anyone's ever said to me."

It wasn't, actually, even close, but it got him a laugh. "You wanna get out more, mate. So are you a local, then? Cos you don't sound like it."

"Public school from the age of seven tends to do that to you." Jory said it lightly. It was an old wound now.

"Yeah? How come you ain't in Westminster running the country with all the other Old Etonians, then?"

"There *are* other public schools. And . . . it's complicated. Family issues."

Mal nodded, like that made perfect sense to him.

"You're here on holiday?" Jory rushed on.

"Kind of." Mal's smile was twisted. "Work issues. I'm staying at the Sea Bell—me mate's little sister is the barmaid there. Tasha, you know her?"

"I . . . don't tend to drink in pubs." Jory had seen her around, though. A pretty girl with pale tan skin and extravagantly bushy brown afro hair. Mrs Quick, who volunteered at the museum in the off season and liked to keep abreast of things all year round, had pointed Tasha out to him as one of her previous guests at the B&B. She'd given a strong hint that her hospitality had been instrumental in getting the girl to relocate to Porthkennack.

"You *really* need to get out more." Mal finally took a biscuit and bit into it. "Hey, these are great," he said with his mouth full. "Cinnamon, right?"

Jory nodded, distracted by waiting for a shower of crumbs that never came.

Mal looked pleased and swallowed. "So I was thinking, you ought to come down the pub tonight. Let me buy you a drink to say cheers and all." Again, there was a vague hand wave. Presumably this one was referring to the tea, biscuits, and sympathy, rather than the naval museum as a whole.

"I— There's no need."

"Yeah, there is." Mal gazed at him sorrowfully. "You wouldn't leave a bloke to drink alone the day his rat died, would you?"

It wasn't a dilemma Jory had ever been faced with before. "I . . . No. Of course not."

"Brill. See you at the Sea Bell at seven, then?" Without waiting for an answer, Mal stood up and grabbed a couple more biscuits from the tub, flashing a smile in Jory's direction. "Couple for the road."

He winked. Then he was gone.

He hadn't drunk his tea. Jory took a cautious sip from his own mug and realised why. The milk had, in fact, turned.

Ye gods, that was awful.

CHAPTER TWO

The high from a successful pickup—or a successful invite to the pub at any rate, which was almost the same thing—lasted all of thirty seconds after Mal stepped out of the dusty air of the naval museum and into the bright sunlight.

Hermione. He was fucking well going to miss her. She'd been the best rat a bloke could have. The *best*. And yeah, he still had Rose the Third and Luna from her last litter, but it wasn't the same with them. They were great rats, course they were, but him and Hermione, they'd been through *so much* together. He'd cried on her fur that night after—

Shit. *Not* gonna think about that. Mal got down to the road, and wondered which way to go. Back to the Sea Bell? Tasha was pretty good at knowing when a bloke needed a hug. And it was literally the ideal place to get a stiff drink to toast Hermione.

Trouble was, Tasha wouldn't stop at the hug and the drink. She'd want to know what was wrong, and Mal wasn't sure he could handle talking about it. Not yet. Not without blubbing like a baby, and no way was he going to do that in front of his best mate's little sis.

He turned towards the cliffs instead, making his way down the lane and then onto the footpath over the grassy clifftop. It was quiet up here, except for the gusting of the wind, the crashing of the waves on the rocks below, and the screaming of the seagulls . . . Actually, come to think of it, it was bloody noisy up here, but they were *quiet* sounds. Like, non-people sounds. You didn't get those in London. Mal liked a bit of his own company, every now and then, which was one reason he hadn't wanted to stay in customer service . . .

Mal shivered and wrapped his arms around himself. Nope. Not thinking about work. Think about . . . Think about Jory, instead. Yeah, that'd do.

He didn't really know why he'd bothered to pick up the shy museum bloke with the dodgy mugs and even dodgier milk . . . Okay, that was a lie. Mal didn't have a type, exactly, but tall and built would pretty much do it for anyone, wouldn't it? And yeah, he liked the contrast between the way the guy looked and the way he spoke and acted. Like he had no idea how fit he was. It was cute, the way he somehow managed to stand and sit like he was apologising for his height all the time.

Mal left the footpath and sat down on the grass overlooking the bay. Over to the right, as he glanced down, were some vicious sharp rocks jutting out to sea. His tourist map told him they'd been named after Voldemort's mum and judging from those jagged edges, they'd probably caused almost as much trouble. On the plus side, they were dead handy for the lifeboat station. Mal couldn't see it from this angle, but he knew it was there from walks with Tasha.

He'd been kind, too, Jory had. Mal liked that in a bloke.

And anything was better than hanging around the pub on his tod for another night with Tasha being *nice* to him. Christ, Dev and Kyle couldn't get here fast enough for his liking. They'd be here in a week, staying at that cottage on the cliff that Kyle had had last summer. It was only a short distance from Roscarrock House, so they could lean out of the window and shout *Fuck you* up the hill anytime they wanted. Although Dev kept saying he was well over all the shit that had happened last year.

If he'd said it a few less times, Mal might even have believed it.

He squinted along the cliff and could make out the big house up on the high point at the other end of the bay from where he was standing. He'd visited yesterday, basically cos he was a nosy sod but also cos he liked a bit of history. Always had. He'd been the one member of the family who'd actually enjoyed it when Mum dragged them round to yet another ancient pile when him and Morgan were little. Later, when Morgs was old enough to put her foot down, it'd just been him and Mum. Well, fair dues, his dad's shifts hadn't always allowed him to come along.

Mum would like this place, he'd thought as he traipsed round the place with a load of other tourists, keeping an eye out in vain for anyone who looked vaguely like the old ancestral portraits. The family must keep out of the way on days when it was open to the public. Mum had offered to come down here with him, but Mal was a big boy. He didn't need his hand held, and more to the point, Morgan was the size of the bloody Gherkin and about ready to pop her first sprog. She needed Mum with her.

It'd given him an idea, anyway, visiting Roscarrock House. Something to do while he was here. Take his mind off things. Mal had overheard one of the volunteer guides talking about Mary Roscarrock, and it'd rung a bell, so he'd stayed to earwig. It was when the old bloke mentioned she'd been a bit of a goer that he twigged—Kyle had said something a while back about her being his great-great-whatever-grandma or -aunt or whatever. Allegedly. And okay, Roscarrock might be a four-letter word round him and Dev's, but Mal still reckoned Dev would probably be glad to find out more about her.

Maybe it'd even help him. Show him the family weren't all straitlaced snobs, that kind of thing.

And Mal owed Dev and Kyle. They'd been fucking great to him since . . . since he'd had to take time off work, and hadn't been coping too well on his own. They'd let him camp out at theirs as long as he wanted, no problem, despite how it must've cockblocked them something chronic, and then Dev had set it all up so Mal could come down and stay here with Tasha.

It'd be good to have something to tell them when they got here.

So he'd stayed to listen while the old bloke went on about Mary Roscarrock from the early sixteen hundreds.

"She was a very spirited young lady," the guide had said. "It's said she was disowned by the family for some misdeed, the details of which have been lost to time."

That alone made Mal glad he'd stayed. After the crap that family had given Dev . . . Yeah, anyone disowned by them was definitely worth knowing about.

"Was she up the duff?" he butted in.

The guide glared at him over the tops of his glasses, which were the wire-rimmed sort and made him look like a pissed-off professor. "The details of which have been *lost to time,*" he repeated pointedly.

Mal wondered where the naughty step was, and if he should go and sit on it now or wait to be told.

"Didn't she become a pirate?" The woman who'd spoken was a wiry old girl with grey hair and pale but sharp blue eyes. She reminded Mal of the husky one of his neighbours had owned when he was a kid.

His ears pricked right up. A pirate in the family? Dev'd be well chuffed to hear about that.

The guide nodded. "Oh, yes. You might say she learned the trade at her father's knee—Sir John, who built this house in which we now stand, sailed with Sir Francis Drake on the *Golden Hind*. Came home with a fortune in Spanish gold."

Mal frowned and tried to remember his history books. "Wasn't he supposed to be a hero? Drake, I mean. Saved us from the Spanish Armada, and all that."

"To the English he was a hero, yes." The prof gave him a slightly more approving look. "To the Spanish, whose ships Drake captured and stripped of all their treasures, he was nothing but a pirate, for all he was sponsored by the crown. Indeed, if it hadn't been for the constant attacks by English privateers, King Philip might never have sent the Armada to invade England."

"Huh. So what about Mary Roscarrock?"

"She became captain of her own ship, crewed by men—and women too, or so they say—from down in the village."

"What, so Lady Mary from the manor goes down to the village and is all 'I say, you chaps, one is going to become a pirate, what larks, who's with me?' and they all go 'Yeah, why not, we ain't got nothing on today'?"

The husky lady laughed, and so did a few other people who'd stopped to listen in. The prof seemed to thaw a bit—Mal reckoned it'd made the old boy's day to get this big an audience. Now he had them, it'd probably take one of those cannons they had out on the lawn to get him to stop talking. "Ah, but you forget how close-knit communities were in those days—and with no welfare state, the poor relied on the kindness of their landlords. Plenty of those villagers would have had very recent memories of Mary Roscarrock herself helping their families or friends out in times of need. And, of course, attitudes to the laws of the realm were, ah, we'll call it pragmatic, shall we? There's many a family kept food on the table by a bit of smuggling on the side, or wrecking—although it's never been proven ships were deliberately lured onto the rocks around here, needless to say." He tapped the side of his nose with a wicked smile.

Mal found himself grinning back. "Bet the rest of the family were dead chuffed. You got any more information about her? She sounds well cool." He could see her now, dressed up in men's clothes, a pistol in each hand—if they'd had pistols in them days. Maybe just a cutlass—and forcing some rich entitled bastard to walk the plank.

"There's a book," the guide said dismissively. "Romantic codswallop, if you want my view. All about her running off to be with one of the village lads, too lowborn for the family's taste."

Mal had picked up a copy of *The Beautiful Buccaneer* in what passed for a gift shop anyhow, and had read a couple of chapters since then. He kind of liked it, but it was pretty clear the author hadn't been aiming for historical accuracy. Lots of corsets and heaving bosoms, which Mal didn't have a problem with, but he was fairly sure posh young ladies who'd persuaded their brothers to give them a quick fencing lesson one afternoon weren't *actually* able to fight off ten hardened swordsmen at once, all while sailing a ship single-handed cos the crew had gone and got themselves captured again.

The old boy's parting suggestion had been a trip down to the naval museum and a poke around in their local history archive, which was why Mal had headed there today. Not that he'd made it very far before getting that phone call from Mum . . .

Ah, sod it. Sometimes you just needed a hug even if it meant you'd have to talk about stuff.

Mal got up and took the lane back to the Sea Bell.

Tasha was on her own behind the bar when he got back, so Mal didn't go straight over to speak to her. He could wait until her boss had come back from the cellar or the gents' or wherever the hell he'd got to. Jago Andrewartha was a slow-moving old bastard who ruled over the pub like he was King Arthur himself, which must make the locals on their barstools his knights.

Mal had a little snigger at the thought of that lot on horseback, armour gleaming in the sun. For his eleventh birthday, his mum had taken them down to Hever Castle to watch the jousting. His sister had whinged on about it being boring and stupid and why couldn't she have spent the day with her boyfriend instead, but Mal had loved it. He'd wanted to try it himself, but Mum and Dad hadn't had the money for horse riding lessons even if they'd been able to find anywhere local that did them. And anyway, round where he lived, poncing about like you reckoned you were posh could get the shit kicked out of you if anyone heard about it, so it was probably just as well.

Rats were his thing, not horses. Grief for Hermione slammed into him again. Shit. Maybe he wasn't in the mood for company after all—

"Mal!" Tasha yelled out, waving at him. She held up a pint glass with a clear question in her eye. Half the Round Table had turned to look, like they hadn't just seen him at lunchtime—seriously, didn't some of these old codgers have homes to go to?—so there was nothing for it but to nod at Tasha and head on up to the bar.

She was already pulling him a pint of Rattler Cyder, which Mal had tried on his first night here and decided he liked better than the local beer. Plus, it had to be healthier, didn't it? It had proper Cornish apples in. Hermione had liked apples . . .

"You all right, babe?" Tasha asked.

Jago loomed up behind her like he'd come from nowhere. He'd been in the cellar, then. "You've got a face on you like a wet weekend," he rumbled before Mal could answer.

"So? He don't have to be all happy-smiley if he don't wanna." Tasha gave her boss a pointed look.

Fuck, Mal was sick of this. "Had some bad news from home," he said shortly.

"Sorry to hear that." Jago gave him a nod and moved deliberately to the other end of the bar, where the locals were clustered.

Tasha leaned on the bar, her eyes wide. "What's up?"

"Mum called. Hermione's died."

"That's one of your rats, innit? Oh, babe. Come here." She leaned even further and gave him a hug. It'd have been a lot more comforting if they hadn't had the bar between them, but then again, Mal could feel tears pricking at his eyes already. Shit.

"'S all right. 'M all right." He pulled back and tried to smile. "Hey, I met a bloke at the museum. He's coming here tonight."

"You don't hang about, do you? What's he like? Fit?"

"Not bad. Tall. Blond. Got a beard. Sorta geeky."

"That your type these days?"

Mal shrugged. "Haven't got a type, have I? I'm an equal-opportunities lover."

"Everyone's got a type."

"Yeah? What's yours?"

Tasha made a face. "Bastards, mostly."

"Yeah? What about you and Ceri? Been wondering about you two for, like, *years*."

"We ain't known her years. Not even one. And we're mates, that's all, you got that? Now are you gonna drink that drink, or just sit and watch the bubbles all night?"

Mal could take a hint. She'd been a bit touchy about Ceri lately—something to do with her going off to work abroad for six weeks with her college mates when term ended, Mal reckoned. "Gimme some dry roasted to go with it?"

"They'll make your breath stink, they will." She still handed over the bag of nuts. "Make sure you clean your teeth before you snog Tall, Blond, and Geeky."

"Yes, Mum."

Tasha gave him the finger, then went to serve a customer with a smile like butter wouldn't melt.

CHAPTER THREE

Seven o'clock. At the Sea Bell. That was what Jory had agreed to — or at least, he hadn't managed to say a definite no, so he should probably go, shouldn't he? It would be rude not to.

Stepping out of the museum at ten past five and locking the door behind him, Jory considered his options. The obvious thing to do would be to walk home, grab something to eat, maybe have a shower and change his clothes . . .

No. God, no. He was reading too much into a simple invitation for a drink. This wasn't a *date*.

Is it? Jory wondered as he took the path along the cliffs. The museum was only half an hour's walk from Roscarrock House, so he never drove unless the rain was coming down in torrents and sometimes not even then. Today the weather was glorious, with hardly a cloud in the endless blue sky and the sea breeze taking the edge off the lingering heat of the day. It promised a warm, pleasant evening, which, given they were only a week or two past midsummer, would last for hours. Below him, the beach stretched out, golden and inviting. On another day, Jory might have gone for a swim—might even have called Kirsty and asked if Gawen would like to come to the beach for some father-son time, although today being Sunday, he'd probably been out with his mother already. Time was too tight today if he wanted to arrive punctually for his date.

Or not, as the case might be, although Mal had definitely seemed to be flirting. He'd *winked*. Who actually did that these days? Or any days, come to that?

So it *might* be a date.

Then again, Mal had just suffered a bereavement. Perhaps he hadn't been thinking clearly. Simply going through the motions.

Perhaps he was one of those people who flirted with everyone. For all Jory knew, Mal might be straight as an arrow.

But he'd winked. Did straight men wink at other men?

He *could* ask his brother . . . Except that no, he really, really couldn't. Bran wouldn't be at all pleased about him having a date. Especially with a man. Maybe he could get away with asking the question, and not mentioning the invitation to the pub?

Because of *course* Bran wouldn't smell anything remotely rodent-like about Jory mentioning he'd been winked at, and then disappearing out for the evening.

Bugger it. He'd just have to play it by ear. Right, well, a quick shower wouldn't hurt in any case. His sister, Bea, had sniffed the air when she got home from work one evening a week or so back and accused Jory of smelling of *museum*, which she'd informed him meant *dust and dead things*.

They didn't even *have* any dead things in the naval museum, but better safe than sorry.

As the path got steeper leading up to Big Guns Cove, Jory found his pace increasing, the exertion helping to calm his nerves. Silly of him. Mal was obviously a tourist, so he wouldn't be here long in any case.

Long enough, perhaps, a sly voice that came directly from his id whispered in his mind.

Roscarrock House had been closed to visitors today, so there were no last stragglers to weave his way around as Jory made it through the gates, which was how he liked it. He didn't know how Bran could stand working from home while strangers poked and pried through the rooms open to them, laughing at the family portraits and occasionally speculating loudly on Great-uncle Lochrin's paternity. And Jory's, come to that, when they got to the photographs.

Every time he came back, Jory had to get used to it all again. Perhaps after a year or two of living here full-time, he wouldn't even notice, as Bran seemed not to. And Bea, for that matter, although Jory had always found it impossible to tell what Bea thought about anything.

Jory managed to avoid Bran on his way to the bathroom. Bran had a way of making Jory feel like he should be asking permission to go out, which had perhaps been reasonable when he was seventeen and they were newly orphaned, but was a little ridiculous now he was thirty-two years old.

Showered and changed into jeans and a polo shirt Kirsty had once complimented him on, Jory headed down to the kitchen.

There was something about being back in Porthkennack that gave him an appetite. Maybe it was the sea air, or maybe it was just the association with childhood and big family dinners. At any rate, Jory was starving, so he dumped a generous portion of pasta into a pan and set it on to boil. There was half a jar of sauce in the fridge, and enough ham and vegetables to pad it out a bit. Plenty for one person. He'd given up trying to persuade Bran and Bea they should all eat together, even one day a week. Their schedules never seemed to match—Bea in particular was always home late from the office, or off at some social event that was more about business than pleasure, like today. He had a strong suspicion that she didn't much like eating in company. Maybe she was worried about looking too human.

Jory gave his wrist a mental slap. He wasn't being fair. And it was time to put the sauce on.

Halfway through his meal, it occurred to Jory that the pub most likely served food. Would Mal be planning to eat?

He'd said, *Come for a drink,* but maybe he'd meant *with the option of dinner afterwards*? Oh hell. Why did life have to be so impossibly complicated? Making a snap decision to hedge his bets, Jory put down his fork and shoved an upturned plate over the rest of his meal. He could always microwave it later.

Then he jammed his feet into his trainers, checked his reflection in the hall mirror for sauce splatters, and set off out, all without having bumped into Bran, miracle of miracles.

The Sea Bell was down a country lane, not far from St. Ia's church. Jory hadn't been there in years. In fact, the last time he'd had a pint in there had probably been over a decade ago, back when he was a student home from uni for the summer. He hadn't remembered it as being quite so . . . unwelcoming. And that was just the exterior. There were no baskets of flowers hanging outside to entice the tourists, and no blackboards advertising quiz nights or football matches or whatever else went on in pubs these days. Just the pub sign itself, a painted rendition of a ship's bell, creaking gently as it swung in the breeze. The salt-laden air had wrought havoc on the paint, which was starting to peel—as was the sober green paint on the doors and windows.

And yes, Jory could stand outside all evening cataloguing the depredations of time on the place, but that rather defeated the object of coming here, didn't it? He took a deep breath, squared his shoulders, and pushed open the door.

The inside of the pub was rather of a piece with its exterior. A row of men of indeterminate age sat at the bar. One of them glanced around at him, stony-faced, then turned back to his pint. Jory swallowed the urge to flee. For God's sake, it wasn't like he was some interloper. He was Porthkennack born and bred. He was a Roscarrock, damn it.

Mal was sitting at one end of the bar chatting to the barmaid they'd spoken of earlier. Jory hesitated, not wanting to barge in, but she spotted him and said something to Mal, who turned round and gave him a wave.

Feeling slightly less awkward now, Jory walked up to him.

Mal smiled in welcome. "Good to see you, mate. Tasha, this is Jory, yeah? The bloke from the museum who made me tea and stuff. His biscuits are well tasty." He winked again.

Oh, bloody hell. Jory tried to will himself not to blush. "I . . . Thank you. Um. Can I get you a drink?"

"They're on me," Tasha said firmly. "What you drinking?"

"There's no need—"

"Don't be daft. You took care of Mal, didn't you?"

Mal, Jory couldn't help but notice, was looking more and more exasperated. "Pint of cider," he said quickly. "Please."

"Rattler, Strongbow, or Scrumpy Jack?"

Just what he needed. Further choices. "The first," Jory said, trying to sound decisive.

Mal grinned and held up his half-full glass. "Good innit? That's what I'm on."

Jory wasn't sure what made him glance round as Tasha pulled his pint. Some kind of sixth sense that he was being watched, perhaps. A man in his sixties or so was working at the other end of the bar—at least, he was on the working side of the bar, although he was in fact perched on a stool and drinking a pint of beer. He looked vaguely familiar, and his gaze was fixed firmly on Jory.

As their eyes met, the man put down his pint and, without hurrying, got to his feet. He headed down to their end of the bar.

He wasn't smiling.

Jory startled as Tasha put his drink in front of him with a "There you go, babe."

"Th-thanks." He took a gulp, hoping to steady his nerves.

"Well, well. We don't often see the likes of you in here." The barman's tone was gruff and not precisely welcoming. He turned to Mal, who seemed as confused as Jory felt. "Surprised to see *you* drinking with him."

"What? Why?"

"Tell you his name, did he?"

Mal frowned. "He's Jory. Works up at the museum."

"Actually that's just temporary—"

"He's a Roscarrock." The barman said it flatly. Coldly. As if it was a *bad* thing. "Brother to Branok and Beaten Roscarrock."

Jory swallowed. *Everyone* was staring at him now. "Ah, well, yes." He wondered desperately what his family could have done to provoke such hostility. Jory had an idea that Bran could be a little ruthless when it came to property, but surely that was all business?

This seemed *personal*.

"Didn't tell you that, did he?" the barman went on.

Mal's face had changed, and not in a good way. "No, he didn't."

"You didn't ask! I mean, we didn't exchange surnames. W-what's this all about?" Jory *hated* how his stammer came back in times of stress.

"My bruv," Tasha snapped. "Mal's best mate. Devan Thompson."

Jory frowned, baffled. "Who?"

Mal pushed away from the bar and walked off a couple of paces. Then he turned back, his face hard. "Not funny, mate. Seriously, not funny."

"I'm not trying to be—"

"Can I bar him?" Tasha asked the barman. "Can I?"

Jory just stared at them, wishing he'd never come. How the hell had it all gone so wrong so quickly? He should have stayed at home with his books and his computer. Or gone to see Kirsty and Gawen. Not accepted invitations from good-looking strangers. When had that ever ended well for him? He should go, now, but his feet seemed rooted to the spot.

"I think you'd better leave," the barman rumbled, and that broke the spell.

Jory fled.

When he got back home, Jory scrambled through the house until he ran down Bran in his study. "Who's Devan Thompson?" he demanded.

Bran glanced up briefly, then returned his gaze to the file he'd been leafing through. "Who?"

"Don't play games with me. He's the man who just got me thrown out of a pub, despite the fact I've never even met him." Jory's face was hot with remembered humiliation.

"What?" Bran's face darkened as he stood up. "That's an outrage. Which pub? Was it the Sea Bell?"

"I . . . It doesn't matter." The *last* thing Jory wanted was to cause any more bad blood.

"What were *you* doing in a pub?"

Oh God. Jory should never have started this. "Tell me about Devan Thompson," he said quickly.

Bran's glare deepened for a moment, but then he let out an exasperated huff and leaned back in his chair, folding his arms. "I suppose I'd better tell you. I don't want you bothering Bea about this. You won't remember—you were just a baby—but when Bea and I were in our teens, there was a . . . regrettable incident with a boy visiting for the summer. Devan Thompson was the result."

Jory stared. "He's Bea's *son*? Our nephew?"

"Only in the strictest sense. He has no claim on us. I thought all of that would have blown over by now. And you *have* met him," Bran added. "You were the one who let him into our house in the first place."

Jory recoiled at the accusation in Bran's tone. "I— What? When?"

"Last summer. When he came looking for Bea."

"Last *summer*? And neither of you *told* me?" Jory desperately tried to recall the occasion. He'd met his nephew and he hadn't even known?

"It was nothing to do with you."

"Nothing... He's *family*, for God's sake."

"No, he's a mistake."

"How come nobody forced *her* to get married?" Jory couldn't keep the bitterness out of his tone.

"She was far too young for that, and there was no question of her keeping the baby." Bran's tone was brusque.

"How old was she?"

"Does it matter?" Bran made an impatient noise. "He was born when we were sixteen."

Sixteen... Jory would have been seven. In his first year of boarding school... "Is that why I had to spend Easter in London with Aunt Sarah?"

Bran nodded. "Mother took Bea away for the final months, and Father didn't want to be left with you running around underfoot."

Jory couldn't believe it. He could still remember the rush of hurt and bewilderment when Aunt Sarah came to pick him up from school instead of his mother, and told him only that his parents had thought it best that he didn't go home. He'd been devastated at not seeing his best friend from Porthkennack, Patrick.

By the time summer holidays came around, Patrick had found a new best friend. One who wouldn't be away for the greater part of the year.

And Bea had been . . . Well. Bea. Perhaps a bit quieter than before? Jory honestly couldn't have said. Maybe Bran had been a little angrier—but then he'd never had a great deal of patience with his much younger brother in any case. "What about the baby?"

Bran shrugged. "Given up for adoption, obviously. She really should have got rid of it, but you know how girls that age are about babies."

It. As if *it* hadn't grown into a young man since then.

Christ. Jory had a nephew only seven years younger than he was. That was less than the age difference between Jory and the twins. And the barmaid at the Sea Bell was that nephew's sister, and Mal—the young man Jory had been *interested* in—was his best friend.

Jory didn't often drink, but right now he felt the situation justified it. He marched out of the study without another word and headed straight for the dining room, which was where Bran kept his very expensive single malt whisky.

Bran wouldn't be happy about Jory drinking it, which would make it taste all the sweeter. Christ, he'd known Bran was . . . how he was, and of course Bran didn't have any children of his own, but how could even he be so callous about this poor unwanted child? Jory grabbed the decanter, poured himself a generous few fingers of whisky and tossed back a gulp. Smooth as it was, the burn of the alcohol didn't hit him until after it had gone down. Jory shuddered and put the glass down, blinking a little. Maybe he'd drink the rest later.

Maybe he'd chuck it down the sink. He needed to think what he was going to do.

He was still sitting there when Bea returned home.

Jory heard her get in before he saw her. Not because he'd been listening for the door, but because Bran didn't catch up with her until she was directly outside the dining room, and angry whispers tended not to stay whispers for long.

They came in to talk to him together, as they always did. Jory had often wondered how much of the united front was just that—a front—but they were no closer to giving anything away tonight than they ever were. The whisky churned uneasily in Jory's stomach. He wished he'd finished his pasta instead.

Bea spoke first. She had what Jory thought of as her networking clothes on: a sleek, expensive navy dress that still looked crisp and uncrumpled despite the heat of the day. "We're not going to fight about this."

"Nice of you to let me know," Jory snapped back.

"You're making a fuss about nothing," she carried on coolly. "The matter was dealt with last year."

"The *matter*. That's an interesting way to refer to your own flesh and blood." Chair legs scraped against the stone floor as Jory stood without conscious decision.

Bran stepped forward, putting himself between Jory and Bea. As if Jory were a *threat*, for Christ's sake. "Don't you think Bea's suffered enough in all this, without you adding to it?"

Guilt stricken, Jory slumped back down into his chair, his head in his hands. "I just can't believe you didn't tell me."

He heard a chair being pulled out beside him, then Bea's cool, even voice. "We thought you had enough on your plate, what with Gawen's troubles."

Jory's head snapped up. "And what about Gawen? Don't you think he deserves to know his cousin?"

"No." Her tone was firm and final. She softened it when she spoke again. "There would be no advantage for Gawen in getting to know Devan Thompson. How is Gawen, by the way? I haven't seen him for a while. Is the schoolwork still going well?"

It was a blatant attempt to change the subject. Jory hated himself, a little, for succumbing to it. "Very much so. He's pretty much certain to get the maths prize this year."

"And Kirsty?"

"She's fine."

"And are the two of you any closer to . . .?"

She left it hanging. Jory looked away. "I wish you'd leave that alone. It's not going to happen."

"But if you—"

"Just leave it, all right? How do you think you'd feel if it was you and this Devan's father?"

Bea recoiled as if he'd slapped her.

Jory felt as wretched as if he *had*. "Oh God, Bea, I'm sorry—"

Bran was gathering Bea up from the chair like a child, and she was letting him. "Christ alone knows why you even bother to live here with us," he snapped, his tone clipped and vicious. "You've got no sense of family, of obligation . . ."

Jory couldn't look at his sister as he stumbled from the room. He needed to get out of the house—he couldn't breathe in this place. Almost without conscious decision, he found himself outside the back door, staring over the old kitchen garden, where he could dimly remember his mother tending her fresh herbs.

Bran had had it grassed over years ago. Jory had been vaguely surprised he hadn't just poured on concrete; after all, even lawns required a bare minimum of nurture.

The path behind the house was an old friend, leading up to the pinnacle of Big Guns Cove, where the cliffs jutted proud into the sea, jagged rocks guarding their base like merciless sentinels. The clifftops calmed him, as they always did. Perhaps it was because Bea and Bran never came this way. How many Roscarrocks had stood here before him, maybe watching for a light or a glimpse of sail that told them their ships were coming home, laden with spoils?

Jory stood for a long moment right on the edge, staring down at the waves far, far below as they crashed on the rocks, sending up bursts of spray. He crouched down, wanting to feel the scrubby grass, softer than it looked beneath his fingertips, the crumbling of the cliff edge as he ran his hand over and down onto the stone. Gulls shrieked around him. The souls of dead fishermen, he'd been told, but just as likely, those of long-gone smugglers and pirates, or hapless sailors, their ships lured onto the rocks by a falsely smiling lantern.

He'd often thought of getting his climbing gear out of the old stables and abseiling down these cliffs . . . but he could picture Bea's and Bran's faces, and knew he'd never do it.

Up here, he felt far closer to his father than he ever had when the old man had been alive. Perhaps he'd been more of a family man when the twins were small, but to Jory he'd always been a distant figure, stern and, if not quite disapproving, always seeming on the verge of it. So different from his friend Patrick's father, who'd played cricket with them on the beach, flown kites, and let the smaller children ride on his shoulders.

Perhaps bad parenting was in the blood. Or perhaps the Roscarrocks had simply never learned how it should be done.

Jory turned to look back at the house, solid and unchanging for centuries.

No. He wasn't going to do this Bea and Bran's way.

He was going to seek out this Devan Thompson, and . . . be an uncle to him.

Whatever that might mean.

CHAPTER
FOUR

Mal still wasn't sure about it all when he got up next day, had a stretch and a scratch, and wandered over to the bedroom window to see what the weather was doing. It was midmorning, cos he'd had a rough night. Bad dreams. *Really* bad dreams, but he wasn't going to think about them, and he didn't need to anyhow, cos he had to sort out what he was going to do about Jory sodding Roscarrock.

On the one hand, he was a bit pissed off about being made a fool of, but on the other, the bloke had had a point about nobody ever bringing up surnames. And on the *other* other hand, Mal hadn't finished all he'd wanted to do at the museum, cos of being interrupted by Mum's phone call, which he *also* wasn't going to think about, so he could do with going back there. And on the other other *other* hand—seriously, people should have more hands, it'd make all this a lot simpler— Sod it, he'd forgotten what he was thinking about now.

But anyhow. The bloke had seemed pretty decent, up until Dev's name had been mentioned, when he'd denied all knowledge. Mal wasn't sure what he thought about that. He'd assumed the bloke was telling porkies, because how could he not know about Dev? But if he had been lying, he'd been doing a bloody good job of it. Mal could have sworn that look of total bewilderment had been genuine, which meant Jory was blameless, didn't it? Course, there was the Roscarrock thing, but it wasn't like he could help that any more than Mal could help *his* name, and—

—and Jory was *right there*, over the road and leaning on the wall, which Mal could see from the window, and shit, he probably ought to put some clothes on cos if Jory looked up now, he was going to get a proper eyefull. Mal yanked the curtain back into place, stumbled across the room, and pulled on his jeans from yesterday. T-shirt, T-shirt . . . did he *have* any clean T-shirts? Oh yeah, there. Pile on the dresser. Ironed and everything. Tasha was still being nice to him, bless her. Mal pulled one over his head, grabbed a couple of socks at random from the heap next to the shirts, and put them on too.

Then he jammed his feet into his trainers and was down the back stairs and halfway across the lane before his brain caught up and asked him what the bloody hell he thought he was doing.

Jory gave him a nervous smile as he approached. "Hi."

"What are you doing back here?" Mal asked. "Uh, don't mean to be rude, but, yeah. 'Sup, bruv?"

"I didn't know," Jory said earnestly.

"What, that Dev's me mate? Yeah, I kinda got that."

"No, I mean . . . I'm aware this is going to sound incredible, but I honestly didn't know about . . . Dev, you called him? Not Devan? They never told me."

Mal gave him a sidelong look. "Seriously, mate? Cos my sister's up the duff right now, and trust me, it's the sort of thing you notice."

"I wasn't here. Boarding school from the age of seven, remember? They kept me away from it all." Jory took a deep breath. "I want to meet him."

Yeah, right. "No, you don't."

Jory frowned. "Yes, I do."

"Yeah? What about your brother telling Dev he'd have the law on him if he kept hanging round the family?"

"He *what*? Oh God. I'm so sorry about Bran. He gets very, um, concerned about the family's reputation."

"Wasn't only him, though, was it? How do you think Dev felt when his own mum—your sister—told him to fuck off?"

Jory closed his eyes briefly. "I don't know. I can't imagine it. I'm sorry. I didn't *know*."

"See, that's where I don't get it. I asked about you. You're their brother, aintcha? So how come?"

"We've never been close. There's nine years between us and, well, they're twins."

"But you live with them, right? In that big house?"

"I do now. Last year, when Devan came to see her, I was only visiting."

"But you were there?"

"Yes, but I didn't know anything about it. Bran just said . . . Honestly, I can't remember what he said. Probably something about it being a business matter. Bea's very involved with various local enterprise initiatives." Jory rubbed the back of his neck. "If I'd known Dev was my nephew . . . I can't believe I opened the door to him and I didn't even know."

Yeah, Mal was having trouble believing it and all. "You must've heard them talking. I don't care how thick the walls are in that old pile."

"I didn't, I swear. Have you got a picture of him?"

"On my phone." Which was upstairs on his bedside table. Mal hesitated. "Look, you can come in, all right, but keep the noise down or you're gonna have Jago and Tasha to deal with, and it ain't gonna be pretty."

He led Jory up the back stairs, desperately hoping Tasha wouldn't choose this precise minute to stumble out of bed, and breathed a sigh of relief when they made it to the box room Jago had cleared out for him.

It felt weird, having Jory in his bedroom, standing six inches away from his unmade bed. And yesterday's kecks, which he'd stripped off last night and let fall on the floor. Mal managed to kick them under the bed when he went to grab his phone.

He turned back to Jory, who was standing around looking awkward and way too big for the room, and scrolled through his photos until he found a picture of Dev and Tasha. "There you go." He handed Jory the phone.

"That's him?" Jory shook his head slowly. "I . . . It seems awful, but I don't remember him at all."

He gave the phone back. Mal didn't know why he did it—maybe cos the bloke seemed so sad—but he flicked through until he found another shot of Dev, this one with Kyle. "That's him and his bloke."

"He's gay?"

Mal nodded, and Jory smiled, like he was pleased about it. Mal's stomach did a weird thing, sort of fluttered. He needed to get some breakfast down him. "That's . . ." Jory trailed off, and just as Mal was about ask what he'd been going to say, he spoke again. "It's odd . . . the other man seems more familiar, somehow."

"Yeah?" Mal shrugged. "You probably saw him around last year. He was renting one of them cottages down the cliff from your gaff."

Jory's frown cleared. "Yes! I remember now. He came to introduce himself as a neighbour. I'd just had a godawful row with Bran about— And I wasn't feeling very sociable right then. And, well, I wasn't living here at the time, so I let Bran deal with him. He must have thought I was terribly unwelcoming." The frown was back.

"Where were you then?"

"Edinburgh. Up at the university."

"Bloody hell, couldn't you find one any further away?"

Jory screwed up his face. "It was just a few years . . . Can you give me his number?"

"What, Dev's?" Mal managed to bite back the *Fuck, no* that had been on the tip of his tongue. "I'd have to ask him about that first, mate."

"Would you?"

Mal slumped down on the bed and ran a hand through his hair. Christ knew what he looked like. It was way too early for all this. "Yeah, see, it really fucked him up, what your sister did. I mean, he said he didn't give a shit, but he's my best mate, right? I know him."

Jory seemed a shedload more oversized and awkward from this angle. "I'm sorry," he said. And yeah, he sounded like he meant it, but Christ, how could he have been there all along last summer and not known?

Trouble was, Mal was going to have to say *something* to Dev, wasn't he? He'd be here in a week, and what were the chances of him and Kyle flying under Uncle Jory's radar then? Only a crap mate wouldn't warn him.

Even if it meant him and Kyle might change their plans and not come here after all, and fuck, Mal *really* didn't want that to happen.

He wasn't sure he could face it if Dev didn't come down.

Sod it. "Listen mate, if I ask you for a favour, will you do it?"

"I, ah, well. Depending what it is."

Mal couldn't blame him for being cautious. "Stay away from Dev until I give you the go-ahead, right? You gotta promise me you'll do that."

"But—" Jory looked well confused.

"Yeah, I know you ain't got his number or his address or anything. But you could get it, couldn't you? *She's* got it. Your sister. But I'm saying, you leave him alone until I tell you."

Jory nodded. "Fine. Of course. But—"

"See, the thing is, he's coming here. In a week. So you're gonna see him around. But you keep your distance, or I'll . . . I'll let Tasha post dog turds through your letterbox."

Mal wasn't expecting Jory's laugh at that, and maybe Jory hadn't been either—he sort of snorted, then looked embarrassed about it, as if he'd farted or something. "I, ah, sorry. Rough night."

"Yeah, you and me both." Mal found himself smiling. A week was a long time. Plenty long enough to find out a bit more about this Jory bloke, and whether Dev was going to want to know him. Mal patted the mattress, about to make some crack about Tasha having stuffed it with rocks, but Jory must've misunderstood, cos he sat down next to Mal.

Okaaayyy. This wasn't awkward at *all*, him and Jory sitting on his bed with the duvet still rucked up from last night. "So, yeah, you lived here all your life?"

Jory nodded. "Apart from when I was at school. And university. And doing postgraduate work."

Mal had to laugh. "So basically, you just come here every summer like a bloody grackle?"

Jory's face screwed up in a frown. It was well cute. "I think you mean *grockle*? A tourist? Isn't a grackle some kind of bird?"

"Fuck if I know. And there was me thinking I was speaking fluent Cornish."

"*Grockle* isn't even a Cornish word. It's general southwest dialect. *Emmet* is more specifically Cornish." He went a bit pink. "But you probably don't want the whole lecture."

"That what you used to do in Edinburgh? Lectures and stuff."

Jory nodded seriously. "Particularly the stuff. An essential part of any university curriculum, *stuff*."

Mal grinned. "Fuck off. I coulda gone to uni if I'd wanted to, you know." He could have and all. He'd had the grades. Straight As, and fuck you very much to all the teachers who'd predicted him Ds just cos he liked to have a bit of a laugh in lessons. He hadn't fancied the crippling debt, that was all.

Okay, so there might have been a bit of peer pressure in there too. His mates would've thought he was totally up himself if he'd gone to uni, especially seeing as he hadn't needed a degree for the job he'd wanted.

"I'm sure you could have," Jory said politely, which wasn't most people's reaction when he told them that. "Academia isn't for everyone."

"That why you left and came back here?"

"I . . ." Jory gave a weird, awkward shrug. "Family. Are you staying here long?"

Mal could take a hint. "Not sure. Gonna see how it goes."

"Between jobs at the moment?"

Jory's tone was sympathetic, which made Mal feel worse about lying to him, but he wasn't ready to go there. "Something like that. Old Jago said I can stay as long as I want, long as I pull me weight and don't leave the place looking like a pigsty."

"Kind of him."

"Course, if he finds me hanging about with you . . ."

Jory swallowed. "It's not just about Devan?"

"Nah. Your big bruv screwed his mate's family over some property or other—I didn't get the details. Chucked 'em all out when the old bloke died, was it? Tasha's mate's grandad, that was. Used to be on the lifeboats. So yeah, Roscarrock's a bit of a dirty word round here."

"Sorry."

"Hey, it ain't your fault." Mal sent him a sharp look. "Least, far as I know."

"God, no. I've never had anything to do with all that. Bran inherited the family interests. Father was something of a traditionalist—primogeniture, and all that." He flushed. "The eldest child inheriting—"

"I know what it means," Mal cut him off, a bit narked. "Just cos I never had a public-school education don't mean I never read books."

"Sorry. But you'd be amazed how many students I've known with frighteningly limited knowledge outside their own field." Jory paused. "So what is your field? You never said."

"Customer service." Mal didn't even feel bad about the lie. People who put you on the spot like that shouldn't expect the truth, right? He stood up. It was good, yeah, getting to talk to Jory, but if they hung around any longer, Tasha might come bursting in, and Mal really couldn't face having World War III kicking off in his bedroom. "Listen, it's been great, and all"—fuck, he sounded like he was trying to ditch last night's one-night stand, and Jory still sitting on his unmade bed wasn't helping—"but I ain't had me breakfast yet and I'm starving."

Jory scrambled to his feet. "I could take you out somewhere? If—if you're willing to give me another chance?"

CHAPTER FIVE

Jory felt like an idiot the minute he'd blurted out the invitation. Mal just stood there, staring down at him. Quite clearly, he'd just been trying to get rid of him. "But you've probably got other plans. Things to do. I'll—" Jory stood up.

"Nah, okay." Mal blinked, giving Jory the absurd impression that he was as surprised as Jory at his response. "Where d'you wanna go? Caff in town?"

Jory hadn't thought that far ahead. "Yes, why not?" After all, the town was full of eating places, and he'd be able to tell at a glance if there was any danger of bumping into Bran or Bea inside whichever one they chose.

"Right. Come on, then." Mal grabbed his wallet and phone, shoved them into his jeans pockets, looked out of the window, and then turned to Jory expectantly. "Ready?"

"Uh . . . Yes." Christ. It was ridiculous how attracted he was to the man. Mal seemed all sharp angles, all spiky class-war defensiveness, but there was a warmth underneath that took Jory's breath away. He was all mercurial changes too—one minute showing tenderness and genuine curiosity, the next slipping back into his cocky, am-I-bothered persona.

And no amount of dithering on Jory's part was likely to make Mal say, *Sod breakfast*, and jump back on the bed with him, and even if he did, Jory was self-aware enough to realise he'd probably run all the way back to Roscarrock House rather than stay and take advantage. But maybe going out for breakfast could be a first step. So Jory forced himself not to smile too widely like a complete idiot. "Yes. Let's go."

Mal nodded. "But keep it down, yeah? On your tippy-toes, and no talking on the stairs."

Sneaking down the back stairs of the pub like a teenager. *Bran would be appalled*, Jory thought. His students in Edinburgh would be amazed.

When they emerged into bright sunlight, both of them were grinning. Mal put a finger to his lips and grabbed Jory's arm, leading him not down the lane but over the fields and through a gap in the hedge to the road. Spiky branches clutched at Jory's clothes, hair, and beard.

Once through, Mal turned to Jory and burst out laughing. "Seriously, mate, you look like a fucking mountain man. How come you're all ripped, anyway? What did you used to teach up in Edinburgh—body-building and 'roid rage?"

Mal was exaggerating. Jory tried not to redden at the compliment, even as warmth flooded through him. "I got into climbing while I was at school. Upper body strength tends to be a bit of an advantage." Especially for those whose genetics had blessed them with a larger-than-average frame that took more hauling about than most when it came to vertical rock faces. Although, to be fair, the reach was a distinct help too.

Building up a bit of muscle had come in handy in other ways too, but he wasn't about to tell Mal any sob stories about being bullied as a young boy.

"Let me guess—your school was the sort that had its own climbing wall?"

Jory gave him a look. "And a fully equipped gym. Am I supposed to apologise for that?" he asked boldly, as they set off down the road.

Mal didn't seem to take offence. "No, but you could try pretending to be a tiny bit sad that mine didn't, yeah?"

"Would you have used it if they did?"

"Fuck, no. I'm a total wuss about heights."

"Heights have never bothered me. It's the depths that get you down." Guilt twinged in Jory's chest. If Bea or Bran heard him speaking of this sort of thing so lightly. . . But they hadn't and wouldn't.

Mal gave him a gentle dig in the ribs with his elbow, apparently far more at ease with casual physical contact than Jory. "Ever go caving? There's a lot round here, aren't there? Old smugglers' haunts?"

Jory hesitated. "A little. But mostly I prefer being out in the open air. Less risk of drowning."

"You got no romance in your soul."

Jory gave Mal a slow, sidelong look. "If drowning is your idea of romance, I may have to seriously reconsider taking you out for a meal." And then he held his breath because, damn it, he still didn't have any idea if Mal saw him that way at all.

If Mal saw *men* that way, full stop.

Mal gave an airy shrug. "Hey, it worked for Leo DiCaprio and whatserface in *Titanic*, didn't it? Nah, I meant, there's legends and stuff about those caves, aren't there? Might even find King Arthur down one of 'em, cuddling up to the Holy Grail while he waits for the second coming."

"Or you could get eaten by a questing beast." Great. Marvellous. Young men with a nonclassical education were always impressed by literary obscurity, weren't they? He braced himself for a *You what, mate?*

Mal just grinned. "Nah, I'm safe. I ain't slept with me sister, and cheers for making me think of that, by the way."

Jory actually stopped dead in his tracks for a moment, and had to force himself to start walking again because, that must look incredibly patronising of him. "You know about the symbolism of the questing beast?" he couldn't help asking. He tried to keep the surprise out of his voice but wasn't sure he'd succeeded.

"Ain't just a pretty face, am I? Course I know. I watched *Merlin* on the telly."

"Oh. I hadn't realised—"

"Nah, I'm yanking your chain. The TV show was on Saturday teatime, wasn't it? So they totally glossed over the whole incest bit so's not to put the kiddies off their fish fingers. I mean, it was all right, but they changed a shitload of stuff from what was in the *Morte d'Arthur*."

Jory's stomach somehow managed to clench and flip at one and the same time, as if his insides were auditioning for some kind of acrobatic act on *Britain's Got Talent*. "You've read Thomas Malory?"

Mal shoved his hands in his jeans pockets—or at least, as far as they'd go, which was about halfway—and gazed off down the road. Was his face redder than before? Jory couldn't be sure in the sunlight. "Yeah, well, Mum used to read me *The Once and Future King* when I was little—you know, the book Disney based *Sword in the Stone* on? Wait, what am I saying, course you know—and I wanted to know where it all came from, yeah? And then there's the name thing."

He was *definitely* red in the face now, and it was unbearably charming. "The name thing?" Jory almost forgot to ask.

"See, Mum was always into all that stuff. Arthurian legends and that. Then she got married to a bloke whose last name was Thomas and, well, Mal ain't actually short for Malcolm."

"Not . . ."

"Yep. Malory Thomas, esquire, at your service, sirrah." Mal sketched a ridiculously overblown bow in the air. "Bet you can guess how that went down at school."

Jory, who'd been laughing, stopped abruptly. "You were bullied?"

"Fuck yeah." Mal put on a snide, mocking voice. "'It's a girl's name, Mallorie, innit?' And that was *before* they found out I got a sister called Morgan. Then it was all, 'Go on, show us which one of you's really the girl.'"

Ouch. Some parents . . . "They didn't tease you about the literary associations, at least, then?"

Mal gave him a look of exaggerated disbelief. "You're giving them gits way too much credit. Most of 'em thought a book was just a posh way of packaging bog roll."

"Did—" Jory stopped, realising he didn't actually want to change the subject right now, no matter how important the question was to him.

"What?"

Apparently there was no help for it. "Did you know Devan then?"

"Dev? Nah, we didn't meet till we were eleven. High school. Had a couple of teachers who used to sit everyone in alphabetical order, yeah? So him being a Thompson, and me being a Thomas . . ." Mal shrugged.

"Thompson . . . that was the family who adopted him?"

"Yeah, but they ain't been around since I've known him. Died."

God, how awful for Devan. Dev. To be orphaned, effectively, twice, before he'd even reached his teens. Jory glanced over at Mal and desperately hoped he wasn't about to hear another tale of everyday woe. "Have you got family, apart from your sister? You mentioned your mum, but . . ." Jory had never been able to think of a tactful way to ask if someone was still alive. Maybe there wasn't one.

Mal seemed to take his meaning anyway. "Mum? Nah, she ain't popped her clogs yet. Hit the big five-oh last year. Her and my dad are still married and everything. Morgan's older than me. Married. Got a kid on the way. Like, any minute now."

It was a rush of information all at once. Jory had to take a moment to sort it out in his head.

They'd reached the edge of town, and the first shops were beginning to appear.

Mal turned to him. "Got a place in mind, have you?"

"Ah, not really, no."

"The Turkish place near the mosque does a wicked coffee—I went there with Dev last year."

Jory blinked. "You were here last year too?"

"Yeah, came down for a week to join Dev. Drove down with Tasha. Missed all the drama though. And we were here again over Christmas, but that was just for a few days."

That was . . . appallingly unfair. Jory could have known him for a year already, if he'd only been in the right place at the right time.

Then again, given what had happened with other members of his family, maybe not. "Um. The trouble with the Seven Stars is that there's an outside chance we might bump into Bea or Bran there." Jory couldn't help glancing nervously around in case he'd somehow conjured them up.

"Gotcha. Tell you what, we'll go down the front. They ever go to the Square Peg?"

"Is it touristy?"

"Just a bit." The way Mal said it clearly implied a place crammed to the rafters with families eating cream teas, half of them pronouncing *scones* incorrectly and the other half putting the jam and cream on in the wrong order.

Perfect. Neither Bran nor Bea would be seen dead in a place like that. "Then no."

"Right, that's where we'll go, then. Tasha's mate Ceri used to work there," he added as they turned down a side street.

The Square Peg Café, when they reached it, turned out not to be quite as tacky as Jory had imagined, but it was every bit as touristy. He wondered how long it had been here, considering he hadn't even known about it, but was afraid to ask.

"Do you mind if we take this table?" He gestured to one set back against the café window and shaded by the awning. It'd give them some cover in case anyone who knew them happened by. Jory was damned if he'd avoid Mal just because his brother and sister wouldn't approve, but he didn't fancy having a public argument about it. And the last thing he wanted was to get Mal in trouble with either Tasha or Jago Andrewartha.

"Yeah, with colouring like yours, the sun ain't your friend, is it? I freckle and burn like a ginge anyhow if I don't slap on the sunblock, so it's no skin off my nose sitting in the shade." Mal grinned. "Literally."

They sat down. Jory took a couple of cheaply laminated menus from the stand in the centre of the table and passed one to Mal, who took it with a smile and a brush of fingers that Jory was almost certain was deliberate.

Almost. He looked down at his menu quickly.

"Now, what I want to know," Mal said with an air of significance that had Jory tensing up automatically, "is, are you eating? Cos I don't want to sit here stuffing my face while you try and make an espresso last half an hour."

"I had half a slice of toast for breakfast several hours ago, so yes, I'm eating." He'd woken up early and been unable to either get back to sleep or force much food down. Nerves.

Sometimes he envied Bea's way of remaining untroubled by strong emotion.

"In that case, the full Cornish sounds good to me." Mal shoved his menu back in the stand.

Jory did likewise, and managed to catch the waitress's eye so he could give their order.

"You don't know her?" he asked a few minutes later, as she bustled away from them. She was a pretty girl, with bleached-blonde hair up in a doughnut on top of her head. It made her look curiously doll-like, and her ivory-and-pink makeup seemed designed to accentuate the impression of unreal perfection. Her name tag had read *Aurora*.

"What, her? Never met her before. Why?"

"Oh—I thought maybe she was a friend of your . . . friend's friend. The one you said used to work here." Jory frowned. Put like that, the connection seemed embarrassingly tenuous.

"You mean Ceri? Nah, she ain't got a lot of friends round here." Mal, who'd been fiddling with his phone, turned back to Jory and grinned. "Why, you fancy her or something?"

"What? No. I, um, I don't really . . ." The heat was rising in Jory's cheeks, and he hated it. "I'm not looking for a girlfriend."

"No? Nah, you're probably right." Mal's voice was off-hand as he flicked through messages on his phone. "I'd be shit-scared she'd bite my balls off if I messed up her hair."

Jory swallowed. Did Mal realise the sort of imagery he was conjuring up? Was he doing it on purpose? Jory wasn't sure how to respond.

And then he didn't have to.

"Well, fancy meeting you here," a familiar voice said in ringing tones that had half the occupants of the café turning to stare.

Jory's stomach lurched. Kirsty was beaming down at him. She was alone, which was the smallest of mercies. Her hair was up in a headscarf, wrapped African style, and she was wearing a pair of voluminous harem pants printed with brightly coloured elephants. Her shoulder bag looked like she'd crocheted it, possibly while drunk, and incorporated little mirrors that caught the light and flung it back at him, accusingly.

Oh God, why now? This was *terrible* timing. "Kirsty. Hi. Um. Yes. Fancy." Jory cringed internally at himself.

Kirsty pulled out a chair with an obnoxious scrape on the ground, and sat down. "So who's your mate?"

"Oh, this is, um, Mal." Jory swallowed.

Kirsty leaned forward on the table and smiled up at him. "Mal? Now, would that be short for Malachi, Malcolm, Malik . . . or something I haven't thought of?"

"More fun to keep you guessing, innit?" Mal, who didn't seem the slightest bit bothered by her appearance, flashed her a wink that left Jory feeling even less at ease. "So how do you know Jory, then?"

"Me?" she said with an easy smile. "I'm his missus. Been married twelve years, we have."

CHAPTER SIX

M al had had half his mind on how he was going to answer his latest text from Dev, and if he ought to mention meeting Jory just in case Tasha did. He hadn't thought twice when the woman had joined them.

Well, all right, maybe he had. Stuff like, *Huh, she's not what I'd have expected one of Jory's mates to be like.* And, *So how come he ain't that pleased to see her?*

Then she dropped her bombshell, and it was like, *What the actual, literal, honest-to-God fuck?*

He stared at her.

She made a face. "Aw, you're gonna be one of those blokes who don't go for married women, aren't you?"

"We're separated," Jory blurted out, loud and awkward and all red in the face, and shit, this woman really *was* his missus, wasn't she?

Mal stood up, cos while there were some things you could deal with on an empty stomach, finding out the bloke you fancied—even if you'd been trying not to on account of reasons—who you'd spent the whole morning talking to about childhood and families and all that shit, had somehow forgotten to mention he was sodding well *married* was not one of them.

Kirsty stood up too. "Oh my God, were you two on a date? Oh my God. Fucked that right up, didn't I? Seriously, though, who goes on a date at eleven o'clock in the morning? Oh my God, it's a morning after, innit? Jory, you sly shit. You never told me you were seeing someone."

Okay, so yeah, that fit with the whole *separated* thing, but why the hell hadn't Jory just *told* him about her?

"It's not— We're not seeing each other," Jory said, looking so bloody miserable Mal almost started feeling sorry for him. Bastard.

She arched an eyebrow. "Uh-*huh*?" If the sarcasm had come any thicker, they could've slapped it on a scone and served it with a nice cup of tea.

"It's…complicated," Jory told the table, cos he still wasn't meeting Mal's gaze.

"Too fucking right it is," Mal had to agree. He wasn't sure whether to sit down again or just get out of this mess, but then the waitress turned up with a couple of piled-up plates of full Cornish breakfast. His stomach decided it was giving the orders, and his bum hit the seat before his brain could get a word in edgewise.

"Will you be eating too?" the waitress asked Kirsty.

"Oh no. I'm out of here. You two have a good time. Jory, I'll catch you later." She hitched her bag up on her shoulder and walked off.

Jory was staring down at his plate as if he was worried another ex-wife was going to jump out from behind a slice of bacon and shout, *Surprise!*

"So, anything else you forgot to mention to me?" Mal asked, then tucked into his food, just in case this all went even more tits up and he ended up walking out before they'd finished.

Not that he'd, like, had any experience of that sort of thing happening.

Jory's face was defeated when he finally met Mal's gaze, and when he spoke, his tone matched it. "You mean, apart from the fact I'm married with a child?"

Mal choked on his sausage. "You got a kid?"

"Gawen. He's twelve."

"Bloody hell." *Twelve?* She hadn't been joking about how long they'd been together.

It was well weird when Jory answered the thought. "We're not together—we never have been."

"Uh, yeah, mate. See, that don't exactly fit in with the whole having-a-kid thing. Way I've heard it, that usually takes at least a little bit of togetherness. And yeah, married? This ain't 1950, and she don't look like the sort who's got a dad with a shotgun."

"No, that was Bran."

"Seriously? Your big bruv came over all big brother on you?" Then Mal's brain finally managed to do the sums. "Hang about, how flippin' old were you twelve years ago?"

"Nineteen. Kirsty was twenty-one." Jory pushed a fried egg around his plate. The yolk broke and started to spill all over the white. "I was in my first year at uni, and I met her when I was home for the holidays."

"You mean 'met' as in 'shagged,' don't you?" Mal threw up a hand at Jory's flinch. "Nah, don't tell me. None of my beeswax, innit?"

"Yes, it is." Jory's eyes were wide, and his gaze fixed on Mal. His expression was open, honest, and vulnerable all at the same time, and it did weird things to Mal's insides. "I should have told you."

Yeah, he should have. Except . . . should he? Because if they were just . . . just two blokes, going for breakfast together (and the voice inside Mal that said *When does that ever happen if it ain't a date?* could just fuck off right now, yeah?), it shouldn't matter if he was married, divorced, or living in poly bliss with the entire cast of the latest Pirelli girlie calendar.

Which meant . . . Jory must've thought this was a date. Or he'd wanted it to be one.

Mal wasn't sure how he felt about that. He'd been working bloody hard to flip the mental switch from *bloke I want to shag* to *Dev's long-lost uncle.* All that stuff with Jory in his bedroom had been doing a number on his head, not to mention other bits, but he'd thought he was safe once they got out in the open. And okay, yeah, he'd been having a bit of a tease when they'd talked about the waitress, but that had just . . . That had just been passing the time, that had.

Kind of.

"So tell me about it now," he said, cos at least if he got Jory talking, that'd give him time to think.

"There's not much to tell. We . . . I . . . They were having a party down on the beach, the one below our house. Kirsty and her friends. Although to be honest, I think she'd only just met them . . . Anyway, I went for a walk, and she invited me to join them."

"Got you pissed and had her wicked way with you behind the beach huts?"

Jory winced. "Behind the lifeboat station, actually. It was a couple of years before they built the new one." He must have caught Mal's *WTF?* look. "The old slipway wasn't on stilts, like the new one. So. More cover. I think. I don't remember it all very well."

His face was so red it made his hair and beard stand out bright blond in contrast, reminding Mal of some old negatives his mum had shown him once from back when she was young and people had taken photos with actual cameras with film in them. Mal felt bad for him but, well, he was supposed to be vetting the bloke, wasn't he? To see if he was the sort of uncle Dev would want to get to know.

Shit. His kid was Dev's *cousin*. Dev wasn't going to want to let that go, was he? Despite the fact that he had about fifty of them on his dad's side. The Malakars, up in Sheffield. Dev had been up there and met half of them, and he'd said they were all welcoming and that. Even his dad's missus, who might have been a bit pissed off about proof that her husband had been shagging around when they'd been as good as engaged, had cooked Dev a big meal and told him to visit anytime.

He'd been a bit quiet when he came back home, though. Showed Mal a couple of pics of him and his half brothers, who were all younger than him and doing really well in school. When Mal said how much they looked like him, he went even quieter.

Mal hadn't wanted to push him on it, but . . . it'd been like when they'd been at school, him and Dev, and he'd come round to Mal's for tea. Mum had always done her best to make him feel welcome, but Dev had always been sad afterwards. Maybe it wasn't the same, but it had sort of reminded Mal of when he'd been little and had dreams he could talk to his rats, like properly talk to them and understand what they said, and sometimes even be their size and go on adventures with them. And then he'd woken up and remembered he couldn't. He'd always felt a bit flat for the rest of the day.

"I'm not doing a very good job of persuading you to trust me, am I?" Jory said. "I'm sorry."

Mal realised he must have been silent too long. "Just . . . it's a lot to take in, yeah? So tell me about your kid. Gow—uh, Gavin?"

"Gawen. It's an old Cornish name." Jory smiled, looking genuinely happy for the first time since Kirsty had left them. "He's great. Brilliant, in fact. Already doing GCSE standard maths. The school wants him to take his exams early."

Great. Another perfect cousin for Dev. He was going to love that.

"So how's it work with you and his mum? You're not living together, right?"

"No. She has her own house. That was part of the deal."

"'The deal'?"

"Bran offered her a house in Porthkennack and financial support, in exchange for her agreeing to legitimise Gawen." Jory stared out across the street. "So we got married, and then I went back to university."

Mal laughed. "Bet your mates were surprised."

"Nobody there ever knew."

Okay, so now he wasn't laughing any longer. "So it's always been your dirty little secret?"

"It's not . . ." Jory made a jerky gesture and knocked over the brown sauce. It landed on the edge of Mal's plate with a clatter of jumping cutlery. "Oh God. I'm so sorry."

He sounded wrecked.

"Hey, chill, bruv. No harm done. I get it, yeah? You were young, you didn't wanna let it cramp your style."

"That's not . . . I was ashamed of myself."

Mal looked at him sharply. "For sticking your dick where you shouldn't of? Mate, we've all been there. It's part of being a bloke, innit? The little head wants what it wants."

"For . . . for lots of things."

Jory didn't seem to want to go into details, which was fair enough. Mal had another bite of sausage while he thought about what to say next.

Jory beat him to it. "I hope this hasn't changed the way you feel about me getting to know Dev."

Had it? Mal wasn't sure. Except, yeah, he really was. "Nah, it's okay. But that's it, innit? You ain't got no more kids stashed away somewhere?"

"No. I can say that with the utmost certainty."

Translation: Kirsty's was the only vag he'd ever shagged. Well, either that or he had shares in a major condom company. Mal grinned, and it was only a little bit forced. "Then we're golden. You gonna eat that?" He pointed at the toasty-brown slice of hog's pudding Jory had left untouched on his plate.

"Uh, no. Feel free."

"Cheers." Mal slid it onto his own plate. "Ain't had this since I was down here last year staying at Mrs. Quick's B&B. I keep trying to get Tash to cook some, but she says she's trying to save my arteries from myself."

"Tash . . . She's Dev's sister, you said?"

"Yeah. Well, foster sister. They ain't blood. Been through a lot together, though."

"What made her move down here?"

"Liked it, I guess. And she had a bit of grief with the last place she was living, so . . ." Mal shrugged. He wasn't going to mention Ceri. That was Tasha's business, not his and Jory's.

"Landlord not maintaining the place properly?"

Mal had to laugh. "Something like that." But not very. He finished up the hog's pudding with his last bit of fried egg, then put his cutlery together on the plate. "You working today?" Maybe Jory could show him around the local history archive, help him dig out some stuff about Pirate Mary.

"No. The museum's closed today."

Bollocks. Maybe not, then. "So what do you do on your days off?"

"It depends."

"On?"

"On whether I've got company or not." Jory gave him a direct gaze.

Mal appreciated that. "Let's say you have, then. What'd you fancy getting up to?"

"If I had company, it'd be up to my guest."

Mal bit his tongue before he could blurt out, *Right, shagging it is, then*, because seriously, did his dick have it in for the rest of him or what? "What's the castle round here like?" he said instead. "Worth a look?"

"It's . . . okay. It's not Tintagel, though."

"I've always wanted to visit there," Mal said with a pang. "Come on, who wouldn't want to see the actual place where King Arthur's dad got his mum up the duff with him?"

"While he was magically disguised as her hours-dead husband. I feel I ought to point out that the historicity is a little suspect."

Mal could picture the bloke in front of a class of students, one eyebrow raised and with a funny, sceptical twist to his mouth just like now. He must give great lectures. "Yeah, yeah, I know. And the castle was built a few hundred years too late. But it's s'posed to be really atmospheric. Inspiring, and all." He tried not to sound too sad about it, but to be honest he was gutted at finally being so near the place and with no means of getting there.

"Why don't we go, then?" Jory said. "Today. It's only about an hour's drive from here. Well, in the winter it is. Maybe a bit more if there's traffic. Um. Maybe it'd be better to make an early start tomorrow."

Mal almost laughed at the way Jory's voice started out all enthusiastic and then trailed off, but he was too busy fighting the hope that had surged up in him. "Yeah, but, whatever day we go it's gonna take most of the day, innit? You've got to have stuff to do." He wasn't sure if he was protesting to be polite or . . . because of the other thing. But whatever it was, it came out sounding pretty unconvincing.

"I'm not working tomorrow either, and Gawen will be at school. There's nothing else I need to be doing." Jory took a deep breath. "I'd love to take you there. I'll be happy to drive, unless you'd rather?"

Mal avoided his eye. "Nah, I, uh, left my car in London. Flew in to Newquay."

"Oh? Most people prefer to have transport available while on holiday in Cornwall." Jory shrugged. "Trains and buses can only take you so far."

"Dev told me about the planes. It ain't a bad service." Mal swallowed, and went for it. "So, uh, yeah, we could take your car."

Jory, who'd been frowning more and more as Mal spouted that load of disjointed bollocks, broke out into a smile. "That's great."

Mal couldn't help smiling back, even if it did feel a bit wonky. He'd be fine. Honest.

And tomorrow was another day. It was, like, famous for it, even. "Right, so that's settled, then," Mal babbled on. "So how about we have a butcher's at the local one today, so we'll have something to compare it to?"

Jory beamed. "Why not?"

CHAPTER SEVEN

The waitress came with the bill at that point, which was a fair hint that if they weren't going to order something else, they should cease and desist squatting on prime café real estate. Jory ignored Mal's protests and paid, leaving a generous tip because the poor girl didn't look like she enjoyed her job over-much.

Had there been something odd in Mal's manner just now? Jory wasn't sure—if there had been, he seemed to have fully regained his equilibrium as they walked away from the café, cracking a joke about how the British on holiday always seemed way more British than usual.

"Maybe that's why we go abroad," Jory suggested. "To be confirmed in our Britishness. Innate nostalgia for the days of empire."

Mal gave him a raised eyebrow. "Nah, mate. Us Brits go abroad to get a tan, get wasted, and get laid."

"It can't be both?"

"Course not. Who wants to multitask on their holidays? Me, I don't even wanna uni-task."

"Or as most people would say, *task*. If they were in the habit of using nouns as verbs." Jory tried not to wince at himself. Next he'd be pulling Mal up on incorrect usage of *who* versus *whom*.

Mal just grinned. "You got a problem with nouning?"

Jory *did* wince then.

Mal burst out laughing. "Lemme guess, you're the sort of bloke whose *sexts* have, like, commas and capital letters in 'em."

Jory barely stopped himself from saying, *You'll just have to wait and see.* Appalled at the near miss, he bit his lip hard, in case the words somehow spilled out anyway. Christ, how did Mal have this effect on him? He was supposed to be trying to convince the man he was capable of being an upright, decent uncle, and he'd thoroughly blotted his copybook once already. And that was just this morning.

Jory was glad when they got caught up in a cluster of meandering tourists who ambled along the side streets and dawdled by every shop window. It made conversation difficult, saving him from any further faux pas.

When they finally broke free from the town crowd and set out upon the coastal path, he felt all the more exposed for it.

Mal stopped to stare far out to sea, hands on his hips like a fishwife. "It's weird, innit?" he said after a moment. "You live in a city, you forget how fucking big the world is." He spun to face Jory, eyes bright with sudden enthusiasm in one of his mercurial changes of mood. "If you could, I dunno, teleport or something, anywhere in the world, where would you go?"

"Right now?" Captivated, Jory couldn't think of anywhere he'd rather be than here, with Mal.

But he could hardly say that.

"I don't know," he hedged. "There are so many places I'd like to see. What about you?"

"Petra," Mal said without hesitation. "You know, that city or temple or whatever in Jordan they carved out of rock like two thousand years ago. I've always wanted to go there ever since I saw it in *Indiana Jones*. And yeah, I know there ain't actual Grail knights there, but fuck it, that place don't even need 'em. You been?"

"No, but I'd like to one day." *With you*, Jory was careful not to add. "Um. Shall we get on?"

They walked along the path, their hair blown by the sea breeze and the sun hot on their shoulders. At least, Jory walked. Mal seemed to alternate between a relaxed amble and a sudden lunge as his attention was caught—by a view, a flower, or a spot where the cliff edge had crumbled, as might be. For the latter, he'd sidle towards it with a sort of nervous bravado, stay an instant, then dart back to the path, pride apparently satisfied. As if he'd fought the cliff and won.

When they came to the Round Hole, one of the local sights, Jory expected a lengthy detour, but Mal made as if to walk straight past, ignoring it.

"Don't you want to take a look?" Jory asked.

"Seen it. Twice. Dev's got a thing about that hole." Mal grinned. "Dunno if it's the size"—the hole was easily a hundred feet across—"or the way you get seawater spurting out. Either way, I reckon it's a metaphor."

"I can't imagine what for." Jory answered Mal's smile with one of his own.

For a moment their gaze held and seemed to communicate something shared. Something intimate. Then Mal's expression faltered, and he stared out to sea once more. "Can I ask you a question?" He went on without waiting for permission. "Earlier, when we were in the caff, you said you were, like, ashamed of yourself?"

Technically, that wasn't a question, but it still dropped a lead weight into Jory's stomach. The silence lengthened as he tried to muster an answer that wouldn't show him in a bad light.

Then he thought, *To hell with it*, and just told the truth. "I had this stupid idea that if I could sleep with Kirsty, I could be straight. Or, you know, straight enough." He wasn't going to admit the most embarrassing part—that he'd have slept with her anyway, simply because she'd so clearly wanted him, and he'd been so desperately unused to that.

Mal gave him a baffled look. "What's the big deal about being straight?"

Jory felt a stab of envy so sharp it was a physical pain in his chest. "Being gay . . . It was just another way I was different."

"From who?"

"From everyone. Oh . . ." Jory turned away, completely unable to meet Mal's gaze as he spoke. "The usual teenage angst, really. School was . . . difficult. I wasn't sporty, and I wasn't loud, or confident."

"Yeah, but you're, what, six one? Six two? Can't see a bloke your size getting picked on." Mal's tone was soft. Sympathetic, despite his words.

"You didn't see me at age seven. I was the shortest boy in the class until I was fourteen. Apart from Clemens, who had dwarfism. And still managed to be about twice my weight. And better at rugby."

Mal laughed. "Bastard. So what happened? You just shot up one summer? That must've been well cool."

Not as much as you'd think. Jory didn't answer.

"What?" Mal prompted. "No, seriously, didn't you go back and they were all like, 'Whoa, easy dude, you keep your lunch money'?"

"We didn't have lunch money. It was a boarding school." One glance at Mal, and Jory could hear him thinking, *Oi, mate, stop stalling me.* "It . . . didn't make it easier at home."

"Why not?"

"You haven't met Bran, have you? He and Bea take after Father—dark haired, and on the short side. I'm a bit of a throwback to an earlier generation." Jory caught Mal's look and shrugged. "Suddenly his little brother was towering over him. Who's going to like that? And later on . . . Bran's always had a strong sense of responsibility."

"What, he felt like you being taller was threatening his authority or something? Jeez, issues, much?"

"I don't know, really. Maybe it wasn't that at all. We never have got on particularly well. And I'm sure he was only doing what he thought was best for the family." Jory tried, but couldn't keep the bitterness out of his voice.

"Meaning, not what was best for you, right?"

"He had a point, though. Gay people face discrimination, even nowadays. Even in this country."

"Yeah, but you still gotta live your life. The only reason things are as good as they are now is cos of people who stood up for themselves and didn't hide in the closet."

"Oh, I know that now. Back when I was in my teens . . ." Jory closed his eyes briefly. Christ, he'd been so young. "Would you believe, I actually suggested to Kirsty that we try to make a go of it for real?"

Mal barked out a laugh. "Yeah? How'd that go down?"

"She told me to eff off and find myself a nice boyfriend. She said it kindly, though," he added quickly. He didn't want to give Mal the wrong idea about her.

"Has she had other blokes? Or, you know, birds? Whatever floats her boat."

"Not many. She's very protective of Gawen. But there have been lovers—although none of them have lasted long."

"So no one likely to get pissed off about you?"

"Not anyone that I've heard of."

"What about you? You must've had a few flings at uni."

Must he have? Jory remembered his undergraduate years mostly as a time of keeping his head down and his nose in a book, still reeling from unexpected fatherhood. "There was someone," he admitted. "Rafi. Up in Edinburgh. We were together for nearly three years."

"Three years? Blimey, that's practically married and all. But you split up? What happened?"

"Gawen was having trouble at school. Being bullied." And there was no way Jory would leave him to deal with that on his own. Not when Jory had first-hand experience of what it was like, to go into school every day and be made to feel utterly worthless. "Kirsty was worried about him. I needed to be here."

"And this Rafi bloke didn't want to come with you?"

Jory half shrugged, half just slumped. "It would have been career suicide. I mean, look at me: working part-time in a museum nobody visits. I hear he's accepted a post as a professor in America."

It had been more complicated than that, of course. Things always were. Jory hadn't suspected how much Rafi had resented him not getting divorced from Kirsty, but it had all come out in their final, bitter row. How Rafi had been sick and tired of making excuses to his mother for why they didn't get married, spending weekends alone while Jory visited his wife and child, and listening to his friends tell him Jory would never commit to him and he should move on. If only he'd *said* something . . . There had been a time when Jory would have done anything Rafi wanted him to. But he'd never asked.

When the end had come, it had all been too late, and they'd both said too much that couldn't be unheard.

Jory startled as a warm arm slipped around his shoulders. Meant as comfort, he realised even as every muscle in his body tensed. He drew in a breath—

—but Mal was already backing off. "Whoa, sorry, dude. So, uh, hey, I think I can see the castle from here? We oughtta get going."

He loped off down the path, leaving Jory to curse himself and follow.

Jory had seen Caerdu Castle many times before, of course. One of the things he'd missed out on by being sent away to boarding school was the annual educational trip there that almost all the local schools seemed to organise, so for a few years, he'd made a point of going there by himself every summer.

He'd thought the place had nothing new to offer him. And strictly speaking, it didn't—but what was new was seeing it through Mal's eyes, and his imagination. Mal climbed every crumbling wall—even the ones with *Keep Off* notices on them—and staged mock sword fights on the fragments of spiral staircases that remained.

Apparently his wariness of heights didn't kick in until above second-storey level. Jory couldn't help but be drawn in, finding himself somehow in the role of French invader fighting against Mal's valiant Cornish defender. As they were armed only with imaginary swords, it might have been a little hard to tell who was winning, were it not for Mal's spirited narration that made it clear that the Cornishman had the upper hand. Jory spat out half-remembered Old French insults and, finally, staggered back to die supine on the rough grass, having been disarmed and run through by Mal's nonexistent weapon.

A smattering of applause made Jory open his eyes. He looked up to see a small crowd of fascinated children and their laughing parents, some of them filming him with their mobile phones. Mal was taking a bow with a courtly flourish.

For a moment, the embarrassment was paralysing—Bran would be *livid* if he found out Jory was making a spectacle of himself like this—then Jory thought, *To hell with it*, and stood up to take his own bow.

"Do I wanna know what you were calling me?" Mal asked as they walked off, grinning like idiots, to take a breather.

"Uh . . ." Jory was glad he'd expunged *fils a putan* from his limited vocabulary of insults. "Gluttonous, base evildoer. That sort of thing."

They sat down side by side in the shade of the highest wall of the castle, and Jory resolutely didn't stare as Mal lifted the hem of his T-shirt to wipe his forehead.

"'Gluttonous'? Hey, that ain't fair. I *asked* if you wanted that hog's pudding." Mal nudged Jory with his shoulder.

It was a companionable gesture, nothing more. Jory knew that. He couldn't help the way it made him want to lean into the contact, though.

Maybe Mal wouldn't mind? Would welcome it, even? Maybe—

Mal stood up. "So, uh, yeah. 'S been great. Think I'd better . . . I'll see you tomorrow, right? If you're still up for it? Cheers."

And he was gone before Jory could work out what had just happened.

CHAPTER EIGHT

Mal was an idiot. A total, gormless prick-led *idiot*.

He lay on his bed, hot and sweaty from practically running back to the Sea Bell, and screamed into his pillow. Really quietly, so Tash wouldn't hear and want to know what was up.

That look on Jory's face, when they'd been sat down together . . . Mal had been *this close* to leaning in and kissing him, and that would've arsed things up good and proper, wouldn't it? Imagine explaining that one to Dev. *Yeah, mate, I met your uncle. And fucked him.*

Yeah, that'd go down so well. Especially when Mal mentioned what'd happened next, what would *have* to happen next, which would be Jory finding out what a fuckup Mal was these days, ever since the thing at work, and backing off so far he'd be halfway to America to join his ex. There was literally no good way Mal could explain himself. *Oh, yeah, soz mate, turns out I'm a total head case and I lied about my job, but you still wanna go out with me, right? Right?*

Jory would decide he should've listened to his brother all along, and tell Mal *and* Dev to piss off.

Except . . . Mal stood up and stared out of his window at that spot he'd seen Jory only this morning. He couldn't believe Jory would be like that. Yeah, not wanting Mal once he knew the truth, that was a given . . . but punishing Dev for it too? He wouldn't do that.

Jory was a decent bloke. So he hadn't mentioned the missus and the kid, so what? He'd have got round to it eventually, most like.

Which was more than Mal could say for his own nasty little secret . . .

Shit.

Mal threw himself back down on the bed. He should never have agreed to go out tomorrow with Jory. Maybe he should call and cancel . . . Bollocks. They hadn't even swapped phone numbers. Of course, he could always call directory enquiries and get the number for Roscarrock House. Mal laughed bitterly, imagining how that conversation would go. *Hi, is that Bran Roscarrock? Yeah, I'm Dev's mate, calling for your bruv . . . Hello? Hello?*

Was it going to happen anyhow, them meeting up? They hadn't said when, or where. That *See you tomorrow* was a fucking classic, that was.

Mal sat up, bolt upright. Jesus, how could he have been so stupid, leaving it like that? At this rate, he was never going to see Jory again . . .

But hadn't that been what he'd wanted like thirty seconds ago? Mal slumped back down on the pillows, except he misjudged the angle and banged his head on the headboard on the way down. And that was just aces, wasn't it?

At least the throbbing headache took his mind off the dull pain in his chest.

There was a thundering knock on the door, and Mal sat up again, startled.

"Oi, Mal? You all right?"

Shit. Tasha. "'M fine. What do you want?"

"Nothing. 'Cept, there was this really loud bang, and before that your bed was creaking. Like, a *lot*. Oi, you're not shagging someone in there, are you?"

Christ, chance'd be a fine thing. "No! I . . . Didn't sleep well last night."

"Maybe you should try doing a bit of work, then. Tire you out for tonight. Instead of buggering off all day without telling anyone where you were going." Even muffled by the closed bedroom door, that last bit sounded narked.

Mal sighed. "Who died and made you my mum? I'll be out in a mo, and I'll come and give you a hand downstairs."

There was a pause. "You don't have to. Not if you're feeling—"

"I'm *fine*. See you in a mo."

Mal unloaded and reloaded the dishwasher, wiped down tables, and restocked the fridges, and he actually felt a little better afterwards. Which was kind of depressing, cos no offence to Tash but he really hoped that working in a pub wasn't going to turn out to be his vocation. His mum and dad would be paranoid that he'd end up like his uncle Bob.

"So what did you get up to today?" Tasha asked during a quiet spot at the bar.

"Got breakfast in a caff, then checked out the castle."

"Yeah? Bit boring, innit? Just a load of old stones."

"Just a 'load of old stones'? Lemme guess, if you'd been in charge of planning, they'd have run the A303 right through the middle of Stonehenge."

Tasha grinned. "Well, yeah. All they'd have to do is widen a couple of the arches, and you could literally drive through it. It'd be dead cool." She squealed and ducked as Mal threw a bar towel at her.

"Now then, we'll have none of that," old Jago rumbled from his stool down the other end of the bar, where he'd been holding court again.

"Sorry." Mal shrugged. "What can you do? She's got no respect for ancient monuments, this girl."

Jago frowned. "Now, that's not true. She always speaks very politely to Charlie here." He nodded to one of the locals, a toothless old geezer who always made a pint last out the night.

Charlie looked up and smiled. "That's right. Lovely girl."

How Jago kept his face straight Mal would never know, cos him and Tash were pissing themselves laughing.

Of course, as soon as Mal got in bed that night, the doubts returned. Shit. What was he going to do tomorrow?

One thing was for certain—it'd be too risky to wait in for Jory to turn up here. They'd got away with it once, but twice would be chancing it. No, he'd have to ... What? Turn up at Roscarrock House?

Bollocks. Maybe he could, like, camp out on the cliff just outside? In disguise? Maybe there was an army surplus store around here where he could get some camo gear? Mal grinned into his pillow. Full-body armour would be pretty handy and all, in case Bran saw him. And a rocket launcher.

But what was he going to even say to Jory?

Shit. Mal stuck his head under his pillow and desperately hoped that his subconscious was on the case.

CHAPTER NINE

A s he walked along the cliff path that skirted Mother Ivey's Bay the following morning, Jory asked himself what on earth he thought he was doing. Was he going to just march into the Sea Bell and ask to speak to Mal?

Well, it'd probably be the best opportunity he'd get to witness an angry mob at close quarters. Not to mention the last.

And why the hell hadn't he brought the car, anyway?

He knew the answer to that one, at least. Because if he'd brought the car, it would have looked as though he was blithely expecting today's excursion to Tintagel to go ahead, and that was far from the truth. In fact, he wasn't at all sure Mal was even planning to speak to him, yesterday's *See you tomorrow* notwithstanding.

He'd racked his brains overnight, trying to work out what he'd done wrong, and come to one inescapable conclusion: Mal knew how Jory felt about him.

And he didn't reciprocate.

It was a bitter pill, but if he wanted any kind of relationship with his nephew, Jory was going to have to choke it down.

Seagulls swooped and cried, and for a moment, Jory envied them. Things were so simple for them. None of this agonising about whether the object of their affection liked them back: all they had to do was walk up to a bird they fancied, show off their dance moves, and get either accepted or rejected.

Then again, Jory had zero confidence in his dancing skills as a human, and he couldn't imagine webbed feet making an improvement.

He was aware of the tall, lean shape approaching him along the path for a long while before he had any idea who it was, but gradually the form and features resolved into someone familiar.

Jory's heart clenched almost painfully, and he half stumbled.

It was Mal, walking straight towards him.

Jory fought to keep his pace from becoming unnaturally fast or slow. It was extraordinarily difficult when he felt so under scrutiny. So much for dancing—he seemed to have forgotten how to walk.

"I wanted to apologise," he said when they'd finally met, before Mal could open his mouth. "I think I made you feel uncomfortable, yesterday. I'm sorry."

"What?" Mal looked, if anything, even *more* uncomfortable now. "Nah, mate, it's just . . . I was just having an off day. Too much sun. Or something. I oughtta be apologising to you. You know. For running off like that."

"No, not at all." So they were going to pretend Mal hadn't noticed Jory's unrequited crush on him. Jory could do that. Would *have* to do that if they were to remain friends, and although it might not be what he wanted, it was the best option in the circumstances. "Um. So, er, what did you want to do about today? Do you still want to go to Tintagel?"

Mal hesitated, shoving his hands in his jeans pockets and hunching his shoulders up tight, as if he were trying to squeeze a decision out by force.

"We don't have to," Jory said quickly, his heart sinking. Perhaps *friends* wasn't an option after all. "It was just a thought. I'm sure you've got—"

"No," Mal cut him off. "I mean, yeah. We should go. That is, I want to. If you want to?"

He still didn't look precisely happy, but Christ, Jory was only human. "I'd love to. Um. We'll have to walk back up for my car."

Mal let out a long breath, his shoulders relaxing. "That's cool."

Jory turned, and they walked a few paces up the path in silence while Jory desperately tried to think of what to say.

Mal beat him to it. "So, have you read like all the Arthurian legends? Like Geoffrey of Monmouth, and that French geezer, and the rest of 'em?"

As olive branches went, it was quite a fruitful one, and Jory accepted it gratefully. "I haven't dipped into Chrétien de Troyes or the Vulgate Cycle since my undergraduate days, to tell you the truth.

Or the Mabinogion, for that matter. But Geoffrey, yes. You're familiar with his *Histories of the Kings of Britain*?"

"Uh . . . I wouldn't go that far. But I've read the Arthur bits." Mal smiled, for the first time this morning. "Crazy to think he was writing about Tintagel, like, a thousand years ago and we're going there today."

A weight lifted from Jory's shoulders. It was obvious this trip meant a lot to Mal, and despite everything, Jory felt absurdly privileged to be sharing it with him.

"Have you read Tennyson's *Idylls of the King*?" he asked as they walked on, long strides eating up the distance between them and Roscarrock House.

"Nah, Tennyson, that's poetry, innit? 'Wandering lonely as a cloud' and all that bollocks. I never really got on with that stuff at school."

"Most people don't. Honestly, I'm not sure what the schools are doing, but they seem to be rather good at turning out young adults with a hatred of poetry these days. And the cloud one was Wordsworth, in fact. But if you can manage Malory, you should be fine with Tennyson. It's more of a narrative than a poem." Jory darted him a glance. "Which is not to say you should read them if you don't want to. Sorry. I keep forgetting I'm not actually a lecturer these days."

"Do you miss it?"

"God, yes." Jory hadn't meant it to come out sounding so heartfelt. He sighed. "I miss the atmosphere, and people interested in knowledge for its own sake."

"Museum job not cutting it?"

"It'd be better if the visitor numbers were higher."

"Yeah, you need to put the fun back into that place. Play up the whole smuggling thing." Mal flashed him a wicked smile. "Dress up as a pirate and shiver yer timbers at everyone."

Jory snorted. "I think I'd be a bit of a disappointment to kids reared on Captain Jack Sparrow."

"Nah, don't do yourself down. You'd be great. Go on, gimme your best 'Arr, Jim lad.'" Mal walked backwards for a few paces, gazing at him expectantly.

"Ah. Jim lad." Jory deliberately made his voice sound as BBC English as he could.

Mal burst out laughing and almost tripped over his feet before turning to walk normally. "Maybe not, then. Or you could always tank up on rum first."

"I've actually been thinking about a mermaid exhibit," Jory said, warming to the subject. "We could incorporate local and foreign legends, and I'm pretty sure I can get my hands on a genuine Fiji mermaid."

"Uh. You know mermaids ain't real, right?"

Jory laughed, relief that they were back on a friendly footing making him light-headed. "Genuine in this case means 'really made from the front half of a stuffed monkey sewn to the back end of a salmon.'"

"Fuck me, that sounds well gross." Mal grinned. "Kids'll love it."

"I like the idea of reclaiming the old image of the mermaid as something to be feared, rather than cutesy little teens singing under the sea. The Sirens of Greece, who actually started out as birds, would wreck ships by luring sailors onto the rocks, and mermaids were generally seen as a bad omen. And there's the story of the malevolent merrow, who kept the souls of drowned fishermen in a cage under the sea. Although that one is supposedly apocryphal. Ah, just a fiction." Oh God. Jory wasn't sure what was worse about what he'd just said: that he'd used words Mal might not know, or that he'd insisted on explaining them and thus making it perfectly clear that he thought Mal wouldn't understand.

Mal's smile didn't falter, though. "Aaand again, I'm thinking we gotta have a discussion about what's real and what ain't."

Jory laughed. "Just because you haven't seen something, that doesn't mean it doesn't exist."

"Yeah, and just cos you *have* seen it doesn't mean you shouldn't lay off the alcohol. Or the wacky 'baccy. Or the shrooms. Whatever floats your psychedelic boat, man."

Jory sighed. "Why is all the rum gone?" he asked in what was undoubtedly a terrible impersonation of Jack Sparrow.

Mal laughed anyway, but his smile faded as they reached Roscarrock House. "Sure we ain't gonna bump into your sister or brother here?"

"We'll be fine. Bea's at work, and Bran will be in his study." Jory hoped. "And we don't need to go in the house."

He led the way around the side of the house, unable to stop himself from casting a guilty glance around as they stepped over the low chain that separated the public area of the garden from the private one. Cars were now housed in what had once been the stables—Bea's BMW was absent as expected, but Bran's car, which was almost identical to hers, was parked next to Jory's Fiat Qubo.

Jory gestured at it. "This is mine." He managed to stop himself from adding *Sorry*.

Mal seemed, unsurprisingly, to be struggling to find something positive to say.

Jory put him out of his misery. "I know, it's ugly. It's basically a van in a dress. But I got a good deal on it from a colleague who was leaving the country, and I like the extra head and leg room."

"What? No, it's, uh, they're great little cars, ain't they? I got a Focus, myself, but I left it in London."

"Yes, you said."

"Oh. Sorry."

What had just happened? The easy mood from earlier had been blown away like the spray on the waves, to be replaced with a crushing awkwardness.

Maybe Mal really hated Fiats? Or had realised, on seeing the Qubo, precisely what sort of man he was with? Jory suddenly wished he'd paid more attention to which cars were considered cool. "Um, shall we?"

"Right. Yeah." Mal climbed in and buckled his seat belt. Jory did likewise and then started the engine.

From Roscarrock House, it was an open road until they reached the outskirts of Harlyn, a nearby town with its own beach and, therefore, its own surfeit of tourists.

Mal's conversation had dropped to monosyllables. He fidgeted with his seat belt and opened the window. Maybe he suffered from travel sickness?

They dawdled along the high street through the centre of Harlyn. Jory had avoided the esplanade, thinking progress there would be slower, but he might have saved himself the trouble. Even this early in

July, the road was full of people driving at holiday pace—God knew what it would be like in a few weeks' time when the schools broke up. Jory made sure to keep an eye on the tourists thronging the pavements in case any of them should forget that this particular street wasn't pedestrianised.

He tried to keep the conversation going, but Mal still didn't seem keen to talk. Had he changed his mind, decided the trip was a mistake after all?

Maybe it was *Jory* who was the mistake. Had he been babbling on too much, reminding Mal of his hopeless crush? Maybe he should—

Mal grabbed the wheel, wrenching it violently over towards the centre of the road.

CHAPTER
TEN

Jory's stomach lurched. They were heading straight for an oncoming driver. Even as he wrested back control, his heart beating so hard his ribs hurt, the other driver swerved out of their way and blasted his horn.

On the pavement, heads turned.

And then, seeing that nothing had actually happened, turned away again.

Jory kept his cool, despite his shaking hands. He put the car back on course, drove along the road until he could turn up a side street, parked the car, and then turned to Mal to ask him calmly what was going on.

"What the bloody sodding *hell* was that?"

Okay. Maybe he wasn't quite as calm as he'd thought.

Then he noticed Mal was shaking. "Mal?"

There was no answer. Mal just stared straight ahead through the windscreen, his eyes wide.

Jory was starting to get worried. "Mal?" he said again. "Malory?" He put a hand on Mal's arm.

Mal jumped violently. Then he buried his head in his hands. All Jory could hear was a constant, muttered, "*Fuck, fuck, fuck . . .*" His breathing was fast, shallow, and unnatural. Something was terribly wrong.

Jory clumsily unhitched both their seat belts and stumbled out of the car, almost forgetting to check for traffic first. Then he rounded the vehicle and opened the passenger door wide.

Mal didn't resist as Jory pulled him out of his seat. He didn't do *anything*. His legs seemed to have no strength to hold him, and he and

Jory ended up sprawled on the grass verge. Christ, what on earth was going on? Jory felt helpless. Useless. All he could do was wrap his arms around Mal's trembling, sweaty form and hold him fast.

He realised he was rocking Mal like a small child who'd had a nightmare, and was hit by a stab of embarrassment before he registered that it actually seemed to be helping. Mal's breathing was easing, becoming slower and deeper. "It's okay," Jory told him, not sure what he was referring to. "It's okay."

Mal mumbled something Jory couldn't catch, and he drew back, just a little.

"I thought—" Mal's voice cracked.

Jory didn't want to let go of him, not even for a second, but he knew there was a bottle of water in the car. He loosened his grip on Mal cautiously, then when he'd managed to convince himself that nothing dire would happen, let go entirely and lunged for the glove compartment, where he fumbled until he found the water bottle.

Relieved, he sat back down on the grass and put his arm around Mal's shoulders once more. It made it harder to open the bottle, but he didn't much care.

The water inside must have been unpleasantly warm and stale from sitting in the car for weeks, but Mal gulped it down so fast that Jory ended up taking it from him, afraid he'd make himself ill. "Slow down, okay?"

Mal nodded jerkily. He was staring at nothing again. "I thought he was gonna jump. That kid. Thought he was gonna jump in the road."

"What kid?"

"Dark hair. Metal T-shirt. From Download, maybe? Some festival like that. Don't remember. Just thought he was gonna . . . Shit."

Jory frowned. He'd seen the boy—young man, really. He'd been walking with a girl in a black crop top, and he'd made an exuberant hand gesture, but nothing had made Jory think there was any danger.

Why had Mal thought he was going to jump in front of the car? Why *would* anyone jump in front of a moving car? A toddler might think it was a game, perhaps, but not a grown man. And if anyone actually intended harm to themselves, well, they'd undoubtedly find a more reliable way than jumping in front of slow-moving traffic in a seaside resort.

It's not like there's a shortage of cliffs around here, Jory thought bitterly. It just didn't make sense. "Mal, has something happened to you? A . . . car accident?"

Mal didn't answer for a long moment. "Not car. Tube. Had a one under."

"A . . . what?"

"'S what we call it. When they jump."

But Mal had said he worked in customer services . . .

He hadn't said where, though, had he? And London Underground probably employed thousands of people in customer services. "You saw it happen?"

Mal made a horrible sound then, a sort of sobbing laugh. "Was driving."

Jory felt sick. "Oh God. You couldn't stop?"

"Never can. You slam on the brakes, but . . . yeah. Not a chance. Just gotta wait. For the bang. Takes ages. I mean, it's seconds, yeah. Less? Dunno. But it takes ages. And you just gotta wait."

Jory had both arms around him now, and was holding as tight as he could.

"Is he all right, dearie?"

Jory looked up. Two watery blue eyes were peering down at him from a face that was a mass of concerned wrinkles under feathery white hair. "Um . . ."

"Too much sun, is it? Sweet tea, that's what he needs. You bring him along to mine, dearie. It's only two doors up."

Jory glanced at Mal, who had gone back to staring into space. Sweet tea was good for shock, wasn't it? And Mal certainly seemed like he was in shock.

Somehow Jory found himself getting Mal to his feet and half supporting him as they followed the old lady and her shopping trolley. It had jaunty little sailing ships on it, and a faded sticker of a butterfly.

It was unexpectedly tiring to move at the speed of an old lady. The few yards felt like half a mile.

"You can call me Helen, dearie," she said as she let them into her terraced house.

"Oh. Ah, I'm Jory and this is . . . Malory." Jory hoped Mal wouldn't mind, but she didn't seem the sort of person one introduced people to using their nickname.

"Malory? That's an unusual one. Come on in, dears."

Mal hadn't reacted at all—not to the name and not to the comment. Jory helped him into the house and tried not to panic.

The street door opened directly into a tiny front room. The walls were covered in photographs: laughing, gap-toothed children, young people wearing academic robes and clutching scrolls, and at least three wedding photographs in varying degrees of faded colour and fashion disaster.

At Helen's direction, they sat down on a surprisingly modern sofa. This was probably just as well as what Jory at first took to be a fluffy, if slightly tatty, black cushion on one of the armchairs turned out, on closer inspection, to be a cat. At any rate, that was his best guess, given that he could see it breathing.

"I'll put the kettle on," Helen said, carrying on into the kitchen.

Jory knew he should offer to help—but he couldn't shake the fear that if he let go of Mal for a moment, something terrible would happen. "Thank you," he said, so as not to seem utterly devoid of manners.

He turned to Mal, who was breathing more easily now, thank God. "Are you all right with this? We don't have to stay here if you don't want to."

Mal closed his eyes. "No. 'S okay." He opened them again and smiled faintly. "Think that's her?"

Jory followed his gaze to the oldest wedding photo, in black-and-white, which showed a strikingly attractive young woman with an unimaginably tiny waist, beaming as if overjoyed to be wedded to a rather ordinary-looking man.

"I think so." Jory tried in vain to trace any resemblance between the glowing young bride and the old lady with the shopping trolley, but he didn't doubt it was her.

Helen returned with a mug in each hand. "I hope you don't mind, but I just can't be doing with cups and saucers these days. Young men prefer mugs anyway, don't they?" She bent to put them on a side table, a process that took an alarming amount of time.

She bustled away, returning soon after with a mug of her own and a plate of chocolate biscuits which shook slightly as she held it. Jory hastened to take it from her. She dimpled at him. "They're Sainsbury's own brand, but they're very good."

Helen eased herself down into the cat-free chair and smiled at them. "It's not the sun, is it?" she asked calmly. "Don't you worry. My Peter's boy came back from Iraq with that PTSD. Used to jump at loud noises. He's much better now. Drink your tea, that'll help."

Mal lifted his mug and took a sip. Then he grimaced. "Blimey, you got the EU sugar mountain in here?" He took another mouthful, though, and then a third.

Jory, relieved as he was to hear Mal talking normally, eyed his mug and wished for a handy potted plant and a moment's inattention on Helen's part. But when he took a cautious sip, he found his tea to be strong, sparingly milked, and unsweetened.

Helen caught his eye with a satisfied look. "You should have a biscuit, both of you," she insisted. "I'll never manage to eat them all by myself."

Jory handed the plate to Mal, who took one and demolished it in a couple of bites. "'S good," he mumbled through his mouthful, and for a moment Jory was back in the museum at their first meeting. Christ, had it really only been a few days ago?

"You're not from around here, are you? Oh, I know who you are, Jory Roscarrock," she added, sending a frisson of surprise down Jory's spine. She nodded towards the mantelpiece. "See that picture, with the boy in the stripy top on his dad's shoulders? That's my grandson Patrick with his eldest. I remember when you two were thick as thieves, running round barefoot all summer and covering his mother's carpets in sand."

Jory stared at her for a moment, then after a glance at Mal, he got up to examine the photograph. That was what Patrick looked like now? His hair was thinning, and he had what Jory had seen referred to on the internet as a "Dad body." Jory wouldn't have known him. The child he carried was too small to have grown into recognisable features, but Jory fancied he saw a hint of the young Patrick in his eyes, and his smile.

He felt a sharp pang of loss for that far-off time when the worst thing that could happen had been a rainy day. "He's... doing all right?"

"Very well. He's living in Newquay now. His wife's a lovely girl. A pharmacist. Patrick met her at university."

She didn't ask about Jory's marital status. Perhaps she already knew that too.

"I'll tell him you asked about him. He's a good boy. Rings me every week."

"I, ah, I'm glad to hear it."

"'S important. Family," Mal spoke up out of nowhere.

"I'm sure you've got a lovely family, dear. London, is it, you're from?"

Mal nodded.

"And you've brothers and sisters?"

"Just a sister. Morgan. She's gonna have a kid." Mal, who'd been mostly talking to the carpet, looked up. "I mean, she's got a husband and all," he said earnestly.

Helen twinkled. "Why is it the young always assume the old will be shocked by modern ways? When you reach my age, dearie, you realise there's nothing new under the sun."

"Gay marriage. That's new," Mal said with a hint of challenge that Jory was glad to see, possible offence to their kind hostess be damned.

"Oh, people have always managed to find each other somehow. Now, will you have another biscuit? More tea?"

Mal grabbed another chocolate biscuit and pretty much inhaled it. Then he drained his mug and stood up. "Thanks. You've been— Think I'll be okay now. And... Cheers. Your grandson's a lucky bloke. Nah, don't get up. I'll wash the cups and all."

He collected their mugs—Jory finished his tea hastily before handing his over—and walked out of the room with purposeful stride.

Jory was left with his childhood best friend's grandmother.

She smiled at him. "I always thought it was a shame when they sent you off to school. But from what I hear, you've done well for yourself."

Jory was almost afraid to ask, but—"What have you heard?"

"You're Dr. Roscarrock now, aren't you?"

He shrugged, awkwardly. "Nobody calls me that."

"Perhaps they should. Are you back here for good?"

"Yes. I—" Jory took a deep breath. "I wanted to spend more time with my son. Gawen. He's twelve now."

"His mother's an artist, from what I hear," she said placidly. "Does he take after her? Or is he more like you?"

"Me, I think. In looks as well as temperament." Unnerved by her level of knowledge about him, Jory fumbled in his pocket for his phone, and found a recent picture of Gawen to show her.

"Oh, yes, he's a handsome young man all right. I'm sure he'll be breaking hearts in a few years' time." She patted his hand. "Not that I'm suggesting you'd do anything like that."

"I, er— No." Jory was relieved to see Mal's return.

"You ready?" Mal didn't sit down again, so Jory stood up, not sure himself that he wanted to spend any more time with this uncomfortably astute old lady.

"Yes. Thank you so much, Helen."

"Oh, it was my pleasure. I don't get many visitors who aren't family. There will always be a welcome for you in this house, Jory Roscarrock. And you too, Malory."

Mal nodded, his face a little pink. It was a definite improvement on the deathly pale of earlier. "You take care, yeah?"

She dimpled at them from her chair, obviously expecting them to see themselves out, so they did.

Once they were out on the street, a problem presented itself. Jory hated to ask, but: "Are you going to be all right to get back in the car?"

Mal flinched. "Uh. How far are we from the Sea Bell? Shit. Don't think I'm going to make it to Tintagel today. Sorry."

"You've got nothing to apologise for. And of course we're not carrying on with a journey that's making you uncomfortable."

"Might be okay sitting in the back," Mal said, but he didn't sound all that certain. "'S what I did on the way from Newquay. Jago came and picked me up. Tasha sat in the back with me." He gave a bitter laugh. "Like I was a little kid."

"Or someone who'd had a traumatic experience. Look, we're probably around an hour's walk from the Sea Bell. I'm game if you are. I can come back for the car later."

"You don't . . . Shit. Cheers. That'd be good. But . . . Not straight back, yeah?"

"You want to go for a drink? Something a bit stronger than sweet tea?"

Mal shook his head. "Nah. Not gonna . . . I just need some fresh air, that's all."

"Well, you've come to the right place for that. It's an endlessly renewable resource around here. We could bottle it and sell it." Jory hoped he'd succeeded in keeping his tone light.

"Yeah, how come you don't?" Mal gave him a weak smile. "They sell cans of Scotch mist up in Scotland."

"I'll suggest it to the local enterprise group." Meaning Bea. Maybe not, then. "Are you sure you don't want to go and get a drink?"

"No."

Jory flinched at the unexpected vehemence.

Mal hunched in on himself. "Uh, sorry. Don't wanna start down that road, that's all. I'm fine."

"No, I'm sorry. I shouldn't have pushed."

"Nah, that's good. Maybe we could go down the beach or something?"

Jory thought about it. "Harlyn Bay is closest, but it's a surfing beach so it'll be busy. We could take the cliff path back to Mother Ivey's Bay, though. That'll be quieter. Unless busy is what you want."

"Quiet's good. Not so many people to worry about. Feel bad, though. That's gonna take you past your house, innit? Then you'll have to come all the way back again to get the car . . . Listen, I'll be fine, okay? I can make it back on my own."

"Don't—" Jory stopped himself. *Don't be silly* probably wouldn't go down too well. "Don't worry about it. I like to walk. And the weather's perfect for it." It was: a cool breeze freshened the air, blowing clouds across the sun every now and then to dapple the streets with shade.

Harlyn was a small place—much smaller than Porthkennack—and they were soon out of the town, such as it was, and on to the cliff path that skirted the bay. Mal seemed to breathe more easily once they were away from traffic, thank God. By silent agreement, they cut across the fields to avoid going too close to Roscarrock House, and before long the beach at Mother Ivey's Bay stretched out before them.

Mal got out his phone and glanced at the display. "Huh. That took less time than I thought."

Jory nodded. "It's only about a mile, a mile and a half. It just seems further in the car."

"Yeah, tell me about it."

It was high tide, which meant the main beach was cut off from the smaller ones at the lifeboat station end by craggy outcroppings of rock. They kept to the cliff path until they'd reached that point, and then scrambled down the rougher path to the beach.

As Jory had hoped, it was all but deserted. A man, a boy, and a dog scampered around at the water's edge, and a teenage couple were wrapped up in each other by the cliffs at one end, but nobody paid the slightest attention to Jory and Mal.

Jory bent to pick up a likely-looking stone. "Let's see if I've still got the knack." He skimmed it at the sea, pleased to see it bounce five, maybe six times before sinking into the water.

"Hey, not bad. Let's have a go."

Mal, it turned out, didn't have the first clue about picking good stones for skimming. His first effort disappeared straight into the water with a scathing *plop*. "Crap."

"Try finding flatter ones," Jory suggested. "And round, if you can. Think of it as the difference between a Frisbee and a ball."

"Huh. Yeah, that makes sense." Mal's next few efforts were much better. "Hah—bet I could beat you with a bit of practice."

It warmed Jory inside to see him returning to his usual self. "Let's see you, then."

Whiling away an hour or so out here in the fresh air, with nothing more immediate to worry about than who could grab the best stones first, was just what the doctor ordered. Jory couldn't stop continually glancing at Mal, and the warm feeling grew as he saw the colour return to his face and the brightness to his eyes.

By the time his arm started to tire, Mal was rivalling him for number of bounces. "Do you want to sit down for a bit?" Jory asked.

Mal nodded, and they headed up, closer to the bottom of the cliff. The sand here was bone-dry and scattered with broken shells and dried-up seaweed. Jory sat down first, and when Mal joined him, sitting so close their hips touched, it seemed natural to throw an arm around him, as he had up in town.

Jory wondered if he should talk to Mal about what had happened, but he had a feeling that peace was what was needed right now. Just them, the rush of the waves, the calling of the gulls, and the occasional bark from an unseen dog. The silence felt more intimate, somehow, than any words could have been, although Jory couldn't help a twinge of guilt at relishing a closeness brought about by such appalling circumstances.

After a while, it was Mal who broke the silence between them.

"He died."

Jory blinked. "What?"

"The bloke who jumped under my train. He died. People always wanna know. So. Thought I'd save you asking." Mal paused. "He was a young guy. Depression, they reckoned. 'S a bastard."

"My father killed himself," Jory blurted out, then hugged himself, too late to stop the words escaping. "Oh God. You don't want to hear about that."

"How'd he do it?"

"The cliffs. At the back of our house." Jory couldn't help glancing over in the direction of Big Guns Cove, although the curve of the bay shielded it from view. "They called it an accident but, well. We knew." Probably everyone had known, but the coroner had been an old family friend.

"Fuck."

Jory nodded. "It was . . . My mother died a few months before that. They were everything to each other."

"Christ, that's . . . How old were you?"

"Seventeen."

"And it was just you, your brother, and your sister after that? How much older than you are they again?"

"Nine years." It'd seemed like a lot back then.

"And a year or two later you met Kirsty and had Gawen." Mal said it as though the timing was significant.

Perhaps it was. Jory had always shied away from too much analysis of that time in his life.

Mal's head dropped onto his shoulder, and Jory couldn't help turning to nuzzle his hair. It smelled of lemon and salt, and was softer against his cheek than it looked. Mal muttered something that sounded like *fucked up*, and then he lifted his face to Jory's, and kissed him.

Oh God. His lips on Jory's were demanding, and the taste of him intoxicating.

Jory felt clumsy, oafish in comparison as Mal twisted in his arms and grabbed hold of him, one hand on his jaw and the other low on his hip. Jory opened his mouth to the hot tongue that sought entry, surrendering eagerly to the invasion. His whole body was alive with sensation—and the need for more, damn it.

When they finally broke apart, Jory wasn't the only one breathing hard.

"So. Yeah. That happened," Mal said, drawing back and shifting a few inches away on the sand. His voice was as rough as the craggy granite cliffs that surrounded them. "Uh. Probably shouldn't happen again, yeah?"

Oh. The fizzing inside Jory suddenly went flat.

"See, you're Dev's uncle, and he's my best mate. I don't wanna fuck that up for him. Not just for a . . ." Mal made a vague gesture that seemed to encompass all of Jory in his glorious inadequacy. "Whatever."

"Fine," Jory found himself saying. So that was how Mal thought of him, was it? Just a . . . *whatever*. Well, perhaps it was better to find out sooner rather than later. "No, you're right. That would be . . ." He stood up, feeling cold and very alone. "I'll, um, let you get on, then."

"Jory . . ." Despite the pleading tone, when Mal got to his feet he took a step back, widening the distance between them.

"You'll be okay to get back from here?" Jory asked, his tone harsh in his own ears.

Mal drew in a breath as if to say something—but then stopped and shook his head. "Yeah, mate, I'm good. Cheers for . . . you know. I'll see you around, yeah?"

Jory nodded curtly. Mal paused again, then turned and walked away.

Jory didn't watch him go.

CHAPTER ELEVEN

Shit. The look on Jory's face.

He'd been so fucking great about Mal pretty much having a nervous breakdown in front of him too. After nearly killing both of them—Christ, what had he been *thinking*, grabbing the wheel like that? Mal felt like a total arse as he walked the short way from Mother Ivey's Bay to the Sea Bell.

That was why this thing, him and Jory, had to not happen. Because he was fucked up big time, and if he went into something with Jory, he'd fuck that up too.

And then he'd have let Dev down on top of everything else.

Christ. Mal walked blindly through the pub's back door.

Sometimes . . . sometimes he felt like it should have been him hitting the front of the train with that godawful *thump*, getting carved up by the wheels— Shit . . .

He wasn't supposed to think like that. That was what the counsellor had said. But she didn't get it, did she? He'd *killed* someone.

"Babe?"

Mal glanced up. Tasha was staring at him through the open door of the kitchen, her usual worried expression in place. Well, usual when she looked at him, anyway. Great mate he was turning out to be. "Keep frowning like that and you'll end up with wrinkles," he said weakly.

"Fuck off, you wanker. What's happened, babe?"

"Mixed messages much?"

"Oi. Stop stalling and come and sit down. You want a drink?"

Christ, why was everyone trying to push alcohol on him? He traipsed wearily into the kitchen. "Want me to turn out like me uncle Bob, do you?"

"Is he the one who drank a bottle of Jack a day and had a stroke in his forties? You ain't gonna make it to your forties. Someone'll murder you way before then. Sit down, cos I'm getting you a glass of water and you're either drinking it or wearing it. Your choice." She stepped over to the sink.

Mal sat down at the kitchen table. A moment later, she clonked a pint glass of water down in front of him.

He drank. It felt better than expected going down. Cool and clear. Unlike his fucking head back on that beach.

Tasha slid into the chair next to his. "Babe, if you don't wanna talk, that's okay, yeah? But you just look . . . rattled, yeah? Like something's happened. Are you sure you're all right?"

"I saw that bloke again," he blurted out. "Jory. Roscarrock."

Tasha would make a fucking epic mother tiger. He could have sworn she actually bristled. Maybe even growled a bit. "What did he say to you? What did he do?"

"Gonna send the boys round? Nah, it ain't like that. I think he's all right, you know? He swears he never knew about Dev. And he wants to get to know him."

"Why?"

"Cos he's a decent bloke. He said sorry like a hundred times for what his bruv and sister did."

"And you believed him?"

"Well, yeah. Why's he gonna lie about it? What's in it for him?"

"I dunno. So he can get in your kecks, maybe?"

"No one's gonna go to all that trouble for a leg over."

Tasha shrugged. "True. You ain't that good-looking. And I've seen your kecks. I've *washed* your kecks." She made a face.

"Cheers, love. You really know how to make a bloke feel special. Oi, you still ain't said nothing to Dev about Jory, have you?"

"Not yet. Wasn't sure what to say. But we'd better, hadn't we? What if he gets Dev's address from that cow and gets in touch?"

"He won't. I got him to agree not to. Not until Dev and Kyle get down here."

"You told him Dev's coming down? What did you bloody go and do that for?"

"Come on, they're gonna be staying literally just down the road from where Jory lives. It ain't like he's gonna be able to miss him."

"S'pose. Least it means we ain't gotta rake all that shit up again before we have to. And Dev won't have to worry about it till he gets here."

Mal frowned. "D'you think . . . Do you think he'd, like, not come here if he knew?" The minute he'd said it, he wished he could take it back, cos what if she said yes? Then they'd have to tell him, and maybe he wouldn't come here, and Mal wasn't sure he could handle that.

It wasn't like he *needed* Dev or nothing. But he'd been looking forward to a couple of weeks with his best mate, pissing about, having fun. Like, after he'd had that, he'd be strong enough to go back to London. Maybe even back to work.

"Nah, he'd still come." Tasha said it firmly, but then she turned her face away. "Shit. I dunno. Maybe we oughtta tell him. Give him a chance to make up his own mind. It's just . . . I don't wanna put him off, yeah? I haven't seen him for like months. Am I being a selfish cow?"

Mal gave her a hug. "If you are, that's two of us. Moo."

She giggled. "Fucking moo to you too."

"Mooooooooooooooo."

"MOOOOOO . . . Oh, all right, Jago? Didn't see you there. What you after?"

"Milk," Jago said, deadpan, and Mal and Tasha cracked up.

That night, Tasha barged into the bathroom while Mal was flossing his teeth in his boxer shorts. She stood there with her arms folded and watched for a minute or so before she spoke. "Are you gonna see that Jory bloke again?"

"Maybe. But I ain't *seeing* him."

"Good." She didn't move.

Mal chucked the floss in the bin and got out his mouthwash, thought *sod it*, and offered her a capful with a sarcastic bow.

She made a face. "It's all yours."

"Suit yourself. Dental hygiene's very important."

Tasha waited while he gargled and spat. "Gonna shag him?" Her tone was sharp.

Mal rolled his eyes and shook his head firmly. "No. I'm not gonna risk messing things up with him and Dev. They got enough to deal with, with that bloody family."

"Good."

"Why you got such a problem with him, though? Seriously, he's all right." He was more than all right, which was why Mal needed to steer well clear of him.

"The problem I got is you saw him today, didn't you? And you came in looking worse than you did when your rat died, and don't think I didn't notice you never told me why. So what did he do to you?"

"What? Nothing." Mal caught her disbelieving expression in the mirror and sighed, slinging his towel round his neck. "It wasn't his fault, okay? I was in his car and . . . I had a dodgy moment, that's all. Sorta flashback thing."

"Oh, babe. Did anything, like, happen?"

"No. No thanks to me. Shit. I grabbed the wheel, didn't I? Thought he was gonna hit someone, but it was all in my fucked-up head."

"Fuck." Tasha came up behind him and slipped her arms around his waist. Her hair tickled his neck, and her bare arms were a bit too warm on his skin for comfort. It still felt good, though. Like when he was a little kid and his mum would give him a cuddle.

Or when he was not so little, for that matter. Mum had wanted him to stay with her and Dad while he got over stuff, but he just . . . couldn't.

"I don't get it, Tash." His voice sounded thick. It was from the gargling, wasn't it? "Dad was on the Tubes for twenty years. I know he had stuff happen. But he never . . . He just went for a few pints with the lads and then went back to work next day. How come I'm such a fuckup?"

She squeezed him then, so tight it actually hurt. "You're fucking well *not* a fuckup, Mal Thomas. You ain't your dad, babe, that's all. Everyone's different." Then she loosened her hold, and he could breathe again. So it was stupid how he was sort of disappointed she'd stopped squeezing the life out of him. "Your Jory bloke, was he okay about it?" Her words were hot puffs of breath on his skin.

"Yeah. He was great." Mal couldn't help smiling at the memory.

She stuck her bushy head out from behind him and met his eye in the mirror with a teasing grin. "Looked after you, did he? Give you a little cuddle? Did you manage to cop a feel while he was at it?"

Mal laughed. "It wasn't like that. We had a cup of tea with his old school mate's nan, all right?"

"You're shitting me."

"No, swear to God. There was chocolate biscuits and everything. He's a good bloke, Tash. You'd like him if you gave him a chance." Probably. Tasha could be funny about blokes. "Now are you gonna let me get to bed or what?"

"Yeah . . ." She didn't let go of him, though, and a minute later she spoke again. "Got a text from Ceri."

"She okay?"

"Yeah. Sounds like she's having a great time."

"That's good, then, innit?"

"S'pose." She stepped back, letting her arms fall from around his waist. "Yeah. Imma go bed, now. You sleep tight, babe."

"Yeah, you too. And oi, no having X-rated dreams about me, all right? Don't think I won't know when I see you in the morning."

"You're so full of shit, you wanker." But it got her to smile, which was the main thing.

Lying in bed later, Mal couldn't help thinking about Jory. Christ, he hoped the bloke would forgive him. Kissing him like that—it'd been well out of order when he'd known it couldn't go any further.

Could it?

No. No way. Jory was . . . He was Dev's. In, like, a totally nonsexual sense. Jesus. And Mal's crap handling of it all showed he couldn't be trusted with anything that belonged to anyone else.

He'd see Jory again, yeah, but just to apologise.

That was all.

CHAPTER TWELVE

Much as he liked walking, Jory hadn't been in the mood to traipse all the way back to Harlyn by himself for his car. He'd called Kirsty and got her to give him a lift there after she picked Gawen up from school. She was good about that sort of thing, and she hadn't pressed him on the reason he needed a ride.

She *had* asked him if he'd had any more breakfast dates, but after Jory's curt no, she'd dropped the subject, for which he was grateful.

The three of them went out for fish and chips down on the seafront once they were back in Porthkennack—Kirsty's suggestion, because it at least meant that Gawen would get *some* fresh air in the day. He seemed happy enough, even though he had to put away his phone because greasy fingers and touch screens weren't exactly a match made in heaven.

When they'd eaten, Jory had a go at teaching Gawen to skim stones. He picked up the technique surprisingly quickly for a boy who hated ball games, and they had a good time while Kirsty combed the beach for interesting driftwood. Everyone was still smiling at the end, which was something, wasn't it?

And if Jory's thoughts kept drifting to another beach, and what had happened there only hours previously, well, he'd just have to carry on finding things to distract himself with, and eventually it would stop hurting, wouldn't it?

After he got home, Jory took his laptop down to the kitchen, made himself a mug of hot chocolate and spent the rest of the evening on the internet, learning far more about suicide by train than he'd ever wanted to know. Apparently between twenty-five and fifty people killed themselves on London Underground every year—sources disagreed on the exact tally. Half of those who tried it survived—maybe that was where the discrepancy arose?—some of whom were left with life-changing injuries. The most popular time, apparently, was eleven o'clock in the morning, which Jory couldn't make sense of at all. The most popular line was the Northern Line. Having travelled on it, Jory could see a grim logic in that.

He wondered which line Mal had driven on. Did drivers have their own routes, like bus drivers, or did they just go wherever needed?

Bran came into the kitchen unexpectedly at one point, and Jory had to close his tabs in a hurry. Of all of them, Bran had taken their father's suicide the worst. Jory had sometimes suspected it was why he'd never married—perhaps he never wanted to be so devoted to one person that their death would send him off the rails like that.

God. More railway imagery. That was the last thing Jory needed right now.

It took him a long time to get to sleep that night, and his dreams were a confused jumble of Mal, trains, and his long-dead father.

The next day dawned grey and overcast. Waking up with a heavy, tugging sense of loss, Jory was glad he had work to go to. If he'd had to spend a day idling around Roscarrock House, he reflected as he braved the drizzle to walk to the museum, he'd have been climbing the walls by lunchtime.

God, he missed climbing. Literal, not figurative. There was nothing quite like it—the steady reliance on one's own body, methodical testing of handholds. The feeling of accomplishment on reaching the top.

Maybe he should find a local club? He'd held off, in the few months since his return to Porthkennack, because he knew Bran would be upset, even though the danger was minimal if proper safety procedures were followed. But he was missing the exercise as much as the challenge, and the sense of freedom climbing brought him. Fingertip pull-ups in the garage really weren't the same.

And there was so much to climb around here. Right on his doorstep. It was almost criminal not to take advantage of it all. Jory allowed himself a wry smile as he let himself into the museum. He could always tell Bran he was bird-watching. Keep the gear stowed in the Qubo.

Yes. What he needed was something to focus on, to take his mind off . . . other things.

The morning passed more quickly than Jory had expected, with a steady trickle of visitors due to the rain forcing holidaymakers to find indoor amusements. There was already a family of four mooching around the exhibits when the door opened just before lunchtime.

Jory blinked and stood up. It was Mal.

He was the last person Jory had expected to walk in. He had on jeans and a slightly too-large long-sleeved T-shirt that made him look a good five years younger than he must be if he was Dev's age. Any resentment Jory had harboured against him melted to see him like that.

"Reduced price entry for coming twice in one week?" Mal asked with an awkward smile that wrenched at Jory's heart. "Or, you know, mates' rates? If we're still mates?"

"I, uh . . ." Jory swallowed. "Don't worry about it. The ticket, I mean. Come in," he added, because Mal was hovering by the door.

He loped in, all limbs today. "So, I, uh, I wanted to apologise. For yesterday."

"The car incident? I told you, you've got nothing to apologise for."

"Yeah, well, it put you right out, didn't it? Having to leave your car there and all. And anyway, it wasn't just that." Mal ran a hand through his hair. "About the beach . . . I didn't have me head on straight. What happened was out of order. So I'm sorry."

He shoved both hands in his jeans pockets, and looked up at Jory with a sheepish expression, his rumpled hair falling over his eyes.

He'd probably practised that move from an early age to charm his way out of trouble. Even so, something inside Jory twisted and broke at the sight.

"Still mates?" Mal asked with a shy smile.

Christ. Right now, Jory would have happily given him his *soul*.

But mates was good. Better than . . . not mates. He nodded.

Mal broke out into a grin that had relief written all over it. "You're aces, bruv. So how's it going? Caught any mermaids yet?"

"Not yet. But I'm almost certain I'm going to get funding for the exhibition." Jory knew he sounded more positive than the situation really warranted, but he was just so bloody glad to be on a safe subject.

"Yeah? That's great. So tell me about the stuff you've got in here at the mo. I never got a good look around last time. Seaman Staines, here, he got a story?" Mal waved a hand at the dummy dressed in a replica eighteenth-century naval uniform, which Mrs. Quick had provided the museum with in a burst of enthusiasm last winter. It wasn't a bad copy of the real thing, which they had under glass, of course.

"That's Midshipman Staines to you. And yes, but it's a short one—he went down with the wreck of the *Troilus*, apparently." Jory pointed at the painting on the wall.

"Poor bastard. Was that wreckers, then?"

"Just rocks, as far as I know. But we do have a display about wreckers, over here." He led Mal to a glass cabinet containing an eighteenth-century brandy bottle (empty), a flintlock pistol of uncertain antiquity, and a lurid retelling of the story of Cruel Coppinger, who wasn't even local and the tales of whose misdeeds were almost certainly apocryphal. "I don't think there's a lot of historical truth in the legend," he couldn't help apologising. "Most visitors don't seem to care, and it does make a good story."

Mal nodded. "Yeah, it's like all the King Arthur stuff, you know? And Robin Hood, and all that bollocks. Sometimes you just want to hear about heroes. Like, it's, uh, aspirational?" He said the word as though unsure he was using it correctly, and Jory was unwillingly charmed all over again.

"Yes, I think the medieval concept of chivalry was something to aspire to, rather than a code people really lived by." He smiled. "Although in fact the wreckers of Cornwall were probably better, and more humane, than the legends would have you believe. There are as many stories telling how they saved sailors' lives as there are of them causing deaths."

"What about pirates? I mean, have you got anything on Mary Roscarrock? Uh, the one what ran off to be a pirate?" Mal went pink. "If, you know, you don't mind talking about it. Her being family."

"She lived four hundred years ago. I think you can safely say we weren't close." Jory paused. "We haven't, actually, and now you mention it, I'm not sure why. A local legend like that is just what we could do with here."

"Yeah? Sure your big bruv wouldn't close you down? Bringing the family name into disrepute and all that?"

Jory cast a glance around for the visitors and was relieved to see they'd wandered into another room. "Bran may like to think he controls everything in Porthkennack, but I can assure you, he doesn't. I'll ask Mrs. Quick about it. She's been involved with the museum a lot longer than I have."

Mal frowned. "Yeah, I been meaning to ask—she related to the old admiral there?" He nodded towards the bust of Admiral Quick over by the desk.

"Doubly, in fact. She's the descendant of a cousin, I believe, and obviously she married a Quick." Jory shrugged. "You get a lot of that sort of thing around here. Or, at least, you used to. These days everyone is a lot more mobile than they used to be."

Mal grinned. "Yeah, I bet you miss the good old days with horses and carts and inbreeding and all that shit."

"Thanks. I'm thirty-two, not a hundred and two."

"You keep telling yourself that, Grandad."

Jory was spellbound by the easy intimacy of the moment. It was as if nothing awkward had ever happened between them. It would be so easy to lean forward and kiss Mal's lips—but then the front door creaked open and the sound of voices interrupted.

Mal's trainers squeaked on the floor. "Looks like I'd better let you get back to work."

Jory swallowed. "Yes. Right." He hurried back to his post at the desk and busied himself with the new visitors, handing over a family ticket for the princely sum of five pounds.

Mal dawdled around the museum a while longer, but Jory didn't feel he ought to leave the desk and go chat with him while there were other visitors who might need his help.

It was probably better not to in any case. He didn't want Mal to think he was following him around like a lovelorn sheep.

At length, Mal came back to him. "What time do you finish tonight?" he asked in a low voice.

"Five o'clock." The surge of relief that Mal hadn't simply waved and gone on his way left Jory a little giddy. "Would you like to go for a drink or something? Um, possibly not in the Sea Bell?"

Mal chuckled. "Yeah, maybe not. I'll see you back here, and we can decide then, okay?"

"Okay."

And it will be okay, Jory told himself. Just two men, having a friendly drink.

He could do that.

The heady rush of having more than half a dozen visitors to the museum all at the same time didn't last, of course, but for once Jory didn't mind. He was glad of the free time to consider plans for the evening.

He was less glad for the leisure to second-guess the purpose of tonight's . . . well, he'd call it a date, except that Mal had been so adamant that kissing him had been a mistake, hadn't he? But planning, planning was good.

And anyway, if Mal was *that* set on not kissing him again, he wouldn't have arranged to see him the very next day, would he? Jory's heart leapt at the possibilities. He'd have left it a few days at least. Even if he'd felt compelled to apologise as soon as possible, he wouldn't have asked Jory out for the evening too. Not unless he . . .

But this was getting Jory nowhere. Except determined to have a concrete plan for the evening. Something for them to do, so there wouldn't be any awkward silences.

Something fun, so Mal would enjoy their time together. Would want to see him again . . .

Oh hell. Jory might as well admit it to himself. He wanted to make Mal want to kiss him again. To realise that what there was between them—what there *could* be between them, at any rate—was strong enough not to pose any threat to Jory's future relationship with Dev. What would be the best way of doing that? He needed something special. Something . . . something personal. Maybe if he showed Mal a little more of himself, he'd . . . Okay, there was a fifty-fifty chance

Mal wouldn't actually *like* what was revealed, but wasn't all of life a gamble? Jory took risks every time he climbed—hell, he'd taken risks as a small child, scrambling along what remained of the smugglers' tunnels through the cliffs of Big Guns Cove with Patrick.

Jory stood up from his chair with such an abrupt move the bust of Admiral Quick wobbled on its plinth behind him.

That was it. Something personal and fun. He'd take Mal down there.

CHAPTER THIRTEEN

Mal turned up at the museum ten minutes early but decided it'd be awkward if he went in and Jory couldn't leave. Especially seeing as there probably wouldn't be any visitors, just him and Jory watching the clock.

So he wandered around a bit, having a gander at the place from the outside. It was . . . Well, maybe it was the old-time equivalent of a midlife crisis flashy car? All big and show-offy, as if the bloke who built it was all, *You think this is impressive? Wait till you get a butcher's at my dick.*

Then again, Mal drove big long trains into tunnels all day for a living, so it wasn't like he had much room to talk.

When he stepped through the door dead on five o'clock, Jory was already there waiting, leaning against the front of his desk, hands in his pockets. He glanced up, and fuck, that smile ought to come with a health warning, cos it was doing some serious damage to Mal's heart.

"Are you up for something physical tonight?" Jory asked, stepping away from his desk.

Mal took a step back before he knew what he was doing, and threw a furtive glance around the place in case there were any late visitors still there. "Uh, mate, see, I thought we weren't gonna—"

"I didn't mean . . ." Jory swallowed, his face redder than the worst sunburn Mal had seen in his life, and he'd spotted a few classic English lobsters on the beach only this afternoon. "Caving. I thought we could go caving."

Oh. Mal wasn't disappointed. He fucking *wasn't*, all right? He turned and led the way out of the museum to cover his embarrassment. "Uh, yeah. Sorry, bruv. One-track mind, me."

"I suppose it helps when driving a train," Jory deadpanned as he locked the door.

Mal's laugh was a bit higher pitched and more girly than he'd have liked it to be, but at least it let out some of the tension. "Mate, that was terrible. Seriously. Never, *ever* give up the day job." He coughed. "So, uh, caving? Don't we need like equipment and stuff for that? Or were you talking about the tourist caves?" He'd picked up a leaflet about them in the tourist information place, all floodlit and a bit, well, tame if he was honest.

Jory looked smug. "There are some old smugglers' caves almost directly under Roscarrock House that have never been open to the public. I used to explore them when I was a boy. And I didn't have any special equipment then."

"Weren't your mum and dad worried you'd, like, get buried alive or something?"

Jory gave a shifty glance to the side as they walked along the path. "Um. I might have neglected to tell them *exactly* where I was going."

"Bloody hell. My mum always had to know where I was going, who with, and when I was gonna be back. To the minute."

"You grew up in the city though. Dangers around here are different—or at least, people used to think they were, back then." Jory gave a twisted smile. "And maybe kids were different. These days you don't worry about letting them run around freely so much as count yourself lucky if you can get them out of doors at all."

He must be thinking about his kid. Gawen. Mal wanted to ask what he was like—except there was an ugly feeling twisting his chest and he worried he'd end up saying something he didn't mean. "So . . . we going straight there?"

"Actually, I was planning to get changed first." Jory's tone was apologetic as he glanced down at his posh chinos, and yeah, Mal really ought to try thinking before he opened his mouth. "You should probably do that too. Wear clothes you don't care about—the tunnel should be dry, this time of year, but just in case. And we'll need torches, of course. Um. I could pick you up from the Sea Bell if you like, but . . ."

Yeah, no. It was bleedin' obvious why the bloke wouldn't want him in his car after yesterday. "No worries. Long as it ain't too far."

"It's just past Roscarrock House. How about we meet up halfway there, say in about an hour, hour and a half? I'd say sooner, but I walked to work today. Sorry. If I'd had your number, I'd have called to tell you not to waste a journey to the museum."

Huh. Mal stopped in his tracks. "Seriously? We ain't swapped numbers yet? Gimme your phone."

Jory, who'd stopped when Mal had, dug into his pocket and handed over the latest iPhone. Mal snorted.

"What?"

"Ah, nothing." Mal tapped in his number and saved the new contact, then handed back the phone. "Just, I wouldn't have put you down for an Apple sheep. If I'd had to guess, I'd have thought you'd have one of them ancient flip-out things with buttons and a battery that lasts three weeks."

"I did. This was a Christmas present from Bea." Jory—well, if he'd accused the bloke of it, he'd probably have denied it to his dying day, but Mal knew a pout when he saw one. "I *liked* my old phone. This one's always running out of charge because I forget to plug it in overnight."

Mal grinned. "Yeah, my dad's always doing stuff like that. Having a senior moment, he calls it."

Jory gave him a filthy look. "Just because I haven't become totally enslaved to technology doesn't mean I'm *senior*, thank you."

"Apart from, you know, literally." Mal laughed. "What? You're older than me. It's a fact. Get over it."

"Not that much older. Seven years, if you're the same age as Dev."

"Not like you've been counting or nothing."

"It's an odd thought that I'm closer in age to my nephew than to my sister," Jory said, with a smile Mal couldn't quite read. "Um. I should get moving."

"Right. Yeah." Mal jammed his hands in his pockets. It brought his hand into contact with his phone, which jogged a memory. "Uh, you should text me or something. So I'll have your number."

"I'll text you when I'm on my way out again, how about that?"

"Yeah, fine. See you in a bit, yeah?"

Jory walked on up the path, and Mal turned to go in the other direction, back to the Sea Bell. It occurred to him a moment later he could have carried on walking with Jory for a while, cos he had bugger all else to do for the next hour, but he'd have felt a right dick running after him now.

Nah, it was fine. He'd see plenty of Jory later.

Mal ended up spending the time drinking tea in the pub kitchen and making sandwiches, cos Jory hadn't mentioned anything about food and Mal wasn't taking any chances.

"You're hungry tonight," Tasha said pointedly.

"I'm a growing lad," he shot back.

"You'll have a growing arse at this rate, and then what you gonna do when no one fancies you?"

He shrugged. "I'll always have me rats." Mum had called earlier to let him know that they were all okay and she'd dug Hermione a nice little grave in the park, with a lolly stick cross with her name on like they'd used to do when he was a kid. She'd asked how he was, and he'd said he was fine, and if she didn't believe him, that was her problem, wasn't it? He hadn't told her about the car thing. It'd only worry her.

"Well, I s'pose even sad old cat ladies have gotta have someone to look down on. So you're out tonight, then?"

"Yeah."

"Seeing that Roscarrock bloke?"

"What's it to you?"

"Fuck you and all. So's it serious, then?"

"What? No. I mean, it's not even an *it*, all right? I wouldn't do that to Dev." Shit, had his face gone red?

She shrugged. "Suit yourself. You ain't joined at the hip, though."

"You what?"

"You and Dev. So what if you shag this bloke? It don't mean it'll fuck stuff up for him and Dev. That's *if* Dev wants to get to know him in the first place."

"Uh. Right." Shit. Why did everything have to be so bloody complicated? "This is all seriously doing my head in," he muttered, and let his head sink down to the table.

"Poor baby." Tasha gave him a hug, then a jab in the ribs that made him sit up straight all in a jerk. She laughed. "You got mayo in your hair. Better wash that out before you see him, or he might think you started without him."

"We ain't starting nothing, you got that?"

Tasha gave him a long, hard look. Then she shrugged. "No skin off my arse either way, but you wanna have a bit of fun, you should go for it, right? Life's too short and all that bollocks."

She just didn't get it. And no way was Mal explaining it. Not even to her.

The text from Jory came through at ten past six, so he hadn't hung about. "Right, that's me off," Mal said, grabbing his rucksack. It now held half a ton of sandwiches and a couple of bottles of cider he'd nicked from the bar. Jago had caught him red-handed, cos the old bastard had ninja skills, but he'd just rolled his eyes so Mal was fairly sure he didn't mind. Or he was planning to bill him double later.

Course, if Jago had known one of those bottles was earmarked for a Roscarrock, he'd have shoved it where the sun didn't shine. Mal was going to have to work on that—it wasn't fair, Jago giving Jory shit for stuff his brother had done.

The clouds had blown over to leave a warm, sunny early evening, everything gleaming bright and smelling fresh from the earlier rain. If there was a better night for a picnic, Mal wanted to meet it. It was kind of a shame they were going underground, but then again, they probably weren't going to spend *all* their time in a cave, were they?

He'd made it almost as far as the cottages above Mother Ivey's Bay when he saw a long, lean figure coming out from behind them. He stared as the figure waved. It looked longer and leaner than he'd expected, somehow.

It was Jory, yeah—and he hadn't been kidding about changing his kit.

"Hi, you made good time, then," Jory called as they drew close.

"Fuck me," Mal blurted out. "Are you wearing *tights*?"

Jory was in, like, head-to-toe Lycra: a blue T-shirt that clung to everything—Christ, Mal could see his *nips*; he was going to fucking *dream* about those—and black leggings that hugged muscular thighs and made Mal want to climb him like a tree.

He was going to kill Tasha, putting all those thoughts of shagging Jory in his head.

Yeah, right. Cos there was no way he'd ever have come up with the idea on his own . . .

"Oh, ah, yes." Jory shrugged, looking a bit sheepish. "It's what I wear when I go climbing. They're very comfortable to move in."

"I bet." Mal would be quite happy to move into them right now, ta very much.

"And they're less likely to catch on anything. Being close-fitting," Jory added.

"Yeah, noticed that." Mal was well proud of his voice for not coming out sounding strangled.

"I, um, brought a spare pair. If you wanted to borrow them. It's pretty deserted up there—no one would see you change."

Fuck him *dead*. "Uh, thanks, but I'll stick to me jeans, okay?" At least they, and the baggy T-shirt he was wearing loose over them, had some hope of camouflaging the stiffy that was already threatening to put in an appearance. Christ knew if he'd be able to control himself when he got a good look at Jory's arse in those tights. He'd probably pass out from lack of blood to the brain.

And yeah, wearing Jory's gear was kind of tempting, but for all the wrong reasons.

"That's fine. It's not like we'll be doing any actual climbing."

They walked up towards Roscarrock House, then followed the lane on past for several hundred yards. Jory stopped at a lay-by, where there was a gap in the hedge.

"We'll have to backtrack a bit, but, um, the more direct route goes from Roscarrock House. I doubt it'd improve the evening to run into Bea or Bran."

As far as Mal was concerned no part of the day was likely to be improved by meeting either of those two, but it probably wouldn't be polite to say so. "No worries. Told you I was up for being energetic, didn't I?"

Jory coughed. "Right. Let's go, then." He led the way through the hedge.

"Did you bring them torches?" Mal asked after they'd walked a short way back.

"Better. I brought us a couple of headlamps." Jory stopped, slung his backpack onto the ground, and bent down to rummage inside.

His arse looked every bit as good in those tights as Mal had been picturing.

Fuck my life. Mal squeezed his eyes shut for a long moment, but that just made it worse. It was like Jory's perfect arse had been printed on the inside of his eyelids. Handy for the spank bank, maybe, but not a lot of help right now.

He opened them quick when Jory spoke again. "I've only got one hard hat, so you should take that."

Mal glared at the yellow hard hat Jory handed him. "Uh-huh. I know what this is about. You want me to be the only one with helmet hair."

"Believe me, it's preferable to the other option." Jory pulled on a headlamp to show him, and Mal had to laugh. The straps flattened his hair in weird places, leaving him with a sort of reverse Mohawk.

"Heh, okay, I'll believe you. So do I put this on first, or do you fit the lamp to it first, or what?" Mal put the hat on without waiting for an answer, just to see how it felt.

Jory stepped up close to him. "We can do it either way."

Do it any way you like, mate— Shit. Mal had to stop taking everything as a bloody innuendo. He took a deep breath, as Jory got even closer and reached up to fit the lamp onto his helmet, still on Mal's head. He'd showered, Mal realised—Jory smelled fresh and clean, with a hint of something posh he couldn't identify.

His dick started to stiffen, and Mal desperately tried to think unsexy thoughts. Old women in saggy tights who smelled of Germolene. Dev's farts after they'd had a curry.

Dead bodies on a train track.

Fuck. Mal stepped backwards, breathing hard.

"Mal? Are you okay?"

His stomach threatening a revolt, Mal held his hand up for a mo, then crouched down with his head low until he could speak. "Sorry. Had a . . . flashback thing. Sorry."

"Oh God." Jory was down there with him in an instant, kneeling in front of him and holding him lightly by the shoulders. "Sorry. I should have thought—of course you wouldn't want to go underground—"

"What?" Mal looked up at him, startled. "Nah, mate, it's good. I mean, underground ain't *the* Underground. Like, no trains. That's the main bit."

At least, he hoped not. Now Jory had mentioned it, he was starting to worry—for fuck's sake, if just trying to get rid of a stiffy was going to set him off . . . No. He was good. He stood up, carefully in case he got light-headed, but he was fine. "Come on. You promised me a cave."

Jory's leg muscles did wonderful things as he got easily to his feet. Seriously, Mal was going to find out who made those climbing tights and give them a fucking awesome review. "Remember, we can cut it short anytime you like."

"Gonna give me a safeword and all?"

Yep, one track mind. God, he was so screwed. In the totally nonliteral sense. Fuck his *life*.

Then again, it seemed to have stopped Jory worrying Mal was about to throw a wobbly any minute now. He was smiling, and a bit pink, but all he said was, "Will red, amber and green do?"

"Nah, that's well boring, that is. Tell you what—if I say 'Mordred,' that means stop, and if I say 'Merlin,' that means carry on. And, uh, 'Arthur' means hold up a minute and wait for the second coming." Jesus, where was his brain getting all this shit?

Jory laughed, though, and Mal found himself smiling right back. They just stood there for a moment, and there was definitely *something* going on . . .

Then some old bloke with a dog strolled past and called out, "Evening," and Jory blinked and said, "Okay, it's this way," and they were off over the field, the moment lost.

Which was good, yeah. Because . . . reasons.

Right.

"So how many people know about this cave of yours?" Mal asked, matching Jory's long strides across scrubby grass.

Jory shrugged. "None that I know of. It's on Roscarrock land, and Bea and Bran don't like to walk up on the cliffs."

Shit. Mal had almost forgotten what Jory had told him about his dad, and how much of an arsehole did *that* make him? "You don't mind?"

"No. I like it out here." Jory turned to Mal. "We weren't close, and if it was the only way he was going to find peace . . ."

Mal swallowed and nodded. He wondered if that poor sod on the tracks had found peace. Couldn't quite see it, not with . . . Shit. Not going to think about that.

"I only found it by chance," Jory went on briskly, which Mal was grateful for. "The original entrance has been lost for a century or longer. Probably caved in, if not deliberately blocked by the authorities. The Roscarrock boundaries aren't as wide as they used to be."

"'The authorities'? That mean the excise men, like in all the stories about smugglers?"

Jory huffed a laugh. "More likely the local council, concerned about possible casualties."

"Yeah? Thought nobody sued in them days."

"Apparently they cared about people getting injured even if it didn't directly cost them." Jory walked past a footpath sign pointing off at a tangent, and opened a gate marked *PRIVATE—NO TRESPASSERS*.

One of those Roscarrock boundaries, Mal guessed. He followed Jory through and closed the gate behind him. "You'd never believe that of the tossers they have in power these days. I don't mean just here. Anywhere you go, politicians are a bunch of smarmy, lying bastards. Don't matter if they're Westminster or local government."

Jory's smile was wry. "Bran was a local councillor, until he decided it was taking too much of his time away from the property business."

Mal gave him a sharp look. "Or he'd made enough contacts already to make sure all his planning applications would go through no questions asked? Shit. Sorry. I know he's your bruv."

"It's okay. You haven't exactly seen him at his best."

Technically he hadn't seen him at all, but he also hadn't seen any evidence the bastard actually *had* a "best," either. Mal bit his tongue on that one. "So how do you know it's a smugglers' tunnel?" he asked instead. "Could it be, like, an old mine, or something?"

"There's no tin in these lands. Or anything else worth having." Jory made a sound that could have been a grim laugh. "You can bet Bran would have exploited it if there was. It's possible the excavations were started in a search for minerals, but nobody knows for sure.

Anyway, there's only one use around here for a tunnel that goes down to a secluded cove."

"Shagging?"

Okay, the next noise was definitely a laugh. Maybe a bit of a splutter. "*Smuggling*. As if you didn't know. Here we are."

Mal stared. "It's a hole. In the ground." It was like some giant had pressed the fingers of both hands into the earth and then pulled them apart, leaving a narrow gap about ten feet long and maybe two feet wide. Or if you saw it another way . . . well, with the grass and weeds growing all around it, it looked like a bloody great green minge. There was even a roundish bit of rock at one end to complete the picture. Not that Mal had anything against minge, but . . . "We're going in there?"

"Don't worry. I've been doing this since I was a boy."

"Early starter, were you?" Seeing Jory's baffled face, Mal went on quick. "Right. Uh, don't we need ropes and stuff?"

"This way into the tunnel was created by a cave-in, so it's pretty steep for the first few yards, but you can easily manage." Jory sounded a lot more confident than Mal felt as they stepped up to the edge.

"Bloody hell, it's like the entrance to the underworld. You sure we ain't gonna meet a welcoming committee of orcs, morlocks, and a bloody great dog with three heads?"

"Not unless they've moved in here since last summer. And I strongly suspect I'd have noticed if so."

"That the last time you were down here?"

Jory nodded. "I was thinking of bringing Gawen, but he'd been having nightmares at the time, and Kirsty thought it might make things worse."

"Did you see a lot of him, back when you weren't living here?"

"As much as I could. Which wasn't really enough."

"That why you moved back?"

"Yes. He's . . ." Jory sighed and crouched down at the edge of the hole, staring into it. Mal tried not to fixate on those muscular thighs, lovingly outlined by the skintight leggings. "He's getting bullied at school. It's always been a problem, but last year it suddenly started getting much worse. Puberty, I suppose. Sometimes I wonder if he would have done better with a private education, but Kirsty wanted him to go to school locally, and I wasn't so sure I wanted to push the issue. That was the one good thing about my school, though. Being bright didn't automatically make you a target." Jory glanced back at Mal. "Did you have that problem? I mean, you're obviously bright and well-read."

Mal blinked. Then he forced a grin. "Nah, mate. Me, well-read? Bollocks. I just remember odd stuff."

Jory raised both eyebrows. "Sorry," he said after a long, awkward moment. "Not the sort of thing you'd want to be reminded of."

"Hey, no worries," Mal said automatically. He *really* wasn't comfortable with the whole topic of conversation. Which was why it made bugger all sense when the next minute he blurted out, "It was crap for a bit, but it stopped when I got friendly with Dev. No one wanted to mess with him."

Jory smiled. "He stood up for you?"

"Nah, it was more, people left me alone cos I was with him."

It was stupid, cos it wasn't even true. Well, it *was*, but it wasn't the whole story. Yeah, hanging around with Dev had pretty much instantly made Mal, who'd been the weediest, swottiest eleven-year-old on the planet ten times cooler, but . . . Shit. No way was he telling Jory the other reason the bullies had laid off him.

"Gawen came up with a different method of dealing with it, I suspect," Jory said, looking away again. "He's never admitted it, but his school grades suddenly went right down last year. I think he was getting questions wrong on purpose in the hope that the less able children would like him."

Mal closed his eyes briefly. Nail on the head or what? Fuck his *life*. "Yeah. I get that." His voice came out rough.

Jory gave him a look that did weird things to Mal's insides, and grasped his arm firmly.

Mal coughed. "Right. We going in, then?"

"If you're ready." Jory switched on his lamp and started to clamber into the hole. It was like watching the world's buffest baby getting born in reverse.

Mal shook himself and switched on his own lamp.

"Careful on this bit," Jory said.

"Don't worry. I'm well careful, me." Mal tried to lower himself into the gap the way he'd seen Jory do it, feetfirst and inching down a steep, uneven slope. He ended up sliding the last few feet on his arse. Jory held out a hand to help him up, which Mal didn't take for a mo because he was so busy looking around.

There was enough light coming from above, and from their headlamps, to show him that they were in a rough tunnel that extended down into darkness. It was sort of man shaped. But bigger. Yeti shaped, maybe? The walls were greyish and uneven, and the floor was only mostly flat.

At least it was tall enough to stand upright, even for Jory. "Ready to go?" he asked.

Mal nodded, the light cast by his headlamp bobbing. "Yep. Lead on."

CHAPTER FOURTEEN

Mal soon realised that following Jory down the tunnel with his headlamp on gave him a fantastic view of that Lycra-covered arse. Trouble was, he also realised he was going to have to be a lot more careful where he looked. Unless he *wanted* Jory to notice there was a big glowy spot parked permanently on his backside. He hoped he'd be able to remember to keep his eyes above the waist when Jory was facing him, or that'd be even worse.

Then again, there was that skintight T-shirt with his nips practically poking through the fabric . . . Maybe Mal had better keep his eyes above Jory's neck. Or not look at him at all.

Right. Eyes on the ground. At least he'd be less likely to fall over anything like old brandy barrels, dead excise men, whatever. "Hey, you ever stumble across a load of blokes in armour snoring away under here?"

"Sadly, no. Nor any sleeping dragons." Jory had turned to answer, and Mal's headlamp showed a tiny smile on his face. "I did my best to find them. After a trip to Tintagel, where I got all fired up on Arthurian legend. God knows what I'd have done if I'd actually found Arthur and all his knights. I think I had some vague idea that they'd teach me how to be a knight, because of course when you wake up from centuries of slumber, your highest priority is going to be the tuition of small boys."

Mal laughed. "Yeah, and you gotta ask yourself, if you wake 'em up, are they gonna be happy about it? We're talking about heavily armed dudes here. And well-dodgy morals. Sod all that crap about chivalry."

"Next you'll be telling me you don't approve of murder, rape, and incest."

"Not exactly my three favourite things, no." Coincidentally, Mal's gaze went back to what *was* one of his favourite things right now. He got his comeuppance a moment later—he tripped and ended up grabbing hold of Jory's shoulder to keep from face-planting on the tunnel floor. "Whoa—sorry mate."

Jory's hand briefly patted Mal's where it lay on his shoulder. "My fault. I should have told you it gets a bit uneven around here."

Mal remembered to let go of him. He was proud of that.

There was silence for a few minutes as they scrambled over a bloody great boulder in the middle of the path—if that was *a bit uneven*, what would Jory call a total cave-in? *Mildly impassable* or some shit?

Then the ceiling got low, and they had to walk bent over. "Oi, you sure you shouldn't be wearing a hard hat and all?" he asked after the third time he'd grazed his helmet on sticky-out rocks.

"Ah . . . Well, I only had the one." Jory's voice sounded guilty as hell. "But strictly speaking, yes. Anyone from my old climbing club would be horrified. So if you ever meet them, please don't tell."

Huh. Not much chance of that, was there? Mal's spirits dropped.

Jory was speaking again. "It's just . . . I've been down here so many times. And there's never been a cave-in in my memory."

"So, what, we're just about due one now?"

"If I said no, it'd be tempting fate, wouldn't it? But fingers crossed."

It felt like they were going down to the centre of the Earth. There wasn't any light apart from their headlamps. And yeah, Mal was used to tunnels, but this was different. It was more . . . real, somehow, feeling his way along uneven ground, rather than sitting in a train cab in stale air that smelled of sweat, packed lunches, and burnt diesel. Here, the air was cold and had a different kind of flatness, the salt of the sea mixed in with a dry earthy odour.

It was well creepy too. So quiet, the only sounds were their own breathing and footsteps. And Mal hitting his helmet on the ceiling, but he was getting better at avoiding that. Every now and then a jagged rock would stick up from the floor like a single broken tooth in the mouth of a monster, or a seam of lighter-coloured rock would flash in the light from their headlamps and make Mal think he'd seen a ghost.

Probably not a friendly one, if it was some long-dead smuggler who thought they were after his booty, and not in a sexy-times way. Or even if it was a murdered excise man, who'd sworn with his dying breath to haunt the smugglers for eternity.

Mal shivered. Didn't they ought to be seeing daylight by now? "You sure this comes out somewhere?" he said, only half-joking. His voice was dry.

"Trust me," Jory said, and right at that moment, they turned a tight bend in the tunnel, and there was more light than Mal knew what to do with. It was blinding, after the darkness underground. He half stumbled out of the tunnel after Jory and found himself walking on soft sand.

He blinked. They were on a tiny beach, in a perfect mini cove. The cliffs curved around the sand in a sort of granite hug, casting long shadows. Even in the shade, the air felt warm and fresh on his exposed skin, with barely a hint of breeze to cool it. Mal took a deep, heady breath.

"Like it?" Jory asked, smiling triumphantly.

Mal shook his head, grinning back. "Fuck me, did they do that on purpose? That hairpin bend just before the end?"

"I think they must have. If by *they* you mean the smugglers who first dug this tunnel. Probably something to do with lanterns not showing out to sea—I expect they used to douse them when they got to the bend, in case there were Revenue vessels out there instead of the cargo they were expecting."

Mal turned round slowly, taking the place in. "It's like . . . There's no way in, is there? You can only get to this beach by sea or by that tunnel."

"Well, given a minimum of gear, I could rappel down the cliffs easily enough. But generally speaking, no." Jory's smile seemed to grow as he pulled off his headlamp, leaving his hair sticking up in cute little tufts. "For all intents and purposes, this is our own private beach."

"And there speaks a man who knows how to show a bloke a good time." Shit, did that come over as suggestive? "Hey, you hungry? I brought sandwiches." Mal took off his helmet and shoved up his sleeves to dive into his rucksack.

"Snap. I've got tuna mayo or cheese—how about you?"

"Yeah, I brought cheese too. But mine's got pickle. And there's ham. And pickle." Mal grinned. "Jago's gonna slaughter me next time they have a run on ploughman's lunches."

"Did you bring drinks? I've got a couple of bottles of Rattler."

"I see your Rattler, mate, and I raise you a couple of packets of—ta-*dah*—bacon fries." Mal pulled them out of his rucksack with a flourish.

Jory laughed. "Okay, I think we can agree we've hopelessly over-catered." He sat down on the sand and pulled a couple of bottles of cider from his own pack, one of which he passed to Mal.

Mal took a long swallow, then breathed out in satisfaction. "Fuck me, that was like liquid gold going down."

Jory gave him a sidelong look. "Except minus all the throat-searing agony you'd expect from *actual* liquid gold."

Mal gave him the finger and took another gulp of cider. "Yeah, stuff's never as good as it sounds, is it? Like, I used to wish Mum had called me Arthur. I mean, if she's so into all them stories, why not name me after the hero, not the bloke who wrote 'em? Then I read *Morte d'Arthur*, and, well." Mal sighed. "He's a bit of a shit, ain't he, Arthur? He's a mass kiddie murderer for a start. There he is, supposed to be this hero, all chivalrous and stuff, but one of the first things he does is kill a bunch of kids—*babies*—cos Merlin tells him one of them'll grow up and kill him in like twenty years' time."

"No, I never much liked the casual way Malory refers to that. But to be fair to Arthur, Merlin was correct."

"Yeah, but he deserved it after that, didn't he?" Mal took a bite out of a cheese and pickle sarnie. It was pretty good, if he said so himself.

"I always felt sorry for Mordred," Jory said, grabbing a sarnie from the opened foil package. "He didn't get a very good start in life. But then again, neither did Arthur, being taken from his mother's arms at birth."

Just like Dev, poor bastard. "Nah, Arthur was fine. His foster family all got top jobs after Arthur was crowned king, so they must have treated him right."

"Still . . . it can be hard, growing up in a family you don't quite feel you fit into." Jory's voice went quiet.

"Yeah, you don't look much like your sister. Dev showed me a picture off the internet."

"Bran's very like her. In pictures of them as children, it's actually hard to tell them apart."

"Was your mum like a second wife or something?"

"Most people just ask if we had a particularly friendly milkman."

Oops. Sore point there. Mal opened his mouth to apologise, but Jory got in again before he could speak, so Mal grabbed another sandwich instead.

"No, it's simply a quirk of genetics. I look a lot like the portrait of my great-uncle Lochrin Roscarrock, as it happens, but the men on my mother's side were tall and fair too. Bran used to tell me I must be a changeling, and the fairies would come back for me one day." Jory gave a twisted smile. "I don't think my mother realised why I always refused to sleep with the window open, even in the hottest summers."

Christ. "The worst lie my big sister ever told me was that the hazard warning lights button in the car worked the ejector seat on the back, and if I didn't stop kicking her seat in the front, she'd press it."

"That seems fairly harmless. Did you believe her?"

Mal laughed. "Course not. Least, that's what I told her. Then one time my dad had to slow down really quick on a motorway cos there'd been an accident, and when he turned on the hazard lights, I screamed the bloody car down. Dad reckons he practically had a heart attack, and they nearly had to send a second ambulance along for us lot."

They ate in silence for a bit, but it didn't feel awkward. More like they were comfortable enough together not to need to fill the gaps with words, and that was such a scary thought Mal gulped down his mouthful and said the first thing that came into his head. "So, you were working at a university before you came back here, right?"

"Yes. I've spent all my time since leaving school in the hallowed halls of academia."

"Yeah? I nearly went there on holiday once, but I didn't fancy the food and I couldn't afford it anyway."

Jory laughed. "That's actually a pretty accurate description of most universities these days."

"Which one did you do your degree at? No, wait, lemme guess. Oxford?"

"The other place. Cambridge." Jory shrugged. "It's traditional, in my family. For a first degree, at any rate. What wasn't traditional was staying there. Bran wasn't impressed. He thought I should be doing something useful, which you can read as either 'lucrative' or 'liable to contribute to the family's political interests.'"

"Huh. My mum would've loved it if I'd gone to uni, but, well . . . Who wants that debt hanging over them? I wanted to be earning, and I didn't really need any more qualifications."

Jory nodded. "That's more or less what Bran said to me after I graduated—the qualifications thing. The fees weren't so bad back when I went to college—they'd only recently started bringing them in."

"So what, you stayed and got a master's or a PhD or whatever?"

"Both."

"That's just showing off, that is," Mal said, because *Fuck, you must be well intelligent* would sound pathetic. "And . . . you were like a lecturer?" He had a vague idea you had to teach if you worked at a university, alongside doing . . . whatever university doctors did.

"And a supervisor for undergraduates. That's the bit I miss most, actually. Teaching small groups, discussing texts with them . . ."

"Don't you hate it in that museum where nobody goes?"

"No, it's fine." Jory smiled. "Knowing it's only temporary makes a big difference. And the place is overdue for a shake-up, so it keeps me occupied."

"You're just doing it for the summer?"

"Yes. I take up a teaching post in September at Gawen's high school. Deputy head of the English Department."

"Yeah? How's he feel about that, then?"

"He's happy, I think. Although whether it's about me working at his school or because it means I'll be staying in Porthkennack, I don't know."

And if that wasn't a timely reminder that him and Jory weren't going anywhere, Mal didn't know what was. "Oi, he ain't hoping you're going to get back with his mum, is he?"

"As we've never actually been together, I doubt it." Jory stared out to sea. "You're probably thinking I'm a terrible father."

"Nah, it wasn't your fault. Shit happens. And you're making up for it now." Which was the main thing. Not like Jory's sister, who'd had a second chance to make things right with Dev and had just chucked it in the toilet. "You should totally bring him down here. Bet he'd love it. Smugglers and pirates and all that crap, kids go for them lot, don't they?"

Jory smiled. "I will."

"Although . . . ain't it a bit embarrassing for the family, knowing your great-great-whatever-grandparents were involved in smuggling? I mean, they had to be, didn't they? No way that tunnel could have been dug on their land without them knowing about it." Mal gave Jory a sidelong look. "That brother of yours, Bran, he's gotta be really pissed off about the criminal past."

"You're not thinking like a Cornishman. Back in those days, *everyone* was involved in smuggling—or free-trading, which is how they viewed it. A lot of people saw it as morally justified. The English taxes were so high, the Cornish people would have starved without the free-traders."

"You say *English* like it's a . . . like Cornwall's a separate country."

"That's because it is. Or was. A separate race, with a separate language. If you go back a few centuries, the idea of Cornwall being part of England was in many ways just that—an idea, not a concrete reality in the everyday life of the Cornish people."

"You, mate, sound far too English to be saying it like you miss them days."

Jory stretched out his arms, his hands clasped together over his head. Mal basked in the view, even better than the one in front of them, as all the muscles in Jory's arms and shoulders stood out sharply, nothing hidden by the thin, stretchy T-shirt. "I may not sound Cornish, but it's in my blood. Sometimes . . . sometimes I wonder how on Earth I ever stayed away so long." He turned to give Mal a sharp look. "I suppose you feel the same way about London."

"What? Nah, I . . ." Mal stopped to actually think about it. "I dunno. I mean, yeah, it's where I've lived all me life, but I dunno about it being in my blood or nothing. S'pose cities are like that. Most people who live in 'em came from somewhere else, even if it's a few generations down the line. You got all this history here, and you can read about it or whatever and think, 'My great-great-grandad was living here when that happened—in the same *house*'—and it's more, like, connected, innit? And yeah, London's got a ton of history, but I ain't got a bloody clue where all my ancestors were when it happened." He laughed and raised his bottle of cider. "Probably in a pub somewhere, though. Cheers."

"Cheers," Jory said, and raised his own bottle before drinking.

"It's weird to think about, though, innit?" Mal nudged a piece of driftwood with his foot. "This place, this actual patch of sand, hundreds of years ago, swarming with smugglers and excise men. 'Brandy for the parson, 'baccy for the clerk' . . ."

"'Laces for a lady, letters for a spy,'" Jory carried on the quote, which Mal was well chuffed about cos he hadn't been sure he'd remembered it right.

"Yeah, and 'Watch the wall, my darling, while the gentlemen go by.'" Mal grinned. "Sounds a bit risky now you think about it."

"I don't think Kipling had that *particular* interpretation in mind." Jory chuckled.

"He was Victorian, wasn't he? They were all a bit repressed. Not good for a bloke, that ain't. You gotta let it all hang out."

"Could let anything you like hang out here," Jory said. "No one's around to see."

Was that a come-on? Mal took another swig of cider to cover his sudden nerves. Then he shivered at a gust of wind, and Jory's arm wrapped around his shoulders and Mal thought, *Yeah, that was a come-on all right.*

CHAPTER
FIFTEEN

"Is this all right?" Jory asked, and Mal really wished he hadn't, because he'd been quite happy ignoring the question and enjoying the moment.

But, shit, it was just a fucking cuddle. Not even with both arms. *Tash* gave him cuddles that were more full-on than this, and there'd been nothing dodgy going on there cos Mal liked his balls where they were, ta very much. "'S fine," he said, relaxing into it a bit.

Jory let out a breath and squeezed him tighter.

"Fuck, I want you." It sort of slipped out without Mal meaning it to, and when he saw the look on Jory's face, there was no way he was going to take it back. And, well, he liked Jory. A fuck of a lot.

One little shag wasn't going to hurt, was it? Him and Dev had screwed around back when both of them were single, and it hadn't ruined anything. They were still best mates. Tash was right. Life was too short.

Yeah. One little shag would be fine. Mal closed the last bit of remaining distance between them, pulling Jory fully into his arms. He felt great there—warm and solid. And he smelled fucking awesome, a hint of fresh sweat from scrambling down the tunnel all mingled in with the briny sea smell that got into everything round here. Mal nuzzled into his neck, wanting more of it, and Jory tightened his grip round Mal's waist before lying back in the sand, taking Mal with him.

Oh yeah. Mal was half-hard already, and when he felt the thick, hot ridge digging into his hip, he was all the way there quicker than you could say, *Fuck me, those tights don't hide nothing.* He ground down on it, and Jory groaned, which turned Mal on even more, like a feedback loop which was going to end up busting the eardrums of the *world*. He kissed Jory roughly, biting his lip and shoving in some tongue. Jory tasted wicked, like cider and pickle and pirates. Mal wanted to eat him whole.

Strong hands were kneading Mal's arse like it was made of dough. Fuck, he wanted those fingers inside him. He scrabbled at his zip, desperate to get his jeans undone.

Jory breathed a word or two that could have been, *Oh God*, and then the world flipped, and Mal was on his back, Jory looming over him like the hottest fantasy he'd ever had. And seriously, all that education was definitely good for something, cos Jory had Mal's jeans open and shoved down his hips in about 0.3 seconds flat. And, and he'd somehow got his own dick out, fuck knew how, magic maybe, and they were pressed together with Jory's big hand wrapped around them both, and Jesus, Mal was gonna die.

It was all going to be over way too soon, so Mal summoned up the dregs of his willpower and pushed Jory a few inches away. "Wanna suck you."

Jory took a deep, deep breath, then rolled off Mal and onto his back on the sand.

Mal raised himself up onto his elbow and drank in the sight. Christ, he was amazing. But not nearly naked enough.

Jory narrowed his eyes. "Need directions?"

"Nope. Just waiting for you to get that shirt off." Mal stripped his own T-shirt off, in case Jory needed a visual cue, and yeah, that seemed to work cos seconds later he was gazing in lust at the glory that was Jory's chest. It was, like, *all* muscle, except for a healthy amount of hair that Mal had the weirdest idea he wanted to floss his teeth with.

Maybe he wouldn't mention that bit out loud.

"God, you're gorgeous," he breathed instead, and fuck him if Jory's nipples didn't tighten as he said it. Mal wanted to kiss them and grope them and rub his dick on them all at the same time. He settled for lying down on Jory, chests together and dicks— Fuck, yeah. "Wanna come all over you," he heard himself say, and judging from how Jory's hands clamped on his arse like a vice, there wouldn't be too many objections coming.

Heh. *Coming.*

Christ. Mal was drunk, but not on cider. He was drunk on Jory. Totally gone, off his head, nuts in the bonce, and away with the fairies. And they weren't touching enough, so Mal pushed his jeans all the way off any old how, and then he peeled Jory's tights down a bit further, and yeah, that was better.

"You're beautiful," Jory said softly, and it made Mal's heart hurt, so he kissed Jory silent, ate his words and was still hungry for more.

Lips were good, yeah, were fucking fantastic, but there were many other parts of Jory he needed to taste, so Mal swirled his tongue one last time around Jory's mouth and then moved down to bite at his neck. Jory bucked up, groaning. And that was, fuck, that had to be the best positive reinforcement in the world, so Mal switched to sucking, right down low by Jory's collarbone, where Jory would be able to hide the mark for work. He was considerate that way, Mal was.

Then he moved straight on down to Jory's chest, because he could be a selfish bastard too, and he'd been gagging to taste one of those rosy red nipples. And jeez, that was good, all hard under his tongue, just asking to be bitten, like the little tart it was. So Mal bit it, just a gentle nip, then he moved on to the other one. And Jory was gasping and groaning, and his hands were all over Mal, stroking and squeezing, as if Mal was a juicy piece of fruit on a market stall. It was so fucking awesome, and he'd known it—he'd known him and Jory would be perfect together—so why the fuck hadn't they done this before?

And okay, maybe he skimped a bit on the rest of Jory as he kissed his way down the treasure trail, but Christ, who could blame him? The first taste of Jory's dick was . . . It was like being plunged into the sea, held underwater until you turned half fish and learned how to breathe down there. It was like seeing colour for the first time, or the piercing bright dawn after working a night shift underground. Too much, far too much—but you still wanted it. Needed it. Mal swirled his tongue around the head because, God, he had to taste it all.

Jory swore, the words all choked up in a sob, and it went straight to Mal's dick, which was just hanging in midair, untouched. And that was a fucking tragedy. Mal shifted position until he was lying on Jory, humping his leg like a husky in heat, his mouth still on that gorgeous cock. Jory's balls fit in his hand as if they'd been made to measure, and he rolled them and tugged on them as he carried on sucking.

"Oh God," Jory gasped. "Going to—" He tried to push Mal's head off his dick, but fuck that for a game of soldiers. Mal held on tight as jet after jet of hot spunk hit the back of his throat, making him gag and swallow. Christ, that was magic.

Mal's eyes were watering by the time he finally let Jory push him away with shaking hands.

Jory's chest was heaving, his eyes glazed. "God . . . That. You."

Sitting back up on his knees, still straddling Jory's legs, Mal grinned and wiped his mouth with the back of his hand. "Oh yeah." He grabbed hold of his dick and started stroking it, slower than he needed, just enough to keep himself on the edge. "You ready for this? Gonna paint you all over."

Jory actually, honest to God, *shuddered*. And, like, not in a bad way, at least not judging from how his hands tightened on Mal's knees, which were the only bits of him Jory could reach.

Mal sped up his hand, jerking himself off for real now, drinking in the sight of Jory laid out beneath him, all sweat-slick and sex-drunk. He was so beautiful it hurt. "Gonna mess you up, make you so fucking filthy . . ." It ended in a drawn-out groan as he shot his load, streams of jizz jetting out and landing in streaks on Jory's chest and, fuck, yeah, on his face too. Christ, that made an awesome picture. Mal was going to remember that till the day he died. Like Jory was Mal's, all his, marked up so no one else would dare to touch him.

He collapsed down by Jory's side, breathing hard, then grabbed Jory and pulled him in for a quick, hard kiss that smeared spunk from Jory's beard all over Mal's chin.

If he hadn't just had sex, he'd think that was well gross . . .

Shit. He'd just had sex. With Jory.

Mal scrambled to his feet and pulled on his jeans, his fingers clumsy. That had been . . . And Jory's *face* . . .

Sitting up and wiping himself down with one of the paper napkins he'd brought with the sandwiches, Jory was smiling like he'd won the bloody lottery. "That was amazing. I knew we'd . . . Listen, I want you to come back to Roscarrock House with me. Meet Bran and Bea. Once they know we're together—"

"Whoa, hey, hold on, mate." Mal's mouth was dry, but he had to shut Jory up, he *had* to, cos every word was like a knife between his ribs. He wished so fucking hard he could be like Jory, could believe this would all end up in happy-ever-after land, but he couldn't.

His stomach was twisted up in knots, and his chest felt bruised inside, like he'd eaten a dodgy curry and come down with pneumonia all at once. Or like that time the dickhead who'd picked on him all through primary school had seen Mal in the park holding hands with another lad, and barged in with his mates to give them both a kicking.

It was all going wrong. It was only supposed to be a shag. It wasn't supposed to *mean* anything.

He hadn't wanted things to change between them. Being mates with Jory, that was good—but he couldn't let himself hope for more. He couldn't. "Look, it was great, but it's just . . . I mean, I'm only here for a holiday, so . . . It was only a bit of fun, yeah? No need to bother your family and all that."

Christ, Jory's face. Mal couldn't look at him, so he turned away and grabbed up the hard hat that was lying upturned on the sand. "We'd better get back, yeah?"

CHAPTER SIXTEEN

Jory couldn't understand it. What the hell had gone wrong?

There was a simple answer to that. He'd been trying to make what had happened on the beach into more than what it was. Christ, he might as well have asked Mal to bloody *marry* him, with all that babbling about them being together and how Mal should meet his family, for God's sake.

"Them that asks no questions isn't told a lie . . ."

He was an *idiot*. A stupid, pathetic, needy idiot. But, damn it, what was he *supposed* to think, with Mal blowing hot and cold all the time?

Jory's rising bubble of anger hit the guilty knowledge that Mal was recovering from a trauma, for God's sake, and punctured wetly, leaving only a hot tide of humiliation in its wake. "Look," he said urgently as they climbed through the dark, the way seeming far longer than it had coming. "I'm sorry about . . . I shouldn't have assumed."

Mal didn't turn. "'S okay."

Jory barely caught his muttered words. He didn't sound okay.

When they finally emerged at the other end of the tunnel to skies streaked with red and pink, Jory tried again. "Back at the beach . . . Just forget what I said. Too much cider. There's no need—"

"You might as well take the short cut back from here," Mal interrupted him. "No point you going out of your way."

"It's no trouble," Jory insisted, beginning to feel desperate and, worse, angry. For God's sake. Did Mal think he couldn't be trusted to keep his hands to himself if they walked together?

"Nah, 's okay. Cheers and all. Here you go." Mal handed over his hard hat, and their fingers brushed. Mal flinched. "I think . . . maybe we shouldn't see each other for a bit."

The words were like a blow to Jory's already churning stomach. "What? No, that's—" He pulled himself up short. He *wasn't* going to be pathetic, damn it. "Fine. If that's what you want."

Mal nodded, then turned on his heel and walked away.

Jory stood there for a long time, just watching the sun set.

Then he walked the lonely path back to Roscarrock House.

CHAPTER SEVENTEEN

Mal's feet were aching by the time he got back down to the Sea Bell, and he felt weary to the bone, even though his rucksack had been a lot lighter than on the way up.

He'd fucked things up good and proper with him and Jory. Like he'd known he would. *One little shag* . . . Yeah, right. Dick-brain. Dick. *Brain*.

He didn't get it, though. Him and Dev had shagged loads of times and never stopped being friends. Why the hell couldn't it work like that with Jory? Why couldn't they just be mates who shagged?

Christ, he wanted Dev here. Not for a shag, cos they didn't do that anymore since Dev had got together with Kyle, but as a mate. His *best* mate. Someone who could tell him why this thing with Jory was doing his head in so much.

All he knew was that he needed to stay away from Jory Roscarrock. That was the only way not to fuck things up even more.

Tasha was behind the bar when he walked in to slump on a barstool. She took one glance at him and rolled her eyes. "What you done?"

"Oi, who says I done anything?"

"Your face. Better not go near any police lineups, cos you look guilty as hell." She took a step nearer, and her nose wrinkled. "Oh my God, you didn't?"

"Didn't what?"

"You know." She cast a glance around before leaning over the bar and lowering her voice. "Do the dirty. With him."

"'Do the dirty'? Since when do you call it that?"

She curled her lip. "Since Jago started fining me a pound every time I swear at work. And don't change the subject. You did, didn't you?"

Mal hung his head. "It just happened, all right? You know what it's like."

"Jesus, Mal, couldn't you keep it in your kecks for once? What happened to 'He's me best mate's uncle'?"

It sounded dead pervy when she said it like that. "What happened to 'No skin off my arse'?"

Tasha glanced over at Jago, then leaned in close and lowered her voice. "Yeah, well, you got me thinking, dintcha? Like maybe it ain't such a good idea after all. Dev's like . . . He needs his family, you know? But he ain't going to choose some uncle he's never met over his best mate if it all goes tits up. And, babe, you got *tits up* all over your face."

"Yeah, well. 'M gonna stay away from him from now on."

"Bit late now, innit? For God's sake, Mal—"

Mal pushed away from the bar and stood up. "Look, just leave it, all right? I fucked up. I know I fucked up. I'm one big fucking fuckup, for fuck's sake." He turned to walk out—and realised he was the centre of a big bubble of silence with everyone in the place staring at him.

There was a loud throat-clearing sound from Jago's direction.

Mal sagged, sat down again, and pulled out his wallet. "How much?"

"Five pounds, by my reckoning," Jago said calmly, and shoved a jar down the bar to him. It rattled on the way from the half-dozen pound coins already in there.

Mal folded up a fiver and bunged it in the jar without a word. Jago's face softened. "Go on, Tasha, give the lad a pint on the house. He looks like he needs one."

A few of the locals raised their glasses at Mal, then went on with their conversations as if nothing had happened.

Mal pillowed his head on his arms and closed his eyes.

Maybe if he wished really, really hard, the world would go away for a bit.

Mal was almost feeling like himself after a pint of Coke had washed away the bleariness from all that cider on the beach. What was it about drinking outdoors that always made alcohol taste so much better, and not seem to be making you drunk until suddenly you were, and it was too late?

That was when he noticed Tash kept darting worried glances at him.

She must have noticed him noticing. "Babe? You okay now?"

Mal forced a grin. "Course I am. Never better. 'Sup?"

She looked away. "I had a call from Dev while you were out."

Unease knifed him in the gut. "Oi, what's happened? He all right? Is it Kyle?"

"It's okay. They're fine— Well, Dev's fine. Kyle had a problem with his meds, it was no big. They changed the brand on him and he had a reaction."

"But he's okay, yeah?"

"Yeah, but . . . they wanna make sure he's fine on the new stuff before they come down, so it's not gonna be Friday night now. Dev reckons maybe the middle of next week."

It was like . . . like having some arseholes give you a kicking, and then getting shat on by a pigeon while you lay there bleeding. Like totalling your car in a crash, finding out your insurance had lapsed, and then getting a final demand from the finance company. Like he was a pumpkin that'd been hollowed out with one of them blunt plastic scraper things they sold around Halloween so the kiddies wouldn't cut their fingers off making lanterns. Mal put his head in his hands.

And he *knew* he was being a wanker, and it wasn't all about him. But . . . he'd been counting on Dev coming down. He fucking needed his best mate, all right?

"Babe?"

Mal scrubbed his face with his hands and forced a smile as he looked up. "I'm good. Bit disappointed, you know? And it sucks for Kyle," he added guiltily.

"Yeah. Dev said he ain't too bad, though. They're just being safe. You want another Coke?"

"Nah. Cheers. Think I'll go watch the telly for a bit."

"Okay. See ya."

"See ya."

Mal had thought they'd finished talking about all the difficult stuff, but Tasha cornered him later as he walked out of the bathroom after his shower. "You weren't the only one looking forward to seeing Dev, you know."

Mal felt like a complete arsehole. He wrapped a mostly dry arm around her shoulders. "I know you've been missing him too. Come on, tell your uncle Mal all about it."

She sniffed. "It's Ceri, innit? Going away like that. Just when I thought we was . . ."

"I knew it! I fucking knew it. Hey, congrats, Tash. Welcome to the bi side, where love has twice as many chances to screw you over like a boss."

Tasha managed a weak smile. "Do I get a membership card?"

"Better than that. Free invisibility cloak and a pack of unicorn stickers." He squeezed her shoulders. "Does she know you like her?"

Tasha shrugged. "Dunno, do I? I never said nothing. But I thought it was gonna happen. Then she bloody well bogs off out of the country without me."

"Maybe she needed a bit of space to think about it. I mean . . ." Mal wasn't sure how to put it tactfully, so he just went for it. "Does she even fancy girls?"

"She never talks about that stuff."

"What? You're girls, aintcha? I thought you talked about everything."

"Yeah, but . . . she don't go out with people, does she? Not no more."

Mal grinned, because there had been a bloody big dollop of West Country in those last few words. Then he saw her expression and kicked himself, mentally speaking. This wasn't the time to tease her about going native. "Well, that's good, innit? Means you ain't got to worry about her getting with someone while she's away."

"S'pose."

"And, like, when she's here, she spends all her time with you, right? Apart from studying and that."

"S'pose."

"So you're sorted, aintcha? Bet she's missing you as much as you're missing her." He gave her a squeeze, which was when the towel round his waist decided to make a break for freedom and fell to the floor.

Tasha squealed and shrieked, "Get away from me, you perv!"

Jago reached the top of the stairs to see her pissing herself laughing and Mal trying to hold on to his dignity with both hands. He had a lot of dignity, all right?

Jago raised an eyebrow and said, "Never mind, my lad. Chances are you're still growing." Then he walked past them to his bedroom.

Well, if nothing else, it cheered Tasha up, Mal thought as he made a grab for his towel and legged it to his room.

CHAPTER EIGHTEEN

Jory had never expected to be so grateful for his stopgap job at the museum, but it was a lifeline over the next few days. He threw himself into organising the mermaid exhibition and didn't think about Mal in the slightest.

The fact that he couldn't seem to keep himself from looking up hopefully whenever the door opened was just . . . just him hoping for more visitors, that was all.

After work, he went for walks on the beach, with or without Gawen. Or he baked. He'd taken to keeping a tin of biscuits on the front desk at the museum now, and offering them to anyone who came in—well, there were only so many he could give to Kirsty and Gawen, and Bea was no help at all in eating them up.

Bran could buy his own biscuits. Jory couldn't help thinking half the trouble between him and Mal was down to Bran having flown right off the handle last year over Dev.

Of course, strictly speaking, he should be blaming Bea too. But he couldn't bring himself to, somehow. She'd been so . . . *quiet* lately. He wouldn't go so far as to say she was sad, because he'd never been any good at telling how Bea was feeling, but she didn't seem particularly happy. As if she was upset by the Dev issue being raised again.

Logic told him he was theorising without evidence. Logic was bloody well overrated.

At five o'clock on a day that had been even quieter than average, Jory shut up the museum as usual. Time to go home. All of a sudden, though, he just couldn't face another long evening in that big, echoing house being ignored by Bran and Bea.

If he was going to be lonely anyway, he'd rather do it on his own, thanks.

Gawen had piano tonight and homework afterwards, so there was no point going round there. And Jory shouldn't rely on his son every time he felt the urge to get out of the house in any case. Gawen had a life of his own. It was past time Jory started building one for himself in Porthkennack.

Walking back up the cliff path, he had the urge to break into a run. He was restless—physically as well as mentally. He needed something more physical to do than just baking his way through the EU flour mountain. Glancing at the craggy shapes of the cliffs gave him his inspiration.

There was a boulder down one end of Booby's Bay he'd been meaning to have a go at for a while, and tackling it would be ideal to ease him back into climbing. Technical enough to take his mind off . . . things, but with zero safety issues. And if he found his stamina wasn't up to a lengthy session, he could simply jump off.

He had all the gear he'd need in the back of the Qubo already, so all he'd have to do was change his clothes and jump in the car. Well, that and avoid Bran, so as not to face any awkward questions about what he was up to. Jory wasn't sure if Bran understood the distinction between bouldering and riskier forms of climbing, and he just didn't have the patience to explain it right now.

Jory made it through the house and up to his room without incident, and miracle of miracles, managed to get back out to his car safely too.

Of course, sod's law meant that when he got down to Booby's Bay, he found the Slanted Boulder, named for its diagonally rising undercut seam, already taken. Jory dumped his backpack on the ground and watched for a while as a skinny young lad—probably around Mal's age, or maybe a bit younger—talked his girlfriend through a rising traverse.

Jory had only been watching for ten minutes when he decided she'd have managed fine without the running commentary—her would-be instructor apparently hadn't even noticed she was quietly ignoring his advice wherever she saw fit.

When she finished the traverse and jumped down, Jory made a point of stepping forward to congratulate her. "Nice job."

"Thanks!" The girl turned to smile at him. Her face was marred by a big scab on the end of her nose. Looking closer, Jory could see other signs of recent minor injury. "It's my first time back—took a fall last week and missed the crash pad. But I made it this time!"

They fist-bumped. Her obvious buzz was infectious, but out of the corner of his eye Jory could see the boyfriend hovering sullenly, and decided he'd better cut this short to avoid causing a row. He turned to the skinny lad. "Are you planning on tackling it now, or can I have a go?"

The lad visibly relaxed at the evidence that Jory was only muscling in on his boulder, not on his girlfriend. "All yours, mate. Think we're gonna head down to the wall now." He sent a questioning glance at the girl, who nodded. "Won't even spray beta at you this time," the lad added, and she gave him a fond smile.

"It helped. Honest."

Jory felt a lot more kindly disposed to him on learning he'd been providing a safety net, rather than simply showing off.

"Just let me clean up," she went on, then brushed away the few patches of white chalk she'd left, packed up her mat and shoes, and left, hand in hand with the boyfriend.

Jory watched them go for a minute.

If only all things were as easy to get over as a fall from a boulder. Would getting back into the driving seat—any driving seat—help Mal? He couldn't help thinking getting over killing a man with a train, however unintentionally, wasn't going to be so simple.

And anyway, hadn't Mal made it clear he didn't want anything more from Jory?

The memory left a bitter taste in his mouth. Jory forced himself to focus, pulling out his crash pad, shoes, and chalk. The problem he wanted to try was a vertical climb up the left side of the boulder, with a sit start. The climbing forum he'd seen it described on had rated it as of average difficulty, and it seemed like a good one to dust off his skills on.

Jory gazed at the boulder until he was certain he had it mapped in his head, then got into the starting position. A soft breeze ruffled his hair and cooled the back of his neck. As he concentrated on the problem and began to climb, the world dropped away, narrowing into the distance to his next hand- or foothold. He could feel his limbs stretching properly for the first time in what felt like ages. He'd ache tomorrow, but he'd have earned it.

His toes slipped halfway up, but he recovered, and after that it was easier, the holds more secure. He'd always loved bouldering— there might not be the heady achievement of a long, difficult climb up a vertical cliff face, but it was freeing, climbing without the heavy tackle of ropes and harness. Conquering nature's barriers by his own efforts alone.

When he reached the top, it felt like too soon. Then again . . . the online forum had described several other problems on this one boulder, including the rising traverse, and when Jory cast a glance down behind him, he couldn't see anyone queuing up to have a go. There were just a couple of tourists watching the spectacle.

Jory smiled to himself, double-checked the fall area was clear, and jumped off.

An hour or so later, Jory slung his backpack onto the passenger seat of the Qubo and changed out of his climbing shoes. He felt better now. Calmer.

And absolutely ravenous. Time to head home.

Traffic through town was light, the rush hour, such as it was, already over, and Jory made it back to Roscarrock House in good time. He parked the Qubo in the old stables and was stowing his backpack and climbing shoes in the boot when Bran walked in, car keys in hand. Jory froze. Damn. Why the hell hadn't he put everything away down at the bay?

Had Bran noticed?

"Off out?" Jory asked, trying to sound casual. He was a grown man, damn it, and he didn't need Bran's permission for his hobbies.

But he didn't have the energy for a row right now.

"Obviously." Bran gave Jory an unreadable look. He was wearing a dark suit and tie, so presumably was going to some kind of business dinner. "You're late back."

"Making the most of the weather." Jory kept his gaze level.

After a moment Bran, turned away and went to his car.

Jory found Bea in the kitchen, staring into the fridge as if hoping a meal would magically spring out and cook itself.

Or maybe merely wondering who'd had the last of the celery sticks. If she'd wanted them saved, she shouldn't have left them so temptingly close to the sour cream dip.

She looked up at Jory. "Oh, hello. You're late."

"Uh, yes." Jory forced himself to go on cheerfully. "I was going to cook—care to join me?"

She blinked and straightened. "All right. As it's just the two of us."

He hadn't expected her to accept. It was an unpleasant shock to realise he'd probably better come up with something a little more "proper" than his half-formed plan of having whatever was in the fridge with pasta and canned tomatoes. Of course, there were any number of ready meals in the freezer, but he had his pride.

In the end, he knocked up a quick risotto, adding a kick with some leftover chorizo, which she eyed dubiously but tucked into well enough with a comment of, "This is actually quite nice."

Jory narrowed his eyes at her over a forkful of food. "You know, it'd be a better compliment if you left out the 'actually.'"

"When did you learn to cook? I always assumed you ate in hall, at your universities. I did."

"That's because you were only there for three years, as an undergraduate. And not every university is like Cambridge. Dining in a medieval college with a high table and Latin grace is one thing. Mucking in with a load of teenagers in an overcrowded student union café is quite another."

She half smiled. "I always did wonder how you managed, living a student lifestyle all these years. Bran used to say he thought you just didn't want to grow up."

"Bran can—" Jory caught himself up short. This friendly atmosphere between them felt like a fragile thing, easily shattered. "Make his own dinner," he finished weakly.

"He does have your best interests at heart."

Did he, bollocks. "I think I'm old enough to judge for myself what's in my best interest, thanks."

Bea frowned. "You know it wasn't easy for him when Father died."

"Uh, no. I'm sure it wasn't." Jory racked his brains for innocuous topics of conversation. Then he had it—something Mal had asked about.

Not that he was hoping to use it as an excuse to talk to Mal again. Obviously.

"Bea, I was wondering—that legend about Mary Roscarrock back in sixteen-oh-whatever turning to piracy. I know we play it up for the tourists, but is there much truth in it?"

She gave him an odd look. "Why the interest?"

"I, um . . . For Gawen. He likes to learn about family history." Jory instinctively felt it would be better not to mention any possible museum exhibits until he knew more about the subject. Bea might be difficult about that sort of thing, and there was no point starting a fight before it was necessary.

"I'm sure he's heard the stories already."

"Yes, but he's, uh, very factually minded. I think he'd appreciate knowing how much of the legend is actually true. Do we have any family records, anything like that?"

Bea put her fork down, although she was only halfway through her risotto, and pushed her chair back.

"Bea?" What on earth had he said to upset her? He put down his own fork, ready to stand up if she did. "What's wrong?"

She shook her head. "It's nothing. . . You should finish your meal. Don't let it go to waste."

That was rather hypocritical of her, as although she stayed at the table, she didn't touch the remainder of her food. Jory had more or less lost his appetite too, but he ate anyway. Maybe it would help her compose herself.

He'd probably given her too much on her plate in any case.

After a few minutes, he was rewarded by her speaking again.

"It brought back some memories, that's all." She had a drink of water, then replaced her glass precisely in the middle of the coaster. "I don't suppose I've really thought about Mary Roscarrock since I was sixteen."

"I don't understand."

"You *do* recall what happened that year?" Bea asked, her tone impatient.

Jory hesitated, then said it anyway. "Dev was born? But I don't see—"

"I needed something to distract me, all those months I was just ... waiting. It wasn't like I could go to school. So I looked up her history. Mummy helped. We sorted through old family letters we found in the attic, and went over parish records. It was something we could do together that wasn't too tiring. Although she did seem better that year. For a while."

Jory had a sudden, vivid image of his sister, visibly pregnant, being kept out of everyone's sight. Locked up in the house like a mad wife in the attic.

It almost, but not quite, banished the sour taste of jealousy that she and their mother had been so close.

"Why Mary? Why not, say, the first Sir John? He sailed with Sir Francis Drake, after all. Or the Jacobite one? I'd have thought they'd have been easier to research—more fully documented, at any rate—if you wanted to fill in some family history."

Bea made an impatient noise, taking him right back to his childhood. She didn't often do that now she was grown-up. "I thought she was like me, don't you see?"

"Like you how?"

"Think about it. She was cast out by the family. What *did* young ladies get disowned for in those days, if not for sexual misconduct?"

"So you assumed she got pregnant? By someone unsuitable?"

She nodded. "A fisherman, I thought. Or someone who worked for the family. Someone poor."

"*Was* that what happened? Or didn't you manage to find out?"

"I was wrong. She didn't have a child out of wedlock, and there was no unsuitable young man from the village." She almost laughed, then, but it had a bitter sound. "She *was* the unsuitable young man. At least as far as I can find out. It's only circumstantial, of course, but there's a fragment of a letter from her sister, Anne, to her husband, which talks of 'my younger brother, the one I'm not to speak of.' But she didn't have a younger brother, not according to parish records.

And there's other evidence in the letter that suggests it was Mary she was referring to."

"So . . . Mary was trans?" Jory was still reeling from the idea of Bea searching for a relative with whom she could feel a kindred spirit. Was it possible he wasn't the only one who hadn't quite felt at home in their odd, amputated little family?

Bea shrugged. "What does it matter, at this distance? Maybe she was just a butch dyke." The words sounded ugly coming from her, but although they made him uncomfortable, Jory wasn't convinced she'd meant them to. "At any rate, she was nothing like me." She picked up her glass of water and took a sip, as if to wash away a bad taste.

Poor Bea. "I wish you'd told me," he blurted out.

"About Mary Roscarrock? Why should you care?"

"No. About you. About the baby."

"You were a child."

"I grew out of it. And then I had Gawen . . ." Jory hesitated, then put a hand on her arm. She frowned at it oddly, but didn't shake it off, which was something. "It must have been hard for you. Another baby in the family."

Bea looked down at her hands, clasped awkwardly in her lap. "We never liked you, you know. Bran and I."

Jory felt as if she'd slapped him.

She didn't seem to notice. "When you were born . . . even before then, Mummy was tired all the time, and she used to say it would get better after the baby was born, and it never did. We didn't know it was because she was ill. We thought it was just *you*." She paused, and when she spoke again, it was in a low murmur, as if she was talking more to herself than to him. "She was always telling us to play with you so she could get some rest, but you were too young to play properly, and you cried all the time, and it was never any fun. I never liked playing with babies, not even pretend." Finally, she looked at him. "You must have thought I was a horrible big sister."

"I . . ." Jory shook his head, still floored by her uncomfortable honesty. He'd always known they'd disliked him, in that sense that one knows something deep inside without being able to explain why. But he'd never expected her to come out and say it. He felt a strange mix of nausea and vindication—and, absurdly, gratitude that she'd admitted it at last.

Equally absurdly, he felt the need to reassure her that it didn't matter—but he didn't know what to say. *I hated Bran more than I hated you* might not actually be a comfort. "It was a long time ago, and we're different people now."

"I know I am."

Jory realised to his shock that she was crying. "Bea?"

"I never wanted children. I knew that from the moment you were born. No, longer. But then I got pregnant . . . You've got no idea what it's like to give up a child. A baby. One you've carried in your womb for nine months."

Jory frowned. "That's not fair. After Gawen was born, I had to go back to college and hardly saw him for months on end. You know that. You and Bran *insisted* on it."

"That doesn't even compare. Someone handed you a baby and told you it was yours and you learned to love it. *I felt that child kicking.* He was real to me for months before he was born. Have you any idea what it was like to give him away the very day I saw him for the first time?"

"Then why—"

"*Because it was the right thing to do.* Christ, you have no idea, do you? It *hurt*, Jory. Like giving birth, only worse. God, how much worse. Like part of me was being ripped away. You know what happens to a woman's body when she gives birth? It turns into a boiling fog of hormones, all designed to make her *suffer* if she loses her child. I made up my mind then, I was never going to feel like that again. Never going to let myself be hurt so badly."

"Dev's a grown man now," Jory said softly, his heart aching for her. All these years he'd thought her cold and in control.

He'd been right, perhaps—but she'd got there the hard way.

"Yes. He is. I'm never going to get my baby back."

"But you could—"

"No. It's too late. He doesn't need me now, so why should he want me? Beyond curiosity's sake. Or for money, maybe. You think we'd all be one big happy family for ever and ever? It doesn't work like that. It never did, even when it was just you and me and Bran and Mummy and Father. He'd take what he wanted from us, and all I'd get would be to lose my child all over again. I *can't* let him in. I can't."

She stood up. "Thank you for the meal. It was very nice. Please don't . . . don't do anything misguided. I don't want any more contact with Devan Thompson."

Jory watched her leave the room, knowing that the next time he saw her she'd be calm, composed, perfect Bea once more.

Apparently he'd missed out on that gene.

What the hell was he doing, living here with Bea and Bran? This wasn't a happy house. It would never be a happy house—not for him, and quite possibly not for them. *Not that anyone's likely to be able to tell one way or another*, he thought bitterly.

Jory needed to get out. Stop taking the easy path and get his own place. Find his own happiness.

Suddenly, he missed Mal so much it hurt. But he couldn't *have* Mal right now.

He couldn't stay here, either, though. Jory glanced at his watch. A little after nine. It wasn't all that late. Gawen wouldn't have gone to bed yet, and Kirsty never minded people turning up unexpectedly.

Yes. He'd go and see them.

Kirsty was always good for an alternative perspective on things.

CHAPTER NINETEEN

Mal found the days after his total fuckup with Jory a bit weird. Tasha took some time off from the pub, even sweet-talking Jago into getting a temp to cover her, seeing as Mrs. Jago, who'd normally help out, was off on a coach trip with the girls.

Mal had met *the girls*, briefly, when he'd first come down here, a bunch of ladies around retirement age who'd done their bit and were damn well going to enjoy themselves now. He didn't envy the coach driver his job trying to keep them in line.

He felt bad, putting everyone out like that, but on the other hand, Tasha deserved a bit of time off and it was nice doing stuff together, like going to the beach and having windsurfing lessons. Okay, one windsurfing lesson. They were both too totally crap at it to bother carrying on, but at least they had a laugh trying. It was all right, but . . . truth was, they were both missing other people, weren't they? And Tash, bless her, couldn't seem to stop treating him like he was gonna break.

She asked him about Jory, one afternoon as they were sitting out on the prom eating ice creams. "So what really happened with you and Dev's uncle?"

"Thought we'd covered that. We *did the dirty*. End of." Mal took a bite of his flake.

"And then what? He told you to piss off cos he'd had what he wanted?"

"No. Fuck, no." He hung his head. "It was me, wasn't it? Jory started going on about taking me to meet his family and all that and . . . it was only s'posed to be a bit of fun, you know?"

"So you're the one who legged it? Babe, I thought you liked him. All that going on about him being a decent bloke and all."

"I do like him. But I just . . ." Mal stood up, walked a couple of paces, then turned round. "I just can't, okay?"

"Can't what?"

Like him. "Be with him. Get involved with him."

"Why not? I mean, shit, babe, maybe shagging him was a dick-brained move but once you'd had him, you might as well of stuck with him, right? I know you were worried about fucking things up for Dev, but I don't see how this is supposed to be better."

She didn't get it. "It ain't just about Dev."

"So what is it about?"

"It's complicated. Look, eat your fucking ice cream before it melts, will you?" He frowned. "Oi, should you be having that? It's got sugar in, innit?"

"What are you, the diabetes police? Relax, babe. I got it." She patted her little backpack with the skulls on, so presumably she had all her needles and stuff with her.

"You gonna need to shoot up? Or, like, stab your finger and bleed on stuff? You're gonna wait till I've finished, aintcha? I got raspberry sauce on this."

Tasha laughed. "God, you're such a wuss. Bloody good thing you ain't in charge of no one's blood sugar."

Too soon, Tasha had to get back to work and Mal found himself on his own for the day. Although he wouldn't miss the mother-henning. Much. He got up late, then wandered down into town to see what he could grab for brunch.

There was a craft fair or market or whatever on the prom today. Tables were set out in a long line, offering all kinds of stuff ranging from cheap shell jewellery to hand-knitted designer sweaters with a price tag so high they ought to throw the rest of the sheep in for free.

Mal ambled on over, cos he quite liked artsy-fartsy stuff, and mooched down the line to a table with driftwood sculptures. His interest pricked up. They were all of sea creatures, some real and some mystical, including one of a mermaid he reckoned Jory would love. It wasn't a cutesy Disney one, or an excuse to show a pair of knockers—not that Mal had a problem with knockers, mind, but he had a feeling they weren't Jory's favourite thing ever. This mermaid was slim and feral looking, not some twee doll or pumped-up Page 3 stunner with a tail tacked on. She was more like the sort who'd lure sailors onto the rocks and then eat them with her sharp little teeth. He couldn't resist running his hand along her tail, with its intricate carved scales. Squamous, that was the word for it. He'd read that somewhere. The wood was warm to the touch, and smoother than he'd expected.

"Oh, hello. Fancy meeting you here."

Mal glanced up and blinked. Shit—it was Jory's missus. Funny to think he'd shagged her husband. Still, he wasn't going to be doing that again. And that was two things they had in common. He gave her a smile. "Kirsty, right? These are dead good. They by a local artist, or are they shipped in from China?"

"You're cynical in your old age, aren't you, love? All made locally by my own fair hands, I'll have you know." She handed him a business card that said *Kirsty Fisher—Art from the sea.*

"You're shitting me. Seriously? These are like epic."

The prices were pretty epic and all, but then Mal didn't have the first clue what the going rate was for driftwood art cos, well, it wasn't like you were paying for the cost of materials, was it? He gave the mermaid a last little stroke in farewell.

Kirsty raised an eyebrow. "Like her, do you? I wouldn't have thought you were the sort to go for mermaids."

Mal grinned. "Mermaids, mermen . . . I'm an equal-opportunities patron of the arts, I am."

"Oh yeah? I'll let you into a secret, then. This is one of my favourites." She picked up a sculpture from the back of the table and held it up. "Like him? I call him AC/DC, cos he's an electric eel. Go on, have a feel. And no, I don't say that to all the boys."

The sculpture was amazing—a snaky S curve of glossy, rich wood mounted on a simple stand. Somehow the eel managed to look like it was alive, and moving, even, swimming through the sea with a flick of its muscular tail. Mal reached out a hand. If he'd thought the mermaid's scales were smooth, this was like touching moonlight. Mal stroked it a few times. It was weirdly satisfying.

"Enjoying that, are you?" Kirsty asked.

Okay, maybe it wasn't all that weird. "Too right. I'd be tempted to take him home, but I bet he's out of my price range."

"Oh, he's not for sale. Who'd I have to keep me company on lonely nights if he went? I could do you a deal on the mermaid, though."

"What kind of a deal?"

"Hmm . . . call her half price, as long as you keep it to yourself. Don't want everyone and his dog thinking I'm an easy touch."

She was still fairly pricey . . . but sod it, what else was he going to spend his money on down here? And maybe he'd give her to Jory to remember him by.

Or maybe he'd keep her to remind him of Jory. Mal got out his wallet. "You've got a deal."

"Lovely. Let me wrap her up for you." She reached down below the table, bringing out bubble wrap and tape, then sat down on the folding chair with the mermaid on her lap.

"How long have you been doing this?" Mal asked as he counted out notes.

"Since I came down to Cornwall, pretty much."

"Yeah, I thought you weren't from here. Where are you from originally?"

"Oh, here and there. Mostly there." She bit off a piece of tape and stuck it down on a neat parcel. "You're a London lad, by the sound of you."

"Yeah, South London. Balham."

"Staying long?"

"Not sure."

"Depends on a certain young Cornishman, does it?"

"What, Jory?" It felt funny to think of him as a Cornishman—he didn't speak like a local, and from what he'd said, he'd spent most of his time out of the county—but he was, wasn't he? "Nah. That's not . . . It's work stuff. I'm helping out at the Sea Bell at the mo. The barmaid there's me mate's little sister."

"I don't get a lot of chance to go to pubs these days." Kirsty sounded sad about it.

"No? I'd have thought blokes'd be queuing up to take you out. Why don't you come round some evening? You can buy me a drink to make up for that hard bargain you kept me to on Ariel here." He gave her a sly wink at the last bit. A middle-aged couple had dawdled over to browse and from the watch on the bloke's wrist they were well minted. Mal didn't have a problem with helping out the redistribution of wealth in society, and Kirsty probably deserved it more than they did.

She had dimples when she really smiled. "I've a good mind to take her back if you're going to call her that. Her name's Zennor, if you want to know. No, I don't like to leave Gawen on his own in the evenings. But you could come round to mine if you like. We could open a bottle of cider. Tell you what, come round about seven and I'll even throw in dinner. Feel free to touch if you want," she added to Mrs. Minted, who was clearly impressed with a leaping dolphin that looked a bit phallic to Mal's mind.

Was it a good idea, going for dinner with Jory's wife? Mal was supposed to be keeping out of his way until they'd both cooled down a bit. "Just you, me, and the kid, right?"

Okay, maybe he was curious to see how Jory's son had turned out.

"You can bring Jory if you want," Kirsty said, like she was testing him.

"Nah. That ain't gonna happen."

"No? All the more for us, then. So, it's settled? Tonight? Or do you have to work?"

He didn't *have* to work any night. And it wasn't like it was folk night at the Sea Bell, when it could get a bit busy. They'd manage fine without him. "Yeah, tonight's good."

"Let me write down the address. I could do you a deal on that one," she added to the punters as she scribbled. "Ten percent off, seeing as I know he'll be going to a good home. If you promise to keep it to yourself. I wouldn't want everyone expecting a discount."

"Does he have a name?" Mrs. Minted asked, already getting out her purse.

"He's Bufeo."

"Boo . . . Could you write that down for me?"

Kirsty scribbled the name on a business card. "You look him up online when you get him home. I think you'll like his story."

"What was that all about?" Mal asked when they'd gone off, smiling, with their own bubble-wrapped package.

"Bufeo Colorado. He's a pink river dolphin from the Amazon Rainforest who turns into a handsome man at night and goes on the prowl for love."

Mal laughed. "Now I'm wishing I'd bought him instead of Zen here." He patted the parcel under his arm.

"Keep it down. You'll hurt her feelings, poor thing. And he wouldn't have done you any good anyway. Bufeo only seduces women."

"That's sexist, that is. And, like, why's he want to cut out half the population like that? Total waste if you ask me."

"But if you know what you like, why not go for it? I'll see you tonight, Mal. Seven o'clock. Don't be late."

In other words, *Bugger off so I can charm some more customers.* Fair enough.

Mal buggered off.

On the way back to the Sea Bell, Mal got out his phone and did a quick internet search on Zennor. It turned out to be a Cornish village with a mermaid legend, around fifty miles from Porthkennack, down near St. Ives, which . . . sucked a bit. Cos the first thought Mal had when he read it was *Wonder if Jory's been there?* Followed by *Maybe we could go together.*

Yeah, right. Even if Mal took a Valium and sat in the back of the car with his eyes shut, which was basically how he'd managed the journey from the airport to Porthkennack in the first place, there was still the thing where spending that amount of time with Jory was a very bad idea.

Sod it.

CHAPTER TWENTY

Kirsty's house suited her, Mal reckoned when he got round there just before seven. It was small, but sort of quirky. The terrace was built on a hill so each house was a few feet higher than its neighbours, and Kirsty's, on the end, was the tallest of the lot. The whole row was painted white with grey roofs so they looked like proper old-fashioned Cornish cottages and they were all weird angles too, which shouldn't have worked but did.

Even if he'd lost the address, Mal would've known Kirsty's house—the front garden was all pebbles, with driftwood sculptures taller than he was set up in it. When he got closer, Mal could see the pebbles were arranged into patterns, with little pools of smaller ones set around plants and sculptures.

There wasn't a door bell, so he knocked on the wood of the front door.

It was opened by a young lad with wire-framed glasses and a serious expression. "Are you Mal?"

"Yeah. Gawen?" Mal tried to make sure he said it right.

The lad was so much like Jory, it kind of hurt to look at him. He was small for twelve, just like Jory had said he'd been himself, and had the same big soft eyes and wary expression. His hair was all Jory too—blond and unruly. Not much sign of a beard yet, but give it time.

"Yes. Mum said you should come on through." He turned and walked down the narrow hallway without so much as a glance to see if Mal was coming too. Amused, Mal shut the door and followed.

They walked literally right through the house and out back to the garden, Mal catching a glimpse on the way of a sitting room that was all bright colours and patterned throws. Kirsty was standing in the garden, a glass of something in her hand, gazing over the fence, where the view stretched out across the fields. She had a skirt on this evening, a long, flowy one in tie-dye shades of purple, as seen on market stalls and students just back from a gap year trekking through India.

"Mum, he's here," Gawen said.

Kirsty smiled. "Found us, then."

"Uh, yeah. Brought this." Mal held up the two-litre bottle of Rattler.

"Snap." She toasted him with her glass and drained it.

"Do you like gaming?" Gawen asked. "I've got the beta version of *Legends of Lorecraft II*. Do you want to play it with me?"

Kirsty rolled her eyes at Mal, then turned to Gawen. "Not everyone wants to sit in front of a computer on a day like this, love."

"Oh." He stared at his feet and didn't say anything else.

Mal felt bad for the kid. "Hey, I got mad gaming skillz, me. See these thumbs?" He waggled them in front of Gawen. "Honed by years of shooting stuff up. So you gonna show me this game of yours, then?"

Gawen looked at Kirsty. "Can I?"

She smiled. "Course you can. I'll start getting dinner on. And no," she added, turning to Mal, "I don't need any help, before you start trying to split yourself in two."

"Thanks, Mum," Mal said to make Gawen giggle, and followed the kid up to his room, leaving the cider in the kitchen on his way through.

Gawen's bedroom must have been amazing for a small boy. Instead of wallpaper there was a mural stretching over two walls, showing a winding trail that led through forests and across rivers and plains to a castle perched high on a hill, the scene filled with animals and mythological creatures. There was a dragon flying in the far distance, and a mermaid in the river—Mal could just see her through the gap in a bookshelf that'd been shoved in front of the mural to hold a collection of sci-fi classics and a haphazard pile of video games. A Star Wars poster was Blu-Tacked half over a faun, and a collection of stickers floated in the sky.

Gawen flung himself down on the floor in front of his open laptop and handed Mal a controller already hooked up to a USB port. Mal grinned. "Come on, then. Show me how it's done."

He lost track of time, playing the game—it wasn't easy, keeping up with the kid—and was surprised when Kirsty poked her head around the door. "Come on, you two. Didn't you hear me calling? Dinner's ready."

Now she mentioned it, Mal could smell it—something rich and meaty, with a strong hint of tomato and garlic. Suddenly he was starving. "Right, yeah—sorry about that. Uh-oh. Think I just died. Gotta work on them dodge-rolls. You ready for your tea, JJ?"

"'JJ'?" Kirsty asked, as Gawen shut down the game and scrambled to his feet with all the grace of a new-born elephant.

"Jory Junior," Mal explained with a shrug by way of apology.

She winced. "Call him that again and you'll be wearing your dinner, not eating it."

"I don't mind, Mum," Gawen said, pushing back his glasses with a finger.

"You're your own man, Gawen Roscarrock, and never forget it," she said, turning to lead the way downstairs.

Dinner was Moroccan lamb with couscous, which they ate with forks sitting out in the back garden around a weathered wooden table. Mal tried not to laugh at Gawen carefully picking out every single bit of dried fruit from his couscous and piling it on the side of his plate. He didn't do too well. Gawen sent him a shy, guilty smile.

"That's all I need, you encouraging him," Kirsty said with a mock glare in Mal's direction as she grabbed the bottle of cider and gave them both a top-up. "I ought to make you eat them instead."

"Hey, no problem. Nothing wrong with getting your vitamins." Mal slid his plate next to Gawen's and scooped the little pile of reject fruit onto his dinner.

The back garden was like the front one, except different. Half of it was paved over and the rest was decking, but there were plants all over in bright earthenware pots, and climbing things growing up the fence on all three sides. It was filled with reclaimed-looking furniture that'd probably sell for a fortune if you shoved it in an antique shop somewhere like Notting Hill. Mal could just see Kirsty scouring auctions and house sales for it. Maybe skips and rubbish dumps too—she didn't seem the sort to worry about getting her hands dirty.

He'd never lived in a house with a garden, so he'd never really got it when people on the telly talked about *outdoor rooms*, but yeah, here, he could totally see it.

"You lived here long?" he asked, fairly sure he knew the answer.

"Since just before my baby here was born." Yeah, he'd been right. Gawen went pink. "Mu-um."

"Get used to it, mate." Mal ruffled Gawen's hair. "I'm twice your age and got me own home, and my mum ain't stopped calling me her baby yet. Hey, this is awesome. Authentic African recipe?"

"Sainsbury's magazine. But close."

A large, fluffy cat with a fuck-off expression and only one eye jumped up on Kirsty's lap. She stroked it absently with one hand, and carried on eating with the other.

"Yours? Or is he only visiting?"

"Well, I feed him, but I think he belongs to himself."

Gawen leaned over to pet the cat in his mum's lap. "He just turned up one day. I call him Tigger."

"Yeah? You sure, mate? He don't look all that bouncy to me. Maybe we should get him on a trampoline."

Gawen giggled. "Have you got a cat?"

"Me? No. I'm a rat man. Always have been."

"Explains a lot," Kirsty said, and cackled.

"Oi, watch it, you." Mal chased the last of his meal around his plate, not wanting to waste any.

"Rats caused the black death." Gawen's voice started off disapproving but ended up like a question.

"Jesus, you cause one little plague that killed off half of Europe, and nobody ever lets you forget it, do they? And it wasn't the rats, smarty-pants. It was the fleas that carried the germs. Wasn't the rats' fault no one had invented spot-on treatments yet, was it?"

"How many rats have you got?"

"Seven. Uh, no, six, since Hermione died. And no, not of bubonic plague," he added pointedly.

"Were you sad when she died?" Gawen asked.

"Yeah. Yeah, I was. She was a good rat."

Mal glanced over at Kirsty, expecting a smart comment, but she just raised her glass of cider. "To Hermione."

He smiled, touched. "To Hermione."

Gawen broke the moment by getting to his feet. "Mum, I need to do my homework now."

"Course you do, love. Don't worry about the dishes. Me and Mal'll clear up."

She didn't make any move to leave the table as Gawen went inside, so Mal topped their glasses up. It was nice sitting here, out in the fresh air with the sky turning pink. "He's a good kid."

"He is." Kirsty stood up, the cat tumbling off her lap without even a yowl, like he was used to it. "Let's go sit on the bench. It's the best place to watch the sun go down. Better make the most of it—I think the weather's on the turn."

Mal grabbed his glass and the bottle and joined her on the bench. It was the old-fashioned wrought iron type, but she'd stripped it down, painted it sky blue, and bunged on a few patchwork cushions. And it faced right at the blaze of colour in the sky as the sun disappeared over the hills. Dev's bloke, Kyle, he'd have loved that sky. He'd done a couple of paintings of sunsets, the colours all way too vivid to be accurate, except they were, Mal realised, gazing at what was in front of him. Funny how your mind did that. Had to turn down the brightness on reality before you could believe in it properly.

"Nice view," he said, and yeah, well eloquent, mate. Embarrassed, he nodded to the wooden shed beside them, painted to match the bench. "That where you keep your driftwood—you know, the stuff you haven't done anything with?"

"The smaller pieces are in there. I've got a garage for the larger bits." She fell silent again.

"Is Gawen arty like you?" There hadn't been much sign of it in the kid's bedroom, unless Mal was doing him an injustice and he'd painted that mural himself, but you never knew.

She half laughed. "Gawen? No. He's not arty." Then she sighed. It was a soft sound, almost lost in the birdsong, the voices of her neighbours, and the far-off traffic noise, but it was there.

"No?" he prompted.

She shook her head, smiling, and stared at the sunset. "I thought he was gonna be like me, you know? Free-spirited, nature lover, bit of a rebel, the sort who doesn't care what everyone else thinks about him.

Then I ended up with this kid who loves school and is like a genius at maths, and he hates parties, and if I didn't drag him out now and then, he'd spend his whole life indoors on his computer. I mean, I love him to pieces, I really do." She looked right into Mal's eyes, her gaze earnest. "I just . . . I just don't *get* him. He's too like Jory."

"What's wrong with that?" It came out sharper than Mal had meant it to. He offered her a top-up as an apology.

She gave him a lopsided smile as she held out her glass. "Nothing. I don't know how to talk to him, though. He's all quantum mechanics and computer games and nanotechnology, and I can smile and nod, but basically it's all *whoosh*." She mimed something flying over her head.

"Yeah, but . . . does Jory know any of that stuff?"

"That's the weird part. He's all into his ye olde knights and damsels stuff, but somehow when Gawen talks, he *gets* it. And if he doesn't get it, he goes away and reads up on it till he does. I wouldn't even know where to start. Like, there was this trading cards game Gawen was obsessed with a while back, and I read the manual three times and I still didn't have a clue, but Jory taught himself in a weekend so's Gawen would have someone to play with."

Mal took a long swallow of his cider. He felt kind of weird, watching her smile get wider and her eyes turn softer as she talked about Jory being this great dad. "You ever wish you and him were, you know, together?"

Kirsty burst out laughing. "Fuck me, no." She shook her head, still giggling. "Don't get me wrong, I love him, I really do, but him and me? Not a chance." She gave Mal a sly look. "Thought you were well in there, though. What happened?"

Mal screwed up his face. He didn't want to bring Dev into it all. He hadn't even told him about Jory yet. It didn't seem right, telling everyone his business. "Ah . . . It's complicated. I . . . I'm not in a good place to start something like that. And there's family stuff going on . . ." It was technically true. Just not Mal's family.

She was nodding. "Know what you mean."

"You see much of his brother and sister?"

"No more than I can help. They don't like me much." She gave another of her little half laughs. "Not sure those two like anyone except each other."

Mal gave her a look. "You don't mean . . . ?"

She frowned—and then burst out laughing, a loud, earthy sound that filled the air and would probably have the neighbours coming round to complain if she kept it up. Or to ask if they could stay and have some of what she was having. "Oh God. Don't even make me think about that. No, God, no. Nothing like that."

"Thank Christ for that." Jesus, what had he been thinking, asking that question? That would've been a fucking fantastic thing to have to explain to Dev about his mum and his uncle.

"Although mind you, I've never seen either one of them with a lover," she said in a teasing voice.

"Oi, don't start. Kinda weird, though, innit? Jory keeps saying how his big bruv's so hung up on Family with a capital F—you'd think he'd be keener to have one himself."

"Would you? I reckon it was the best day of his life when Jory went and provided him with an heir so he wouldn't have to do anything messy like make one himself." She took a gulp of cider. "My Gawen's going to have a lot on his shoulders when he grows up, poor love. I know Bran reckons he's going to take over the family property empire one day."

Anyone would think the poor kid was Bran's, not Jory's. "Sounds like he'll be well minted at any rate."

"I've always wanted him to make his own way in life. Not just follow in his uncle's footsteps." She leaned back on the bench and closed her eyes for a minute. "So what do you do for a living? I bet you didn't blindly go into the family business."

Mal had to laugh. "Yeah, well, that's where you'd be wrong. I'm a Tube driver, like me dad before me." Funny how he didn't mind saying it. She was so easy to talk to. Somehow, as the sky got darker and the warm breeze cooled, Mal found himself pouring out the whole sorry story of his introduction to London Underground's suicide statistics. "It's just . . . you have to sit there, and you know it's gonna happen, and it takes like forever. And afterwards, you think, I had all that time, why the bloody hell didn't I stop it?"

"But you couldn't, right? Trains take, I don't know, a hundred yards to stop, don't they? More?"

"I wasn't even going that fast. I'd braked, coming into the station. He was on the platform . . . Shit. You don't wanna hear about this." He buried his face in his hands.

"I don't mind. If you want to talk about it, go ahead." She reached over and stroked back Mal's hair from his forehead. "I never used to believe in all that time-slowing-down bollocks till I had a scare with Gawen when he was a tot. And it *is* bollocks, cos it's not like you can do anything with all that extra time. You just get to suffer longer."

Mal nodded jerkily. "What happened?" He didn't want to be the one talking anymore.

"He was on a kiddies' slide in the park, see, a big one, standing up right on the top, ready to go down. He was only little, not even two." Kirsty paused to take another drink from her glass. "I was down the other end of the slide, waiting to catch him, talking with another mum, you know how you do. Well, maybe you don't. And I'd been so careful the first half-dozen times he went up and down that slide. Held my arms up by him ready to catch him, and all that. But he'd done it perfectly, each time, climbed up the steps and launched his little self down, and I s'pose I thought he had it down pat. So I stayed at the bottom that go round. There I was, watching him from what, six feet away? And this time, he doesn't sit down on the slide. God knows why, but he just sort of topples off the side of it, six feet up. And all I could do was watch as he fell for what seemed like *years*, head down, about to crack his little skull open on the ground." She took another swallow of cider.

"So . . . was he hurt?"

Kirsty gave a laugh. "Managed to turn himself over, somehow, and landed on his back. I've got no clue how it happened. He hardly even cried after he hit the ground. And all I could think of was that was the longest few seconds of my life."

Mal nodded and raised his glass to that. A few drops of cider sloshed out of his glass, mostly onto his jeans but some of it landing on her skirt. "Whoa . . . Sorry. Got outta the habit of drinking lately. Just call me a cheap date."

"No harm done. Not like it's dry-clean only, is it? And we'll dry off quick out here."

She was probably right, although it wasn't nearly so warm now that the sun had almost disappeared. Mal found himself shifting a bit closer to her. She didn't seem to mind—in fact, she slung her arm around him.

She was warm, and soft, and comforting, and while it wasn't like being with Jory, it felt like it, sort of, cos she was connected to him, wasn't she? She was his kid's mum. Mal snuggled in closer still. Kirsty squeezed tighter and gave him a peck on the cheek, like she was his mum or his nan. It was nice. He ought to tell her that. "You're nice," he said fuzzily.

"So are you." She kissed him again, this time on the lips, and that was okay, yeah, a bit weird maybe, but then it got more intense, and that wasn't what he wanted. Not really. Mal was just trying to work out how to cool things down without hurting her feelings when he heard a voice.

"Kirsty? Gawen said—"

It was Jory.

Jory. Mal pulled back from Kirsty so fast he nearly fell off the bench.

Jory was standing in the doorway from the house, hanging onto the doorframe like it was all that was holding him up.

Staring at them.

There was a horrible silence. All Mal could think of to say was *It's not what it looks like.* And when did anyone ever believe that?

Jory's Adam's apple bobbed as he swallowed. "I . . . Never mind. I'll go."

Before Mal could come out with a single word, Jory turned on his heel and left.

CHAPTER TWENTY-ONE

Mal stumbled to his feet, knocking over his half-full glass of cider which he'd left on the decking at the side of the bench. It didn't break, which was good, wasn't it? Thinking of omens and stuff. "I gotta go after him." The warm cotton-wool haze from the alcohol had left him completely, but his head was still fuzzy, and how fucked up was that?

About as fucked up as his life right now. But he had to talk to Jory. He knew that much.

Kirsty grabbed his arm. "Wait a minute. You told me you and Jory weren't a thing."

"We're not . . . Not exactly. Ah, *shit*." Mal raked his hand through his hair.

"We get detention for swearing at school." That was Gawen, poking his tousled blond head out the back door at them. "Why's Dad gone already?"

"He forgot something," Kirsty said. She was still holding on to his arm, and Mal didn't want to wrench it away from her in front of the kid, but he *had* to go after Jory.

"Look, I gotta go. I'm—"

"I think he's gone now. He came in his car." Gawen was watching them with a weird detached curiosity, like he was going to write it all up for English class later, maybe under the title of *How Adults Fuck Stuff Up*.

Kirsty's hold loosened, and Mal legged it round the side of the house to the front.

There was no sign of Jory or the Qubo.

Mal sank onto the pebbles in despair, his face in his hands. "Shit, shit, *fuck*."

There was the crunch of footsteps. "You going to tell me what all that was about?" Kirsty's voice was thin and tight.

Christ, where to start?

He'd fucked up. He'd fucked up big time.

Shit. He didn't deserve to *live*. The look on Jory's face . . . Mal scrunched his eyes shut, but it only made the image clearer.

Jory'd been so *hurt*.

It was the classic fucking bisexual cliché, wasn't it? *Can't trust a bi bloke, they'll always cheat.* And with the bloke's *wife*, for fuck's sake.

"Christ, I'm such a shit," he muttered into his hands.

But . . . he'd been so lonely, and she'd been so warm, and kissing her had made him feel close to Jory in some totally twisted way. He'd liked her. He'd really liked her. It hadn't been the same—not remotely—as him liking Jory, but for thirty seconds, he'd got confused. And that had been all it took.

And now what the hell was he going to say to Dev when he got here? *Yeah, met your uncle and he was all keen to get to know you, but then he caught me snogging his wife and now he'll probably slam the door in your face just for being a mate of mine?*

He didn't deserve mates like Dev.

He didn't fucking deserve *anything*.

"Come on inside. I'll make some coffee." Her voice was softer now, and a hand dropped onto his shoulder and squeezed.

Mal stood up. "No. I gotta go."

He couldn't stay here, not where it'd all gone so arse-wipingly wrong.

Mal started walking down the road, and Kirsty didn't follow him, thank God. He needed to clear his head. Somewhere no one was going to find him. Christ, he wanted Tasha—but how the bloody hell could he tell her he'd fucked up Dev's one chance of getting to know his mum's family?

At least one thing they had a shedload of around here was empty space. People always said Cornwall was heaving in the summer but it was bollocks. Away from the tourist bits, there was no bastard there. Mal turned his steps in the direction of Mother Ivey's Bay. He wasn't sure exactly where he'd come out, but it didn't matter, did it?

What *did* matter anymore?

He found himself heading up the cliff path towards Roscarrock House. And that was a fucking joke, that was, because Christ, after this evening, there was *nobody* in that house who'd let him in. Unless they planned on shoving him straight through the house and off the cliff the other side, that was.

Maybe he'd even let them.

It'd started to rain, big splats soaking through his T-shirt and making him shiver. He didn't stop walking, though. At some point, his phone vibrated, but he ignored the call. If it was Tash, he'd end up having to tell her what had happened, and he couldn't face that. If it was Jory . . .

Nope. *Definitely* couldn't face that.

Fuck, it was getting dark. To be more accurate, it'd pretty much *got* dark. The rain was coming down harder now, drenching his shirt and running in trickles through his hair and down his face like tears. He should probably stop and find shelter.

Like that was an option. What was he going to do? Bang on the doors of one of the cottages? Break into the one Dev and Kyle had rented and should have been in by now? Besides, if he stopped walking, he'd start thinking, and he just couldn't deal with that. Not now.

Mal carried on walking. Up the hill, and past Roscarrock House, and fuck, Jory would be in there, wouldn't he? Thinking Mal was a total fucking bastard.

He'd be right.

It was so dark, Mal could hardly see the edges of the road. If some git came driving down here with no lights on, he'd be a goner.

"Shit!" Mal screamed into the night. Anything to make the pictures in his head piss off and leave him alone. The rain took his words and drowned them.

If someone hit him, would they care? Would it fuck them up like it'd fucked him up? Or would they get over it, like a normal person would?

Like his dad would?

He didn't so much see the lay-by as notice a change in the darkness at the side of the road. This was where they'd come, him and Jory. It'd all seemed so easy, going down that tunnel. Fun. Going somewhere nobody else knew about—not Dev, not Tasha, not his mum and dad. Nobody. He'd loved it on that beach at the end of the tunnel. It'd been like the rest of the world hadn't existed, just for a while—until Jory had brought him back to earth with a big, messy splat by talking about his family.

Mal stood there for a moment. Rain from his hair ran down his spine and into his kecks, making him shiver. Christ. Where was he even going? At least the tunnel had fucking well been dry.

Sod it. Mal turned into the field. Straight up until he hit the gate, right? He could do that.

He hit the gate literally, walking bang slap into it in the dark and the pelting rain, but that was okay. He was pretty much numb by now. All he had to do was walk on some more until he found the hole. And not fall down it, because that'd be a fucking stupid thing to do.

Mal climbed over the gate, because he bloody well *could*, and carried on walking. His foot turned a few times on the uneven ground—where was a proper pavement when you needed one?—but he managed not to break an ankle.

Visibility was down to *Har har, you're screwed, mate*. Christ, he was going to miss the tunnel, wasn't he? Probably spend the whole night walking around in the rain, if he didn't go straight off the cliff. The buzz from all that cider had left him, and now he felt so. Fucking. Tired.

Maybe he should go back? But if he carried on this way, he'd get to Roscarrock House, right? He was on their land. And then there'd be lights, and he'd know where he was, and he'd be able to . . . to call a cab, or Tasha, or fuck it, Dev, even. Except no, he couldn't call either of them, could he?

Because he'd fucked everything up.

Water was trickling down through his hair, into his eyes, making them sting. God, he just wanted to go to sleep and never wake up . . .

And then the ground gave way.

CHAPTER
TWENTY-TWO

It shouldn't have hurt so much. Not like this. Not like a knife in Jory's chest, slowly twisting every time he thought of Mal and Kirsty in each other's arms—and the image of them together was seared into his brain.

Mal wasn't his. He'd made that plain days ago. Jory had no call to be feeling so devastated. So betrayed. Why *shouldn't* Mal and Kirsty . . .?

Oh God. Jory scrubbed at his eyes as he stumbled into the Qubo. He needed clear vision to drive. There was no Mal to save him from hitting stray pedestrians now, either real or imaginary ones. It wasn't far, back to Roscarrock House. He'd almost walked from there to Kirsty's, instead of bringing the car. Christ, if he had, he'd have got here, what, twenty minutes later?

What would he have walked in on then? Would Mal and Kirsty have been upstairs in bed? Maybe they'd have heard Jory knocking, would have sprung out of bed, tried to put on a front.

Maybe they wouldn't have. After all, what claim did Jory honestly have on Mal?

But he'd hoped—

Jory cut off that line of thought viciously. He was driving. His eyes needed to be *clear*, damn it.

He somehow made it back to Roscarrock House without hitting anything, then sat, for a moment, in the car. Why the hell had he even gone out tonight? So he'd been lonely, stuck in a too-large house with a brother and sister who didn't want him. So what? He could have phoned someone. Christ, he could have gone on bloody *Facebook*.

It seemed like he'd barely kicked off his shoes and slumped into an armchair before there was a ring at the doorbell. Jory ignored it. He wasn't in the mood to be polite to people.

Then it occurred to him it could, possibly, be Mal, and he scrambled into the hallway, only to see Bran beat him to the door and open it as Jory skidded to a halt.

Bran's body, and the angle of the door, shielded the caller from Jory's view.

"Oh, hello. Everything all right?" Bran sounded surprised but not shocked. It wasn't Mal, then, standing just out of Jory's sight.

"Yeah, fine, but I need to speak to Jory, okay?"

Kirsty?

"Come on in, then." Bran gave Jory a suspicious frown as he left them in the dubious privacy of the hallway.

Jory couldn't blame him. Kirsty's face was flushed, and her hair wilder than usual. God alone knew what he himself looked like.

Jory's jaw clenched as he met her gaze. Christ, what was she about to say to him? Ask for a divorce so she could be with Mal? Or was Mal just another of her flings, easily left and soon forgotten? Anger and pain were making his heart ache so badly, he couldn't even tell how much was for him and how much for Mal.

"Is Mal here?" she asked.

"What? No. I thought he was with you. In all senses of the word," Jory added bitterly. He caught a strong smell of alcohol on her breath, and fury flared. "Christ, did you *drive* here?"

"Screw you. You are *not* my keeper. I got a lift from Sam next door, is that all right?"

"What about Gawen?"

"He's twelve years old. I think he can manage in his own home for half an hour. Sam's missus is gonna look in on him if we're not back soon." Then the fight seemed to go out of her, and she slumped back against the wall. "I'm not sleeping with him, okay?"

"What? *Sam?*"

"*Mal*. Nothing happened. Hardly even a snog. And it wasn't his fault. We'd both had a bit much to drink, and I thought you and him weren't a thing."

Jory found his voice, although it didn't sound much like him when he spoke. "No. We're not."

"No? Cos that's not how you've been acting. Either of you."

"I . . ." Jory had to look away. "Mal doesn't want a relationship. Not with me."

"Shit." Her tone softened. "I'm sorry. Honestly. I'd had a few drinks, and Mal's fucking lovely, so I kissed him. That's all."

She made it seem so easy. So natural.

But then, it probably was, for her. If she wanted something—someone—she just went ahead and took it, or them.

"You must have had some idea, though. How I felt about him. You saw us together." He couldn't help the bitterness coming through. She'd always been able to read him so effortlessly.

Her turn to look away. "Christ, Jory, you of all people ought to know I make shit decisions."

"Because I was one of them?"

"Well, yeah."

"Does Gawen know you feel that way?"

"Fuck you, Jory Roscarrock. No, he doesn't, and if you ever tell him one word about it, I'll—"

"Of course I'll never tell him! What the hell do you think of me?" Jory spun and looked away. When he spoke again, his voice sounded broken to his own ears. "What *do* you think of me? Do you really hate me that much?"

"I don't hate you. Not at all. You're a sweet bloke. You should be happy." She was crying now. He could hear it in her voice. *The alcohol*, he told himself savagely, and even tried to believe it. She sniffed. "I just . . . It was never supposed to be like this, you know? My life. I was going to do so much. I was going to go *everywhere*. And then I had Gawen, and he was sick so much when he was tiny . . . And I love him to bits, I really do. I'd die for him, no questions, no second thoughts. But he's not like me. He's like you. And sometimes I look at him . . ."

"And you can't help resenting us."

"You."

Jory turned then and gazed at her tear-streaked face.

She shrugged. "I can't resent him. He's my little boy. My baby. So it all has to go on you."

Should he be angry with her for that? Jory didn't quite have the heart. "And that's why you kissed Mal?"

"That's not..." She glanced up at the sky. "See, you think everyone's like you. Like, they think before they do things. Must be nice. Some of us just . . . I didn't look at you and think, 'Wow, posh boy, nice shoulders, bet he's a virgin. I'm gonna change his whole world.' Maybe that's *why* I did it, but I didn't know it back then. Maybe it's fucked up. But it's how I am. It was like that tonight. I didn't know I was being a bitch. Not then."

Was that really how people thought? How they acted?

Was that how *Mal* thought?

He'd said the same thing, the first time he'd kissed Jory. Something about it being fucked up.

Kirsty was speaking again. "It was never meant to be anything, me and him. Just a bit of fun. A bit of comfort, on a lonely night. Don't blame him for it. He's had a rough time, with what happened at work and all."

"He told you about that?"

She nodded. "Think he was glad to get it off his chest. But you knew, right?"

Stupid, to feel hurt that Mal had confided in her. A better man would be glad Mal had been able to talk about it—glad, even, that he'd found someone he could have uncomplicated fun with, as he seemingly couldn't with Jory.

Jory wasn't a better man. "Where is he now?"

"He left."

"But where did he go? Back to the pub?"

Kirsty shook her head. "Thought he'd come here. After you. He was really upset."

"No. He wouldn't come here." Kirsty raised an eyebrow at Jory's firm tone, but he wasn't feeling up to explaining it all. "He must have gone back to the Sea Bell."

"Right. Well, when you see him . . . Go easy, yeah? Wasn't his fault. And I think you're wrong, for what it's worth. About him not wanting a relationship."

Jory didn't—couldn't—believe it, but there was no point arguing with her.

Again, she seemed to see straight through him. "Don't you dare tell me I don't know what I'm talking about. You didn't see him after you left. Like you tore his heart out and took it with you."

She was being overdramatic. Mal didn't feel that way about him. Did he? Oh God. Was this Rafi all over again? "Kirsty . . ." Jory stopped.

She gave him a questioning look.

"Why did we never get divorced?" he asked.

Kirsty shrugged. "Because you never bothered, and I don't care. What? I never have, you must know that. There's a reason I treat our marriage like a joke, and that's cos it is one. And it's not just us. When did a bit of paper ever make a difference to whether people care about each other or not? The fact that people like you and me can get legally wed shows how fucked up the whole marriage thing is. If it hadn't been for your big brother going all Victorian on us, I'd never have got married to anyone. Would you?"

Jory had never really thought about it. Had never allowed himself to think about it. He was starting to realise what a terrible mistake that had been. "I want us to do it. Get divorced," he added hastily.

She snorted. "Don't worry, I didn't think you meant anything else. Fine. You sort it, I'll sign it. Long as you don't try and pull a fast one about custody of Gawen."

"No. I don't want his life to change at all."

"Good." She was silent a moment. "You should have stayed here, when he was little. I know it wasn't what we agreed—fuck knows, it wasn't even what I wanted, back then—but you should have stayed. He needed his dad, and you were off getting your degree from your posh college, collecting more letters after your name than were bloody well in it, and what was it all for?"

"I don't know." Jory took a deep breath. "If it's any consolation, I think if I'd stayed, we'd have ended up really hating each other."

"Yeah. Fuck it all. Sam's waiting, and I'm going home to bed. You gonna find Mal? Tell him I'm sorry, and I hope he's okay."

After she'd gone, Jory grabbed his jacket—then stopped, irresolute. Should he go and find Mal? Or should he just leave it for the night? Let them both calm down?

He tried to imagine going to bed. Sleeping, with all this still unresolved.

To hell with that. He pulled his jacket on, grabbed his keys, and set off for the Sea Bell.

Walking into the Sea Bell after his reception the last time wasn't the easiest thing Jory had ever steeled himself to do. At least this time he had the moral high ground.

Or had he? He was the one dating while married, for God's sake.

But Mal knew how Jory felt about him. And God, to get off with *Kirsty* . . .

Jory wished he'd asked her more about what Mal had said, after Jory had stormed off without waiting for an explanation—although damn it, what he'd seen hadn't looked like it *needed* explaining. She'd said he'd been really upset . . . Well, guilt could do that to you.

When it came down to it, he only had Kirsty's word for it that Mal hadn't instigated . . . what they were doing. Or even if that was true, that he hadn't been perfectly happy with it all until Jory barged in.

God, this was so screwed up.

Jory walked through the pub to where Tasha was serving at the bar. He probably only imagined that all eyes were upon him.

Probably.

Jago Andrewartha certainly had both steel-grey eyes trained on his every move. He'd got up from his seat the minute Jory set foot inside the place, and had moved to stand by Tasha's shoulder, his presence as solid and threatening as the granite cliffs around Mother Ivey's Bay.

Jory drew in a deep breath. "Can I speak to Mal, please?"

It was Tasha who answered—and oddly, there seemed a hint of sympathy in her expression. "He ain't here. Gone out for the evening."

"He hasn't been back?"

"No." She bit her lip. "Was he with you? He *said* he met some girl."

Jory tried to ignore the stab of pain that caused him. "No. Not exactly. I . . . ran into him. Them."

She gave him a long look—then turned to Jago. "Think I'm gonna take my break now, all right?"

Jago gave a curt nod. "Take it outside."

Jory flushed. Apparently his sort still weren't welcome here. He checked to make sure that Tasha was coming out from behind the bar, then led the way outside.

The wind had picked up even in the short time Jory had been in the pub, and the darkening skies were made gloomier by thick, heavy clouds. He shivered.

Tasha shut the door behind them and folded her arms across her chest. "You and him have a row, then? Over this girl?"

Christ, at least she didn't beat around the bush. "We didn't have a row. We didn't say much at all. I . . ." He swallowed. "I saw them together and left. There didn't seem any point in staying. But Mal was . . . upset."

"How'd you know? You went back? Wanted to have that row after all?"

"No—Kirsty told me."

She frowned. "Kirsty?"

"My . . . ex-wife. The girl," he added, frustrated at her blank expression.

Her eyes went wide. "Mal's girl's your ex?"

"No! It was all a misunderstanding. I think." Jory closed his eyes briefly. "This is all such a mess."

"Tell me about it."

Jory would rather not, thank you very much. Luckily she seemed to have been speaking rhetorically. "But he hasn't been back here?"

"No."

"He couldn't have gone up to his room via the back door?"

Tasha gave Jory a knowing look that made him squirm. "I can check. Wait here." She disappeared around the side of the building, obviously planning to use the back door herself.

Loitering in the lane by the pub door made Jory feel like a child who'd begged an adult to buy him alcohol and cigarettes. The first few fat drops of rain began to fall, adding to his discomfort. A young couple hurried past him, sparing only a brief, curious glance at the idiot standing out in the rain in the dark.

Was Mal out in it somewhere?

Tasha returned, a little breathless and shaking her head. "Not there. Jeez, it's pissing down. Come round the back out of it."

Not without misgivings, Jory followed her back around the pub. They half ran through the back door and into the narrow hallway that housed the stairs going up to Mal's room, where they stood, Tasha hugging herself. She was probably cold—her cut-off denim shorts barely extended past the hem of her oversized T-shirt, which had fallen off one tan shoulder. "So what happened when you saw them? Exactly?"

"They . . . they were kissing."

"Shitfuck." Her eyes widened, and she pressed a hand to her mouth. Taking a deep breath, she seemed to recover herself. "Then what? You have a go at him? Fuck me, what did he even say?"

"He didn't say anything. I just left." Jory forced himself to look her in the eye. "Has Mal confided in you?"

"Why d'you wanna know?" It seemed like a knee-jerk reaction, and after a moment her expression softened. "You mean, about what he wants from you? Look, he's having a bad time right now. Don't think he knows what he wants. Do you really like him?"

"Yes," Jory said, his throat tight.

Tasha pressed her lips together. "And he told you why he's here?"

"The . . . one under. The accident. He's having trouble getting over it."

"Yeah, well, who wouldn't?" The defensiveness was back.

"I'm not criticising him. I'm sure I'd be equally devastated, if not more so. If anything it shows he's got an imaginative, sensitive side."

Luckily that didn't seem to sound as self-congratulatory to Tasha as it did to Jory. She nodded. "Dev said Mal's mum went round his flat and found him in a right state one morning. Said he begged her to take his rats cos he was scared he'd fuck something up and hurt them or kill them or whatever. I ain't supposed to be telling you that, by the way, so don't you fucking dare grass me up. But he's had them rats for *years*. Nobody could look after them better than he does." She paused. "You got any idea where he might've gone?"

"No." When Jory thought of all the places he'd seen Mal . . . half of them were closed at this time of night and the rest didn't seem likely in the rain. Why wasn't he *here*?

She pulled her phone out from her back pocket, scrolled for a moment, then held it to her ear. Jory waited, his stomach churning—would she expect him to talk to Mal? If he'd wanted to do this over the phone, he'd have called himself, for God's sake. He needed to *see* Mal. But after a minute or so, she shook her head and put her phone away. "Went to voice mail. Shit. Look, I'm gonna have to get back to work in a mo. Can't leave Jago to do the bar on his own." She didn't move, though; just stood there leaning against the wall, hugging herself again.

Then she pushed off the wall with an explosive motion. "Fuck it. I ain't leaving Mal on his own neither. Wait here. You got a car, right?" She threw the question over her shoulder as she stomped off deeper into the pub, presumably heading to the bar.

"Yes." Jory took a deep breath. "I'll see you out the front."

He ran back around the building, trying and failing to avoid getting any wetter, jumped into the Qubo and switched on the engine and lights. What a hell of a night. Jory hoped to God that Mal was somewhere safe and dry.

"Have you got an idea where to go?" he asked Tasha when she burst into the Qubo a moment later, slamming the door behind her.

"Thought maybe down the prom. There's a chippie down there he likes. Bit of comfort food, yeah? Where was he when you saw him?"

"At Kirsty's. It's closer to here than to the main seafront. You really think he'd go out all that way?"

"If he didn't wanna talk about tonight, yeah." She sent him a quick look and shivered. "And he probably didn't wanna talk about it."

"Would he go to a— No." Jory put the car into gear and set off for Porthkennack proper.

"What were you going to say?"

"Pub. But it doesn't seem likely."

"Nope. He told you about his uncle, then? The one with the—" She made a drinking-up gesture.

"Yes."

"What did he tell you about me?" she asked suddenly.

Jory frowned, most of his attention taken up by scanning the pavements as he drove past them. "That you're Dev's foster sister. And you mother him a bit—Mal, I mean—although that's not quite how he put it."

"That all?"

"That's all I can think of right now."

"He's a good mate, Mal."

Reaching the promenade, they fell silent. Jory drove slowly along, scouring the seafront for any sign of Mal. "What if he goes back to the Sea Bell?" he asked after a while.

"Jago's gonna call me."

Jory nodded, and they carried on their fruitless search a while longer, both of them, it seemed, too tense to talk. Then another thought occurred to him.

"What if he goes up the back—"

"Left a note on his bed," Tasha cut him off. Jory drew in a breath, but she forestalled him. "'Nother one on the fridge. And the kitchen table, case he misses that one."

She'd apparently thought of everything bar rigging the place with an intruder alert.

Tasha directed him to the fish-and-chip shop, which was brightly lit, had a neon sign advertising the place as *Salt and Battery*, and held nobody who even remotely resembled Mal. Jory sighed.

The longer they drove uselessly around, the more the nightmares crept in.

"He wouldn't . . ." Jory stopped. God, no. Mal would never—

"What?"

"It's . . . No. God."

"*What*? I mean, seriously, *what*, cos you're freaking me out here."

Jory took a deep breath. "Hurt himself. Or . . . worse."

"What? No. No way."

Was she trying to convince herself?

"I'm sorry. I shouldn't have suggested it." Jory swallowed. "It's how my father . . . But that was different. Completely."

"Oh my God. Did he . . ."

"The cliffs. Behind our house."

"Shitfuck. And you still *live* there? Oh fuck. Sorry. But Mal, he wouldn't do that. Never. Swear to God. He knows what it's like, don't he? For people what have to pick up the pieces."

"I . . . Yes. Of course." Jory was silent a moment longer. Then, "I just wish he hadn't been drinking."

"What, Mal? He don't drink a lot. Not lately, anyhow. I mean, he'll have a pint, but that's usually all he has."

Oh God. They'd drunk more than that the day they'd had sex on the beach. Had Jory taken advantage of him? Was that why Mal had fled afterwards? "What did he tell you about me?" he couldn't help asking.

Tasha ignored his question. "Oi, wait a minute. What do you mean he'd been drinking?"

Jory was about to answer when his phone rang. He exchanged a wild glance with Tasha, then pulled over to answer it, his heart jumping into his throat when he saw the call was from Mal. "Hello?"

"Uh. Jory?" Mal's voice sounded off, somehow, but maybe that was because Jory had all but snapped out the greeting.

"Yes. Are you okay? Where are you?"

"Uh . . . I think I fell."

"What? Fell where?"

"Your tunnel. Um. I think I broke it?"

"You bro— What the hell are you doing up there?" Jory's voice was coming out high and strident, but there didn't seem to be anything he could do about it. "Are you all right?"

There was a horrible silence.

"Mal, for God's sake, are you all right?"

"Uh. Yeah. Kinda."

"What the hell does that mean?" Jory tried to slow his breathing down. "I'm coming up there. Stay put."

"Yeah, not a problem."

"Are you injured? Buried?" Christ . . . But no, if he was buried, his phone wouldn't work, would it?

"Uh . . . Bit of both? I'm in the tunnel, and there's stuff on me, but I'm still getting rained on? And my leg hurts. And I think maybe I twisted my ankle."

"I'm on my way."

"Jory?"

"Yes?" Christ, Mal sounded out of it. Dazed by the fall. The alcohol beforehand probably hadn't helped, either. "Did you hit your head?"

"Bit. Jory? 'M sorry. Not just about this. About Kirsty. And being a fuckup."

"You're not a fuckup," Jory insisted, holding the phone between his chin and his shoulder as he started the car and hoping there'd be no passing police to see him driving like that. Then again, he might be glad of some help. "Kirsty explained about . . . you know."

Jory didn't catch what Mal said next, but it sounded something like "wish she'd explain it to me." That wasn't important. What was important was getting to Mal.

Mal spoke again. "Sorry if I made you think I don't care. Cos I do. Care. A lot."

Jory ought to feel elated, but this was starting to sound horribly like a deathbed confession. "You can tell me in a minute, when I get to you. Talk to Tasha." He thrust the phone at her and concentrated on driving.

It took a damned sight longer than a minute by the time he'd parked the Qubo at the side of the road at the nearest point to the tunnel and scrambled round to open up the boot. Jory grabbed both headlamps, pulling one on and thrusting the other at Tasha. He slung the backpack with his climbing gear in over his shoulder—who knew what he'd need?—and shut the boot. Then he vaulted over the hedge, forced himself to turn and give Tasha a hand although everything inside him was chafing at the delay, and then set off at a run, calling out Mal's name.

His voice was probably lost in the rain that was still pelting down on them. Tasha kept pace with him somehow, not once complaining—unless you counted the frequent profanities that slipped out. *Slipped* was the operative word. Jory cursed himself for not changing his shoes. The ones he'd been wearing for work today didn't provide even the scantiest amount of grip. Even trainers would have been an improvement.

He knew from the rise of the ground when they were nearing the mouth of the tunnel. "We're here," he called to Tasha. "Watch your step. *Mal!*"

He thought he heard an answer, half drowned by the rain. Jory cast around wildly in the dark—and glimpsed a light out of the corner of his eye. Mal, maybe, holding up his phone as a beacon? When he turned his head, it vanished. Thinking quickly, Jory turned off his headlamp and looked again.

Yes—there. Thank God. Scrambling over in the direction of the light, Jory almost fell into the tunnel—the mouth of it wasn't as he remembered, the gash in the earth stretching farther than it had all the time he'd known it. "Be careful," he yelled back to Tasha. "The tunnel's collapsed."

God, what he wouldn't give for a moonlit night. Or at least for the bloody rain to stop. Jory got down on hands and knees and felt his way over the unsafe ground.

"Can you see him?" Tasha yelled. "*Mal?*"

CHAPTER TWENTY-THREE

"Over here." Mal's voice was more distinct this time. Closer. Frustrated with his slow progress, Jory got back to his feet and set off in a running crouch. It was a mistake. The ground seemed to fall away suddenly, taking Jory's feet with it, and he landed on something soft that said, "Fuck," and grabbed hold of him with both hands. "Jory?" was gasped out, and his name had never sounded so sweet.

It was Mal.

"Thank God." It came out embarrassingly heartfelt, but Jory couldn't bring himself to care too much. In any case he was busy running his hands over all of Mal he could reach. Damn it, if only he could *see* . . . Oh. Feeling like an idiot, he turned his headlamp back on. That first glimpse of Mal's face, dripping wet and mud streaked, made him dizzy with relief. "Are you hurt? I mean, your leg—how bad is it?"

Tasha stumbled down beside them, half-landing on Jory's shoulder. "Shitfuck. Babe, you okay?" Her voice was high and thin.

"Yeah, I'm good. Chill, Tash."

Chill?

Mal was lying in a depression caused by the collapse of the tunnel, his legs buried. God, how long had this weak spot been waiting for someone to tread on it at the wrong moment? Mal could have been *buried alive* down there. Why the hell hadn't Jory been more responsible? He should have reported it, had it roped off—

"'M okay," Mal said. "Just, there's this rock or something? Couldn't shift it."

Jory dug down around him with numb fingers. There wasn't so much *this rock* as there were a number of large rocks jamming Mal in place. "Tasha, hold on to him," he ordered, just in case he managed to dislodge the one thing keeping Mal from total inhumation.

"Got him."

Her words were confirmed a moment later by Mal's "Ow, fuck, not so tight."

Jory carried on digging, vaguely registering a good deal of swearing along the lines of *You wanker, you do this again Imma cut your balls off with a spoon.*

Tasha was definitely growing on him.

Then he found what Mal had been talking about. A larger fragment of what had once been the tunnel roof was jammed against Mal's thigh. It had to be bloody painful. Jory stared, blinking rainwater out of his eyes. Was that blood on his jeans? Or just dirt?

Either way, he needed to get Mal out of here. "Tasha?" he yelled. "When I tell you, can you try and pull him out—not yet," he added as Mal cursed. "When I tell you." He dug frantically, but it was no use. The fragment was stuck firm, damn it. Jory couldn't shift it—and was scared to try in case he hurt Mal more. He sat back on his heels for a moment, thinking.

"Now?" Tasha yelled.

"No," Jory and Mal shouted back simultaneously.

"I'm going to try digging the other side of you," Jory decided. "Take off the pressure."

It was easier going, digging this side. Relatively speaking. "Have you got him?" he yelled to Tasha as he felt Mal shift.

"Yeah. Want me to pull?"

"Wait . . ." Jory dug further and felt another give. "Okay, now," he ordered, slinging his arms around Mal's body and doing his best to heave him upwards, hoping desperately Mal would have the sense to stop them if they were injuring him.

Mal moved—and then Tasha yelped as Mal landed on top of her, and Jory barely managed to keep from adding his own not inconsiderable weight to the pile.

They all lay there for a moment in the pouring rain, breathing hard—and then Jory realised Mal was laughing.

Thank God. Jory fumbled over to take him in his arms, while Tasha scrabbled away from them with a muttered "You arse." Jory kissed Mal's rain-slick face, tasting dirt and not caring. Mal's mouth found his and locked on tight, even when Jory's headlamp bashed him on the forehead. Jory managed to let go of him long enough to tear it off clumsily and let it fall where it might.

He'd probably regret that later, but right now he didn't give a damn. He was too busy reassuring himself Mal was alive, was okay.

God knew how long they were kissing. Long enough for Tasha to yell a disgruntled "Oi, are we ever getting out of this pissing rain?"

Good point. Jory drew back from Mal, reluctantly. "Can you walk?"

"Dunno. Give it a go, yeah?"

Jory helped him up with hands that, now the urgency had gone, were beginning to feel rather the worse for wear—and almost dropped him when Mal stumbled. Tasha caught him from the other side.

Jory adjusted his hold. "Can you put weight on your leg?"

"Uh. Bit?"

"We just need to get you to the car." Jory hoped to God Mal wouldn't have another panic attack, but making him walk further than he needed to and maybe exacerbating his injuries wasn't an option.

"Come on, you tosser, stop being a baby." Tasha's tone was more sympathetic than her words. "Fuck. Which way are we going?"

Jory took a moment to orient himself. The tunnel was *there* and the ground sloped in *that* direction, so . . . "This way." He didn't need his headlamp, so long as he kept the hedge beside them, and he certainly didn't want to keep Mal out in the rain while he tried to find it.

He took as much of Mal's weight as possible as they stumbled along the field, past the place where the Qubo was parked—he didn't much fancy trying to get an injured man over the hedge—and down to the gap he and Mal had come through a few days ago. It seemed more like months had gone by. Jory pushed the memories to the corner of his mind, alongside the knowledge that, relief at finding him aside, he really had no idea where he stood with Mal.

"Uh, dude, where's your car?" Mal asked as they emerged from the fields.

"Up the road. Sorry. Didn't think it through. Just wanted to get to you as quickly as possible."

Their feet splashed in a river of rainwater as they hobbled up the narrow lane. Fortunately, Jory consoled himself, he was soaked through to the bone already so he couldn't get any wetter. They probably looked like contestants in some bizarrely overpopulated version of a three-legged race, had there been anyone around to see, which, thank God, there was not. Especially since if a car should come along, it was doubtful they'd be coordinated enough to get out of the way in time.

He'd thought he'd been keeping in shape since coming back to live here. The pounding of his heart and the straining of his lungs as he half carried Mal up the hill told him he'd better work harder on his fitness.

Reaching the Qubo, Jory felt like a fisherman who'd weathered the mother of all storms and had at last spotted the harbour lights of home. Fumbling in his pocket for his keys, he had a moment's panic that he'd dropped them somewhere in the fields, before realising he'd left them in the ignition in his hurry to get to Mal.

Thank God the local car thieves were a fair-weather lot.

Tasha was panting hard as they eased Mal into the Qubo's passenger seat. "Fuck me, Mal, you gotta go on a diet."

"Oi, I'm all muscle. Weighs more than fat." Despite his cheery words, Mal's face was pale under its smears of grime.

Jory squinted at him in the sudden brightness of the car's interior light. "How's your leg?"

"Still there. Fuck. Feel a bit sick."

"We need to get you warm and dry." Jory hesitated. "Roscarrock House is closest."

"Nah. Just wanna go home." Mal looked around. Jory wasn't entirely sure he was seeing what was actually there. "Back to the pub. With Tasha."

"You'll be all right going that far?"

"'M what?"

Never mind, then. Jory slipped into the driver's seat and was startled to realise he still had his rucksack on his back. He wrestled it off, Tasha helping from the back seat.

"Oh my God, babe, your hands are a mess," Tasha said, sounding horrified.

Jory was faintly shocked to realise she was talking to him, not to Mal. Since when did he merit a *babe*? "It's okay. I can drive." Although for the first time in his life, he was half wishing he'd bought an automatic. He gritted his teeth and put the car in gear.

It must have been past closing time when they got to the Sea Bell, but you wouldn't have known it from the number of no-longer-young men still propping up the bar. It worked to their advantage in that one of them was Dr. Prowse, a semiretired GP who was able to check Mal over and pronounce him probably able to survive the night without visiting a hospital.

Jago Andrewartha hadn't exactly looked approvingly at Jory when they'd walked in supporting Mal, Tasha's T-shirt plastered to her chest and all of them streaked with mud and dripping on the floor, but at least he'd allowed Jory to take Mal upstairs and help Tasha get him changed into dry clothes and settled into bed.

"I was really fucking careful, you know?" Now coherent, thank God, Mal resembled a teenager, his towel-dried hair fluffing up against his pillow.

Jory knelt by the side of the bed. His clothes had started to dry on him, surprising him with the revelation that yes, they *could* get even more uncomfortable than they had been soaking wet. "You were? I must have missed that bit."

"Watched me step, you know, so's not to fall down the hole. Didn't know I was gonna make a new one."

Tasha snorted. She was in a big fluffy dressing gown with her hair in a towel, as if she'd just stepped out of a bubble bath, the sort that involved scented candles and a glass of wine. "Yeah, and we'll rip you a new one if you ever do anything like that again."

Jory was absurdly touched by the *we* in her threat. "What was so funny, earlier?" he asked Mal. "Remember? You were laughing after we pulled you out of the hole?"

"Fun— Oh. Me. Sorry. Your mum ever read you that fairy story about the enormous turnip? You know, where the whole bloody town and all the animals help pull it out of the ground and end up on top of each other?"

It struck Jory as far more hilarious than it should have. He snickered as silently as he could, probably sounding like some kind of cartoon dog.

"You're an enormous turnip all right," Tasha muttered darkly. "You ever go trying to bury yourself alive again, I'll put you in a fucking pasty."

"Oi, but then it wouldn't be an authentic Cornish pasty. No turnips in one of them. Only swedes allowed."

"You can fuck *authentic.* You can fuck it right up the *arse.*"

"Couldn't do that. Me bloke here would get jealous." Mal smiled at Jory—but then the smile faltered. "Uh . . ."

"I should go," Jory said abruptly, getting to his feet. "You need to rest. And if you still can't put weight on that foot in the morning, go to emergency and get an X-ray. *Despite* what Dr. Prowse said."

"You should stay," Tasha blurted out. "I'll make you a cuppa."

"No. Thanks. I need to . . ." Jory gestured vaguely at his clothes.

Mal made a half-hearted offer to lend him something dry to wear, but they both knew it would have been a very tight fit. Tasha didn't, thank God, suggest lending him something of Jago's.

"Take care," Mal said, grabbing his hand and squeezing it so hard it hurt.

Jory nodded and left.

Back at Roscarrock House, Jory parked the Qubo in the old stables and trudged across the yard. He took his rucksack and Tasha's headlamp with him—he'd need to dry everything thoroughly if he ever hoped to use it again. He was weary to the bone and desperate to avoid bumping into his brother or sister on his way through the house—Bran for one would be bound to ask why Kirsty had been here, and she was one person he really didn't want to talk about right now.

So, of course, as Jory stepped in through the back door, Bran appeared in the doorway from the dining room. Maybe he'd been lying in wait. Jory nodded curtly, hoping Bran would take the hint, and carried on past him.

His hopes of peace were short-lived. "What the bloody hell do you think you've been doing?" Bran demanded.

Jory barely had the energy to spare his brother a glance over his shoulder. "Not now."

He was utterly shocked to be grabbed by the shoulders and yanked around, hard. Christ, where had Bran found the strength? Jory almost fell, but regained his footing just in time. "What are you—"

"Have you been out on the cliffs?" Bran demanded.

"What? Why would—"

"What the hell do you think you were doing, playing at silly buggers in the dark? Are you out of your mind? Don't you give a *damn* about the rest of us?" His face was livid.

Jory shook off his grasp and took a cautious step back. "Bran, you're not making sense."

"Don't be an idiot. I can't believe you'd do this to us. After Father—" Bran's voice cracked.

"What? Bran, I wasn't on the cliffs. Do you honestly think I'd be that stupid? In the dark? When it's this wet?"

"Don't lie to me. I know you've been climbing again, sneaking out when you think I'm not watching. I've seen you. And you're soaking wet and you've got all that . . ." Bran gestured at Jory's hand, from which Tasha's headlamp and the rucksack were dangling by their straps. "That . . . stuff. Whatever you call it."

"I wasn't on the cliffs, okay? I was in the old smugglers' tunnel. There was a cave-in—not while I was in it," he added quickly, as Bran's expression darkened even further. "A . . . friend. He called me and asked for help."

"Why didn't he call the bloody emergency services? And what friend?"

Did they really have to do this now? Fine. Jory stared his brother down. "They wouldn't have known where to find him. I did. And he's someone I've been seeing."

"'Seeing'? You're a married man."

"No, I'm not. I never have been. Not truly. And we're getting divorced. Kirsty and I agreed."

"And you didn't consult me? Gawen is my *heir*, and this is his life we're talking about. You're so bloody selfish." Bran's tone turned spiteful. "You needn't think you're bringing your *friend* here to live with you."

"Christ, Bran, just when I start to believe you actually give a damn whether I live or die—"

"Of course I don't want you to die!"

"Maybe not, but I'm not sure you really want me to live, either."

"Just what do you mean by that?"

"I'm sick of you trying to run my life. I'm not a teenager anymore. I don't need you making decisions for me. I *certainly* don't need you to tell me who I can and can't live with."

"While you're living under my roof—"

"And that's another thing. This house . . ." Jory waved a weary hand. "It's . . ." *Full of ghosts*, he wanted to say, but that wouldn't be fair on Bran. "It's not me. It never has been. I should have got a place of my own a long time ago."

"You're moving out?" Bran's tone was unsure, almost lost.

Jory nodded. "As soon as I can find somewhere. I'll start looking tomorrow. For God's sake, it's not going to be far," he added, exasperated by Bran's wounded expression. "I'm staying in Porthkennack for Gawen, remember?"

"We'll miss you." It came out woodenly. Did that mean Bran was lying, or simply unused to expressing sentiment?

Most likely the former. Still, he'd said it, which was something.

"And this . . . man you're seeing? Will he be moving in with you?" Bea's voice, behind him, made Jory jump, and he turned to face her. How long had she been there, listening quietly?

She flushed, which probably meant it'd been some time.

"I haven't got a bloody clue what Mal's going to do now," Jory said shortly.

He'd had enough. He stepped past Bran, kicked off his squelching shoes and left his headlamp on the hall table, the rucksack finding a home underneath. He could deal with them tomorrow. After a moment's thought, he peeled off his sodden outer garments and left them lying in a heap on the floor.

Then he went to have a shower.

When Jory got back to his bedroom, he found Bea waiting for him, sitting demurely on the end of his bed in her pyjamas.

He tried not to sigh too audibly, but he was almost light-headed with fatigue and desperately wanted to be left alone.

"You shouldn't be too hard on Bran," she said softly. "All he's ever wanted is to do what's best for the family."

"I know." Jory nodded, because he *did* know. "The thing is . . . he's not always *right*, is he? And God knows it's taken me long enough to realise it. I'm sorry, Bea, but I'm not going to let him browbeat me into making the wrong decision again."

Her face closed off, but she nodded. Then she stood and finally, *finally* let him go to bed.

Jory was asleep almost before the door had closed behind her.

CHAPTER TWENTY-FOUR

M al woke up with the mother of all hangovers and a desperate
need to piss. It wasn't till he'd staggered out from under the
duvet, yelped in sudden pain, and promptly fallen back on the bed
that he remembered he also had a dodgy ankle and a shedload of
bruises over a large proportion of his skin.

Trouble was, once he'd remembered all that, he couldn't seem
to stop remembering stuff he *really* wasn't feeling up to coping with.
Crap. Shitting, sodding, bollocking *crap*.

He sat on the bed, rubbing his ankle and wishing he could rub his
life better. He'd made a right arse of himself.

Christ. *Jory*.

What the hell must he think of Mal after last night's little
shit-show?

Oh God. Mal didn't want to think about it. With his eyes shut
so he wouldn't have to meet his own gaze in the mirror, he hobbled
into the bathroom, where he bashed his elbow on the doorframe
and almost fell in the bath.

And then, because clearly he wasn't suffering enough yet, he
walked out of the bathroom to find Tasha waiting for him with the
least sympathetic look *ever* on her face. "Wanna make a bit more
noise? Cos I think there's still people back in London who didn't
quite hear you crashing around up here."

Mal winced. "Keep your voice down, yeah?"

"Aw, we not feeling so good?" Tasha's voice got even louder,
because she was an evil witch who hated him.

"Not so much, no." Mal leaned back against the wall and closed
his eyes again. "Was it as bad as I think it was?"

"Depends. Do you *think* you got shit-faced, snogged Jory's missus, then nearly killed yourself and had to be rescued by the bloke you cheated on?"

"Crap." Mal's eyes flew open of their own accord as another memory hit and jolted him from humiliation to hope. "But he kissed me, yeah? When you and him found me? That happened, right?" Because that kiss . . . He could have dreamed that, easy.

It was way too good to be in Mal's fucked-up life. Just like the bloke who'd given it to him.

Tasha paused. "Look, we were all dead worried about you, you know. Me and him and even her, from what Jory said."

"'Her'?"

"The missus. She went up to see him after you bogged off. Told him you was upset and all."

"Did she tell him it was an accident?" Mal asked hopefully.

"What, you mean like your tongue *accidentally* falling in her mouth? I dunno, do I? We were a bit more worried about *finding* you last night." Tasha folded her arms. "He thought you might've walked off a cliff like his old man."

"Oh fuck, no." Mal screwed up his eyes, then stopped when he realised how much worse it made his headache. "Wait, he told you about that?"

"Weren't you listening? We were out of our bloody minds. So . . . look, the snogging? You and him, I mean. Not her—and fuck, babe, what were you even *thinking*? You gotta not read too much into it. I'm just saying, there's a difference between *Thank fuck you're alive* and *Come back, all is forgiven*."

"I know, all right? I know." But Jory had kissed him like he'd *meant* it. Like he didn't care about all the shit Mal had pulled.

"Thought you didn't think you and him should be together, anyway?"

"I didn't, but . . . Last night, yeah, when he walked in on me and Kirsty? It was like . . . And then when he came to help me when I called him and he was so fucking happy to see me . . . I dunno, babe. It's totally doing my head in."

Tasha put her arm round his shoulders. "You really like him, don't you?"

Mal nodded miserably.

"Then why don't you go for it? Tell him you're sorry you snogged his missus, do a bit of grovelling, and see what happens. I know you're worried about making stuff awkward for Dev, but after last night, how much worse can it get?"

"What if he doesn't like me? Like I like him?"

"Babe. He likes you."

"But how am I supposed to know if he likes me *enough*? Enough to want me back?"

"Well, *duh*. You ask him?"

"Yeah, but . . . What if it's the wrong answer?"

"Then you deal with it."

"What, man up and keep a stiff upper lip?"

"No, you wanker, you come back, have a good cry, and we'll binge-watch *The Walking Dead*, cos there's nothing like zombies for getting over a broken heart."

"Will you make me hot chocolate?"

"For you, babe, I'll even put real sugar in it. So pull up your big-boy knickers, take a headache pill, and go get him, tiger." She paused. "But maybe get dressed first. And brush your teeth cos, seriously, your breath is *rank*."

All right for Tasha to talk, Mal thought moodily half an hour later as he shut the pub door behind him and blinked in the sudden brightness.

She wasn't the one putting her heart on the line. And she didn't know as much as she thought she did.

The day, once he got used to it, wasn't actually all that bright. The weather had well and truly turned. The sky was the colour of a garage floor, mucky grey with blacker splodges like the clouds had been leaking oil. They looked like they were only a rat's whisker from leaking water too. Mal hunched in his hoody and hoped he wasn't going to get another drenching. It was going to be a long walk up to Roscarrock House with a duff ankle. Although the William Morris–patterned walking stick he'd borrowed from Mrs. Jago's hall cupboard (her knees gave her gyp in the winter) was pretty cool. Mal had always liked his pre-Raphaelites, especially the ones with all the knights and the big flowsy ladies falling asleep all over the shop.

A car horn beeped loudly just behind him. Mal winced—paracetamol and codeine could only do so much—and turned to see Jago in his battered old Land Rover, scowling through the side window at him. "You going up to Big Guns?"

"Uh . . ." Right. Big Guns Cove was the name of the cliffs Roscarrock House sat on. "Yeah?"

Jago nodded. "Well, get in, then. I ain't got all day."

Huh. "Thought you didn't approve of them?" Mal got in quick before Jago could change his mind and drive off.

"Think I'm letting you walk up there on a sprained ankle? I'd never hear the last of it from Tasha."

Mal grinned. "Hang about, people are gonna start thinking you care."

"Slander and lies. You going to manage, me driving you?"

Sod it. "One little flashback and everyone thinks I'm gonna flip my shit every time I get in a car. Who told you about that, anyhow?" Not that he couldn't guess.

"Eyes everywhere. And just you remember that."

Pervy old sod. Keeping shtum for reasons of self-preservation, Mal focussed on not actually flipping his shit as Jago pulled out and drove along the lane.

Seeing as (a) the old bloke slowed to a crawl every time they got within fifty feet of any pedestrians and (b) Mal's insides were tied up so tight about Jory he could barely think about anything else, it wasn't as hard as he'd worried it might be. "Cheers, mate," he said as Jago dropped him off at the gates of Roscarrock House.

Jago nodded. "Call me if you need a lift back."

And then he was gone. Mal trudged up the drive, stick in hand and his heart in his mouth.

Roscarrock House was a lot grimmer close up than Mal remembered. Or maybe it was just the weather—the grey stone pretty much blended in with the sky.

Funny to think, if things had been different, Dev could have grown up in this place. Mal would never have met him, or Tasha.

Or Jory.

He swallowed and knocked.

The door was opened by a dark-haired bloke who was shorter than Mal and apparently none too happy about it. Or, well, about anything at all, by the face on him. "Yes?"

"Um. Jory?" Mal wondered where the rest of his words had gone.

Short, dark and grumpy gave him a thorough once-over. He seemed to pay particular attention to Mal's hands which, yeah, were definitely the worse for wear after last night, scratched up and with half the skin off his knuckles. He hadn't managed to get all the dirt out from under his fingernails either. "You're the *boyfriend*," the bloke—Jory's brother, Bran, had to be—spat out at last.

Was he? Mal wished he was half as sure about it. Shit, how much did Bran know about last night? "Can I just—"

"I'll tell him you're here." Bran turned and stomped down the hall, leaving Mal hovering uneasily on the doorstep.

What if Jory didn't want to see him? He had every right to be pissed off at Mal.

But Bran had called him Jory's boyfriend. Not—and Mal reckoned this was a key point and he was going to hang on to it with both hands if it bloody well killed him—his *ex*.

Catching sight of Jory coming down the hall sent a wash of pure relief flooding over him. Particularly when he saw how nervous Jory looked. That had to be good, right?

Or bad. Maybe it was bad.

"Hi," Mal said, his voice coming out in a squeak.

"Hi."

They stood there for about three thousand years, just staring at each other. Jory looked, well, rough—there were dark circles under his eyes, his beard was due a trim, and his hair had forgotten what a comb was for. And his hands . . . "Shit, your hands are worse than mine. You okay?"

Jory glanced down at his hands, spreading them out in front of him like he hadn't noticed that they were all scratched up, his knuckles skinned and nails broken. Cleaner than Mal's, though. "Oh, yes. Fine. Thanks. You?"

Mal shrugged. "Better than I deserve. So, uh, that was your brother, yeah?"

"Bran. Yes. Um. Do you want to come in?"

Mal nodded, relieved, and stepped over the threshold.

Jory seemed to see the walking stick for the first time, and his face fell. "You didn't walk all this way on an injured leg?"

"Nah, Jago gave me a lift. It ain't so bad. Just twisted me ankle a bit, falling." It was sort of true. It'd definitely loosened up since he'd got up this morning. "Got a bruise the size of Ireland on me thigh, though."

"Come in properly and sit down." Jory still seemed jumpy.

"You sure I'm gonna be welcome?"

Jory nodded. "It's fine. Bran and I had something of a heart-to-heart this morning."

Mal laughed nervously. "Yeah? He's got one, then?"

"You'd be surprised. I was." Jory took a deep breath. "Kirsty and I are getting divorced."

"What? Shit. Is that cos of—"

"Only indirectly." Jory half smiled. "But please do come in."

Mal followed him down the hall to a kitchen he hadn't seen on the tour. It was bigger than most kitchens he'd been in—even had room for a proper old-fashioned kitchen table that could seat a family of six easily, though it'd probably been years since it actually had. Jory pulled out a chair for him.

"Tea? Coffee?"

Mal shook his head. "Nah, I'm good." Then he wished he'd accepted, cos it would've given him something to do with his hands.

At least they were in the kitchen. Jory wouldn't bring him to the kitchen to dump his arse, would he? He'd use the front room for that. Keep it formal, shove Mal out the door as quick as he could.

Probably.

Jory sat down in the next chair. And waited.

Shit. Mal swallowed. "Look, I wanted to say I'm sorry. About . . . uh, about last night, obviously, but for fucking you around before too."

"It's . . . okay," Jory said, his tone saying it wasn't really okay, but he thought it ought to be. "Kirsty told me it was her fault, not yours."

There was the hint of a question there at the end. And Mal wanted to say, *Yeah, totally her, what a slapper*, but he just couldn't, all right? It wouldn't be fair. What happened last night had all been down to him not explaining stuff properly, and if things got fucked up between Jory and her, it'd be hard on Gawen. Plus, well, he *liked* Kirsty, so long as she wasn't trying to stick her tongue down his throat.

"I was missing you," Mal blurted out. "I mean I . . . But I never wanted her. She got the wrong end of the stick, that's all."

Jory gazed at him for a long moment, then looked away. "I wish I knew where I stood with you," he said, apparently more to the kitchen wall than to Mal.

It made Mal's heart hurt.

What the hell was he going to say to that? The whole reason he'd come up here was . . . to apologise, yeah, but mainly, if he was gut-wrenchingly honest, to find out where *he* stood with Jory.

Could he do it? Tell Jory how he felt? And risk Jory saying *Sorry mate, last night was the deal breaker*?

Then again, after last night, didn't Jory deserve the truth?

Christ. Mal clenched his fists, his nails digging into his palms. Did he really have the balls to go through with it?

CHAPTER
TWENTY-FIVE

"*I wish I knew where I stood with you.*" Jory hadn't meant to say it out loud.

But maybe it was time they talked about whatever was going on between them? Really talked, without sex or hurt feelings or near-death experiences getting in the way.

"So, what happened with Kirsty . . . Was it just the drink?" Jory took a deep breath. He should let it go, he knew he should; he was harping on about it too much, but he had to be certain. "What *did* happen? Exactly?"

"Think you saw it all. I mean, all of that sort of stuff. We had dinner, we had a few drinks, and then she—then it happened. And ten seconds later you walked in." Mal looked him in the eye. "If I'd known that was gonna happen, I'd never have gone. On me mum's life. And I tried—I wanted to tell you, it didn't mean nothing, but you'd already gone. Wasn't like I could jump in a car and zoom off after you, was it?"

Something twisted unpleasantly in Jory's chest. No, he'd made absolutely certain Mal had no chance to explain himself. But, damn it, it had *hurt* seeing Mal with someone else.

"What would you have said if I'd stayed?" he asked in the end.

Mal stared at him, wide-eyed, like a cornered rabbit. Or any other small, rodent-like creature.

Jory met his gaze, and attempted a half smile of reassurance. He wasn't sure he succeeded—but it seemed to do the trick in any case.

"It's . . . Shit." Mal looked away for a moment and ran a hand through his hair, then turned back to Jory, seeming more fragile even than right after the car incident. More fragile than Jory could have imagined. "I like you. Like, a lot."

Jory's hand clenched into something resembling a fist without consulting him. It sounded good . . . But Mal hadn't finished. Jory could tell. "But?" he prompted.

"But . . . I'm scared, okay?"

"'Scared'?" Jory repeated stupidly.

"Yeah . . . Look, I know this is gonna sound like a really crap ambition to you, but it's all I ever wanted to do, right? Drive a Tube train like my dad. It's the only job I ever done, apart from when I started out in customer service cos you have to, cos they only advertise the drivers' jobs internally. I thought it was gonna be my life, sorted." He screwed up his face as if he was in pain. "Go on, laugh."

Jory was too busy wondering exactly what all this had to do with *them*. And wanting to hold Mal until that pained look had vanished forever. Was touching allowed? Oh, to hell with it. Jory grabbed Mal's hands where they rested on the kitchen table, folding them both in his own. "I'm not laughing. But I don't understand . . . What are you afraid of? You mean, that you won't be able to get over the . . . one under and get back in the driving seat?"

"Yeah. There's that. But then there's . . . Oh, shit a fucking brick." Mal pulled away from him, closing his eyes tight shut. "There's you."

"Me?" Jory's heart appeared to have taken up cliff diving. Did Mal mean . . .?

"Yeah." Mal looked up at him from under his tousled hair. "All that crap I said about not wanting us to get into anything serious . . . Well, it's bollocks, innit? Not the wanting. I mean, the actual thing. Ah, shit. It's too late. I already— You know."

"You're . . . serious about me?" Jory's heart leapt. That was . . . But he could celebrate later. For the rest of his life, if he had his way. Mal was what was important right now. "Then why not?"

"Because I can't deal, okay? I can't deal with it ending."

"Then we won't let it end." Jory tried to put all his conviction into his voice.

Mal was shaking his head. "But you got your kid and your new job coming up, so you ain't gonna want to move to London, even if I did get me old job back, and Christ, I wouldn't ask you to. But if, well, if you wanted me to stay down here, what the sodding hell would I do?

I've only ever been good at one thing, and that's driving trains, and I fucked that up too, didn't I?"

"You didn't fuck anything up," Jory said fiercely. "It wasn't your fault. There was *nothing* you could have done." He was torn between jubilation that Mal had actually got so far as to think about them having a future together, and frustration that Mal had seemingly argued himself out of it before it had even started.

"I don't just mean . . . See, me dad's had his share of that sort of shit, and he never . . . never made a big deal of it. Just got back on with the job. And here's me signed off work for six months and throwing a fucking wobbly every time I sit in a car."

"That's not true. You coped when Jago Andrewartha gave you a lift up here, didn't you?"

"Yeah, but—"

"You're not your father, Mal. No one ever is—I know for a fact I'm bloody well not mine. You can't judge yourself like that. You're not a failure just because something affects you differently than it would him." Jory leaned forward cautiously, afraid Mal might bolt, and laid his hands gently on Mal's. "You're more sensitive than he is, perhaps. Is that supposed to be a bad thing?" He took a deep breath. "From everything you've said to me, it's your mother who's been the greater influence on you."

Mal gave a bitter half-laugh, but at least he didn't pull away again. "Yeah. Proper mummy's boy, that's me."

"Bollocks," Jory said firmly, startling Mal into looking directly at him. "You're not exactly hiding behind her skirts by coming here, are you? I was talking about your interest in history and legend. The way they fire your imagination. That's what I think you get from your mother." He'd wanted to add, *your intelligence,* but was wary of seeming to criticise Mal's father.

"Yeah, well. I let her down, and all."

"Have you asked her if that's what she thinks? Because from what you've told me about her, I very much doubt it." Jory drew Mal closer and wrapped his arms around him, wishing he dared pull him all the way onto his lap. "You should think about counselling, you know. It might help."

Mal shrugged. "Had a bit back in London. Just . . . the woman kept wanting me to *talk* about it, and that's the last thing I wanted, innit? Felt like a total wuss, sitting in her office snivelling into a box of tissues for an hour a week."

"Maybe she wasn't the right counsellor. You could try again with someone you get on with better . . ." Mal grimaced. Jory frowned. "It doesn't make you less of a man, you know, accepting help when you need it. You didn't hesitate last night, did you? You realised you needed help, and you made sure you got it."

"Yeah, but . . . that's different, innit? I was stuck in a hole in the ground." Mal made a face. "And I never said I don't feel like a stupid prat about it."

"Good." Jory almost laughed at Mal's shocked expression, but an unexpected burst of anger flooded through him, drowning the brief impulse. "For God's sake, walking on the cliffs in the pouring rain, in the dark, while drunk, in a place where you know the ground's given way at some point in the past already? That's pretty much the *definition* of being a stupid prat." He took a deep breath. "But calling for help? That was *not* being a prat. And definitely not stupid. So will you at least think about it? Getting another counsellor?"

"I . . ." Mal hunched into himself for a moment, then straightened in Jory's arms. "Wanna do a deal? I'll have another go at seeing someone, and you give the Tintagel trip another try? With, uh, me, I mean. I'll try not to flip out this time." Mal gave a weak smile with more than a hint of desperation in his eyes. "Good job we're both used to me fucking stuff up, innit?"

"Stop putting yourself down." Jory squeezed him tight. "And remind me to point you to some reading on toxic masculinity."

"Oi, you ain't a teacher yet. No handing out homework." Mal's smile strengthened and warmed Jory's heart absurdly.

Then it faltered again. "Yeah, but still . . . how's it gonna work? You and me living hundreds of miles apart?" Mal studied the surface of the table.

Jory leaned forward and took Mal's face in his hand, encouraging him to look up. "We don't have to sort out all the details right now. You're here for a while longer, aren't you?"

Mal nodded. "Six weeks was the plan. I'm not even halfway through that."

"Well, then. We can see how it goes. See what works for us."

"And if it don't?"

"We'll make it work." To hell with it. Jory pulled Mal onto his lap. "If you go back to London after that, I can still travel to see you. And you'll get your counselling, or whatever it takes so you can do your job again, and then you'll be able to travel down here easily. Or we can meet in the middle, or anywhere we want."

"What if I never get okay to be a Tube driver again? And I keep on being a wuss about getting in cars and stuff?"

"If it comes down to it, there *are* jobs here. Um, mostly concerned with the tourist industry, but it'd be a start. Something to do while you think about the next step. Or, well, I don't think the museum has filled the vacancy I'll be leaving yet."

"Don't you have to know stuff to work in a museum?"

"You'd be amazed at the number of serious historical discussions I *haven't* had since I started working there. But you could read up on naval history. You're bright enough— for God's sake, you've read the *Morte d'Arthur*. Most people take one look at the archaic language and decide to watch the Disney film instead."

"I ain't saying it didn't take me a while."

"But you did it. And anyway, that was just an idea. *If* you decide to leave London." Jory kissed him because he could. "Whatever it takes, we'll make it work."

He felt the tension go out of Mal's body, and wanted to punch the air. He'd done it. He'd convinced him.

Then Mal's phone rang.

CHAPTER
TWENTY-SIX

Mal was a bit pissed off when he got the call, cos he'd been on cloud nine and he'd had a feeling him and Jory had been about to have a truly epic snog, but there was a good chance it was Mum ringing to tell him he was an uncle. He dived into his pocket, realising even as he pulled out his phone that the ringtone was "Manic Mechanic." Dev.

Then again, did he really want to miss taking a call from Dev when he was actually sitting in Dev's ancestral seat? Well, on Dev's uncle's lap in Dev's ancestral seat, which sounded dead pervy when he thought about it.

He grinned as he answered. "Yo, bro."

"Hey, how's it going?" It was noisy in the background, like Dev was ringing from a café with hard, echoey floors and a lot of loud people in it.

Mal raised his voice to make sure he'd be heard. "Good, yeah. Fell down a hole in the ground last night and had to be rescued, but apart from that, I'm good." He shared a glance with Jory, who was wincing a bit. Hopefully from the reminder about last night and not cos he thought Mal had a bony arse.

Dev laughed. "Never change, mate. Never change. Listen, I'm ringing from the services on the M5. Me and Kyle are driving down. Set off early to beat the traffic, so we should be with you in a couple of hours."

"What, *today*? Thought it was gonna be middle of next week." It was fucking aces to hear he'd be seeing Dev again so soon—but that was, like, *really* soon.

"Yeah, well, Kyle got fed up hanging about at home when we could be hanging about by the seaside."

"How's he doing?"

"Knackered from the crap meds, but he's good. He says hi. Or he would if he wasn't . . . you know." Mal did know. When a nap attack hit, Kyle could sleep *anywhere*. "So, yeah, we'll be down the pub when we get here, or I will be, anyhow. Kyle's gonna see how it goes."

"Can't wait to see you, mate." Oops. A bit of emotion might have slipped through there.

Dev's voice softened. "How you been? Apart from falling-down drunk?"

"Uh . . ." Mal glanced at Jory. "It's complicated? But, uh, mostly good."

Jory gave him a look.

Mal melted. "Scratch that. Fucking *awesome*."

"Do I wanna know? You can tell me tonight. Tash been taking good care of you?"

"Christ, yeah. For the love of God, tell her to lay off when you get here, yeah? I can iron my own kecks. If I wanted me bloody kecks ironed, which seriously, who even does that? Mum'd have a right go at her for not letting me do it all myself." He hesitated, but if Tasha wanted Dev to know she was pining over Ceri, she'd probably rather tell him herself. "Even old Jago keeps being nice to me. It's doing my head in."

"You love it really. I gotta go, but I'll see you tonight."

"Counting on it."

Mal hung up. "So, that was Dev."

"I kind of gathered." Jory stroked Mal's hair, which was so bloody sweet he could hardly stand it. "I guess I won't be seeing you tonight."

"Not this afternoon, neither. They're only a couple of hours away. Um. I know you wanna meet Dev soon as, but—"

Jory was shaking his head. "I can wait. I've waited twenty-five years. And I'm more concerned about you right now." He paused. "But you'll mention me to him?"

Mal nodded. "Can't promise he'll go for it. That sister of yours did a proper number on him. But I'll do me best, yeah?"

He tried to sound confident, but inside he was a tangled mess of nerves. Yeah, of course he was going to be glad to see Dev again, but . . . timing, much? He'd have felt a lot better with at least a couple of days to get him and Jory sorted before having to introduce the bloke to Dev.

What if Dev didn't want to see him? That was going to be well awkward.

Shit. Mal was starting to remember all the reasons why getting involved with Jory had seemed like a bad idea.

But no way was he going to give him up now.

CHAPTER TWENTY-SEVEN

When Dev walked into the pub around lunchtime, Tasha let out a squeal so loud they probably had complaints about it over in Ireland. "Oi, careful." Mal rubbed his ear on the side nearest to her. "I think I just lost an eardrum."

Tasha shrugged. "Meh. You got another. Dev! Babe, it's been so long."

Dev sauntered over as she slipped out from behind the bar so he could give her a hug, a proper one, her feet off the floor and everything. "Looking good, Tash, looking good."

"Your hair's longer. And, ow, your stubble's got sharper. Oi, lemme go." They were both grinning wildly.

Mal held back, cos Dev might be his best mate but him and Tash were family. It wasn't long, though, before Dev let go of his little sis and turned. "Mal, my man. How's it going? Whoa, check out the pimp cane." He eyed the walking stick propped up against the bar.

"Up yours, mate. And it will be if you don't watch out." They shared a hug that was a lot manlier—no squealing, just bro-type back-slapping—while Tasha ducked back behind the bar and started pouring Dev a Coke.

"Where's Kyle? You leave him back at the cottage?"

"Nah, we walked down together. He'll be here in a bit. Wanted to give Zelley a good run around on the beach after all those hours cooped up in the car."

Huh. Mal kept forgetting some people had pets they could take with them when they went away. "How's he doing? Now he can't hear you telling me."

"He's good. Seriously. He was pissed off about the meds, but he's a lot more chill about that sort of stuff than he used to be." Dev smiled soppily, the big soft git. "So how's it been with you? Really?"

"Uh, good. Well, you know. Swings and roundabouts . . ." Mal dried up. Which was in direct contrast to his hands, which were sweating harder than an overweight pig that'd taken up marathon running. In Hell. He wiped them on his jeans.

Dev narrowed his eyes. "Come on, then, what you done?"

"Uh . . . We don't have to get into that now." Mal crossed his fingers.

"Get into what?" Christ, Dev was like a dog with a boner. Kept humping your leg until he got what he wanted.

"*Tell* him," Tash said. Traitor.

Mal sighed. "I met your uncle."

"That bastard? What did he do to you?"

"No. Not him. Well, yeah, I met him *too*, but . . . the other one. Jory. He's younger. And nicer."

"And?"

Tasha leaned over the bar, eyes bright and her tongue practically hanging out. "And he shagged him, didn't he?"

Mal groaned. "Cheers, Tash. That's exactly how I wanted to break it to him."

Dev stared. "You slept with my uncle? Fuck, bruv, I thought you had *some* standards."

"Oi, he's not like the other one, all right? He's a good bloke, Jory is."

"Uh-huh? No offence, but I'm gonna need evidence before I believe that about anyone called Roscarrock."

"He wants to meet you. Get to know you. And, uh, he's got a kid. Your cousin."

Dev's face had that closed-off expression Mal hadn't seen for a while. Say, since back when Dev had first met the Roscarrocks. "I got loads of cousins."

"Yeah, but Gawen's cool. He's twelve and he's really into computer games. Dead bright too."

"What about his mum?"

"Uh, she's not so cool. Well, she kinda is, but . . ." Yeah, best not going there. "But they're divorced. Uh, getting divorced. They've been separated since like before he was born." Mal realised how that might sound to Dev and hurried on. "But Jory didn't abandon them or nothing. He's a great dad to Gawen. He's gonna be a teacher at his school from September."

"He's all right, honest," Tasha put in. "When we was worried about Mal last night, he dropped everything to drive round trying to find him. *Despite* having reasons not to." She shot Mal a filthy look which, yeah, he probably deserved.

"Oh yeah? And what was all that about, anyhow?" Dev frowned. "You mean you weren't joking about having a fall? What you done to yourself?"

"It was only a little one. I'd've been fine if the weather hadn't been so shit."

"And if you hadn't been pissed out of your skull," Tasha put in flatly.

"Cheers, babe."

"Anytime."

"Oi, you were out on the piss? On your own?" Dev's face was darkening in a way that said brace yourself for thunder, lightning, and all four horsemen of the apocalypse.

"I wasn't on my own!"

Tasha snorted. "Yeah, that was the problem."

"Was this that Roscarrock bloke?"

"No!"

"That was the problem too." Tasha made a face. "Him and Jory was on the outs, and this older woman got Mal drunk and took advantage."

"It wasn't like that," Mal protested, cos it really wasn't fair on Kirsty.

"I tell it like I see it, babe."

Dev shook his head slowly. "Jesus, you two are doing my head in. Look, just tell me about this bloke. My so-called uncle. Are you and him together or what?"

"Yeah. We sorted it out." Mal couldn't help smiling as he thought about Jory.

Dev rolled his eyes. "Right. So now tell me, if he wanted to meet me, how come he never bothered till now?"

"Cos he didn't know. Swear to God. I didn't believe it at first, but that brother and sister of his—" Mal realised he was slagging off Dev's mum and swallowed, but fuck, Dev knew what she was like. "They don't tell him nothing. And they tried to run his whole life. Treat him like a kid even though he's in his thirties *and* he's got a kid of his own."

"You can sorta see why they're all fu—mucked up, though," Tasha said. "Their dad took a long walk off a short cliff right behind their house."

Mal shuddered. "Tasha, do something for me, will you? *Never* volunteer to work for the Samaritans."

"Fu—stuff you. I'd be brill. And stop changing the subject. You gotta meet him, Dev. Well, you're gonna anyway, seeing as him and Mal are in *lurve*."

"It's serious, then, you and him?"

Mal shoved his hands in his pockets. "Pretty much. Yeah."

"So what were you and him on the outs about?"

Aw, fuck. "I told him we couldn't be together."

"Because of me?"

"Yeah. No . . . I've just been really fucking messed up, you know?"

Dev's expression went all soppy again, and he gripped Mal's arm. "Hey, it's okay, bruv. You got every right to be. But this bloke, he makes you happy, yeah?"

"Yeah. Yeah, he does. Still dunno how it's gonna work, but . . . we're gonna give it a go."

Dev sighed, but he was smiling too. "Guess I'll be seeing him, then. And oi, none of that," he added when Mal opened his mouth to say *No, you don't have to do anything you don't want to.* "It's like, word of mouth, innit?"

"Uh?"

"'S how we get a lot of business down at the garage. People bring their cars in, they're happy with our work, so they tell their mates. And then they bring their cars in. So, like, this Roscarrock bloke—"

"Jory," Mal interrupted.

"—Jory, yeah, he's like the garage."

"What, and I'm the car he's serviced? Cheers, bruv."

Dev laughed. "You know what I mean. He's given your engine a good seeing to—"

"Seriously, this metaphor needs to die. It needs to die *right now*—"

"—and now you're recommending his services to all your mates."

"Listen, *mate*, if you even *think* about asking Jory to have a poke around under your bonnet—"

Kyle turned up at that point, which was just as well. He looked good—tired, but good. Zelley was a chocolate brown shadow at his heels. Mal bent down to make a fuss of her, with a lot of *Who's a gorgeous girl, then?* and that sort of thing. Then he grinned up at Kyle. "Oh, you here and all?"

"Good to see you too," Kyle said easily. "How have you been, Mal?"

Dev shouldered in as Mal straightened to give Kyle a welcoming hug. "That's Uncle Mal to you and me now."

"Have I missed something?" Kyle had his lawyer-look on his face.

"Just a bit," Tasha said, and cackled.

Mal threw up his hands. "Jeez, I can't face going through that again. Imma go pee. I may be some time."

"Don't worry, babe, we'll fill him in with all the juicy details," Tasha called after him, as Mal scarpered up the stairs as quick as he could.

After he'd visited the bathroom—he really had needed a pee— Mal escaped into his room and sat down on the bed. He needed a bit of space. Everything had gone good, and now . . . Now he wanted to sit quietly for a mo and try not to think about how badly it could all have gone.

Dev wasn't pissed off about it. He was going to give Jory a chance.

And Jory was going to give Mal another chance. Despite all the fuckups, all the stupid crappy things he'd done, Jory was giving him another chance.

Mal let himself fall back on the bed and lay there, staring at the ceiling. He wondered what Jory was doing.

Then he realised he could just bloody well ask him, grabbed his phone out of his pocket, and sent a quick text: *U there?*

The answer took a little while to come through. *Where else would I be?*

Mal smiled. *Dev here. Up 4 seeing u.*

Waiting for a text to buzz through, Mal almost dropped the phone when Jory rang him instead. "Yo?" Mal's voice didn't shake, he was proud of that, but his heart was pounding in his rib cage as if it wanted to come out and play.

"Hi." Jory's voice on the other end was like the perfect mug of hot chocolate, all warm, rich, and comforting.

"Hey."

"So you persuaded him? I'm . . . I don't know what to say. But thank you."

"Tash helped. And he said if I like you, that's good enough for him. Only, uh, he said it with metaphors."

"Well, as long as it wasn't similes."

"Poncy overeducated git." Mal paused. "Uh, don't take that the wrong way."

Jory chuckled. Over the phone, it sounded all breathy and did weird things to Mal's insides. And other bits. "There's a right way?"

"Duh. There's always a right way and a wrong way."

"So what would be the right way?" Jory's voice was all teasing.

Mal swallowed. "Uh, just to be clear, are we talking about Dev or are we having phone sex?"

"Now that you've brought up my nephew, I think I can categorically say we're not having phone sex."

"Well, shit. Um. So, I haven't, like, made any arrangements, but are you free tomorrow?"

"Would that be for meeting Dev or for phone sex?" The teasing tone was back.

Mal was torn. "You're a lot pervier over the phone, you know that?"

Jory laughed. "That's because you can't see me turning red."

"Oh yeah? How far down does it go?"

"You want me to check for you?"

Mal was going to say *Yeah, baby* in a low, growly voice. Somehow what came out was totally different and all high-pitched and squeaky. "I really fucking wish you were here."

There was a silence that lasted just long enough for Mal to start to panic. Then: "Me too. Funny how far a mile or so can seem. I mean, it's not much further than my walk to work, but . . ."

"Yeah."

"I could come down, but I'm guessing that wouldn't be the best idea?"

Mal tried his hardest to convince himself that Jory coming down to the pub would be the best idea *ever*, but . . . "Nah. Give Dev a chance to settle in. Get ready for it. But tomorrow, for defs."

Mal had planned to give it half an hour and then go back down, but Tasha came up to find him before he got that far. She poked her head around the door with her eyes shut. "Babe? You having a wank?"

Mal moaned loudly. "Oh yeah, that's it, shit, gonna come so hard . . ."

Her eyes flew open. Mal grinned at her from where he was sitting on the bed, fully clothed. Not wanking, cos he wasn't daft. He'd have locked the door for that. "Made you look."

Tasha stuck up her finger. "I knew you weren't really. Wanker. Are you ever coming down again? Cos I ain't bringing your lunch up here."

"Yeah, I'm on my way. I just needed to chill for a bit, you know? You said lunch, right?" He batted his eyes up at Tasha hopefully.

"Ready and waiting. Emphasis on *waiting*, so get your arse in gear, yeah?"

"I'm coming, I'm coming."

"That's what you said before, and I didn't believe you then either." Tasha cackled and disappeared.

Mal heaved himself off his bed and plodded down the stairs. His ankle hardly hurt at all now, and the swelling had gone down. Which was good, obviously, but it made him feel even *more* embarrassed over last night's little adventure. He patted his thigh and, ow, yeah, the bruise was still reassuringly painful. He hadn't been a total crybaby over nothing.

Dev and Kyle were sitting at a side table in the bar, already tucking in to a couple of ploughman's lunches. Mal slid into the empty seat where his own lunch was laid out. "It's all right. You didn't have to wait," he said to be a git.

"Nah, we knew you'd only feel bad about it," Dev said with his mouth full. "You eating that cucumber?"

"Nope." Mal scooped the four or five slices up onto his knife and dumped them on Dev's plate, taking a pickled onion in trade. Kyle would thank him for it later. "So what's the plan for today?"

"Settle in, laze about a bit, hope the weather picks up. You?"

"Not really got any plans."

"Aintcha seeing that bloke of yours, then?"

"Well . . . I saw him this morning. Thought I'd spend the day with you two, since it's been so bloody long."

"Yeah, that's cool. Can't promise we ain't both gonna fall asleep on the sofa, mind."

"No worries. I'll bring my Sharpie."

Dev laughed. "Oi, Kyle's the only one allowed to put a dick on my face."

Tasha, who'd been clearing the next table, made a gagging sound. "Jeez, Dev, you just had to go there, didn't you?"

They all laughed, and then Dev asked out of the blue, "So how are you doing now, about the whole one-under thing?"

Mal choked on his pickled onion.

Kyle patted him on the back, frowning at Dev. "Maybe we shouldn't—"

"What, so I'm not allowed to mention the Elephant and Castle in the room?" Dev's tone was light, but he gave Mal a searching look.

Mal held up his finger and swivelled it for good measure until he could speak. "Prick. It happened at Kennington, and you know it." He took a swig of Coke and almost managed to choke on that. "It's . . . a work in progress."

Dev nodded. "You ever want to talk or anything . . ." He leaned over and grasped Mal's arm. "'M here for you, bruv."

"Yeah. Cheers." That coughing fit had left his throat all tight. Mal took another swig of Coke to cover it.

After they'd eaten, they took Zelley down to the beach at Mother Ivey's Bay. With the skies still grey and threatening more rain, there weren't many people there and definitely no eye candy. A few families were making the best of it, the tots dressed in shorts and anoraks building sandcastles while Mum and Dad huddled together with a flask of tea. It was a real 1950s moment. Well, if you ignored Mum's ebook and Dad's smartphone.

While Dev threw a ball for the dog, Mal and Kyle sat down on the sand. It was cold under their bums, and Mal found himself envying the families—a cup of tea would've gone down a treat right now.

Mal cleared his throat. "So, uh, I guess you heard all about me and Jory, yeah?"

Kyle nodded. "I can't say I've had anything but bad experiences with that family, but I'm willing to keep an open mind. How did you meet him?"

"Local museum. He's gonna be a secondary schoolteacher in September, but he's working there for now." Mal smiled, remembering. "He ain't like his brother and sister. They're all about business and money and keeping up appearances, bollocks like that. But Jory's into learning stuff and passing it on."

"He's younger than them?"

"That you asking me if he's a dirty old man? Yeah, I think they were nine or ten when he was born. So he's less older than me than you are than Dev. Uh, if that makes sense." He thought about it. "Huh. I could just've said he's not as old as you."

"Thanks. Now *I* feel like a dirty old man."

"Anytime, mate."

"So you've been going out with him for a while, then?"

"Uh, well. Um. Not exactly. I mean, we've been out together a few times, but . . . it's complicated."

Kyle frowned. "Oh? I must've misunderstood. I thought from what Dev said that it was a serious thing."

Oh, fuck a duck. "It is, but . . . Fuck it, I really like him, but I'm shit scared it's not gonna work out. Christ, this is the worst possible time for me to meet someone. My head's still all fucked up."

Kyle gave him a look that said *I am older and wiser than you.* Mal would've been well pissed off by it if the subtext, which came across loud and clear, hadn't been *I've fucked my life up more times than you've had hot dinners.* "I understand your worries. Believe me. But things don't always happen at exactly the right time—and if you wait for it to *be* the right time, you could end up missing out altogether. Do you want to take that chance?"

"No." Mal took a deep breath. "It's fucking terrifying, though, you know?"

"Believe me, I know."

"How's it been for you?" Mal blurted it out. "I mean, yeah, you had this high-flying legal career, didn't you—"

"Not *that* high-flying."

"But still, you had to, well, change your ideas about what you were gonna do with your life. When you got ill."

Kyle stared out to sea for a moment. "I'm not going to tell you it's easy," he said at last. "There's always the worry . . . People who don't understand what you're dealing with can be . . ." He sighed. "Don't let anyone tell you you're not trying hard enough. They don't know what they're talking about."

"What if it's me thinking it?"

"Well, that's harder to deal with. But you just have to be honest with yourself. About what you really want, and what you can actually do. About whether your career is really worth the sacrifices you'll have to make for it." Kyle shrugged. "I don't know if that helps at all."

Mal nodded. "Yeah. Yeah, it helps. Cheers, mate." He clapped Kyle on the shoulder and jumped up. "Wanna skim stones?"

CHAPTER TWENTY-EIGHT

It wasn't until late that night that Mal finally got some time to himself. Dev and Kyle had gone back to the cottage, Tasha was serving the stragglers in the bar, the ones who acted like they had no homes to go to, and he'd escaped to his room.

All he could think about was Jory. Well, no, that wasn't quite true. He thought a lot about Dev and Kyle, and how fucking happy they were together too. And he thought about his job.

Driving on the Tubes had been all he'd wanted to do ever since he could remember. To a preschool kid, it'd seemed the coolest job in the *world*—didn't every little kid want to drive a train? And how many actually had a dad who did that job, and who'd tell them spooky stories about the tunnels?

His dad had been so proud when Mal had started work as a driver. For the first time in his life, Mal had felt like his dad saw him as a man. The right sort of man, one he might have been mates with if they weren't family. And Mal had really wanted that. Dad had been so awesome about him being bi, for a start. Like it didn't matter to him who Mal went out with. And yeah, obviously his mum had been the *best*, but that was different, wasn't it? Mal had always felt like he had to work a bit harder to make his dad proud, and the whole *liking boys* thing, it could have gone either way, couldn't it? Dads liked to think their sons were proper manly, and for a lot of dads, being proper manly meant shagging women and no one else. He'd known lads who'd got kicked out of the house for liking cock, even in this day and age. So yeah, *his* dad was awesome, and he deserved a son he could be proud of.

It was doing his head in, so Mal decided to go back to thinking about Jory instead. He'd had the right idea, saying they didn't have to sort everything out at once. They could take it slow and easy.

The thought of him and Jory taking it slow and easy made Mal smile. And start getting a stiffy. He rubbed his dick through his jeans and wondered if Jory would be up for sexting.

Or a plain, U-rated phone call, even. Sod it. Mal just wanted to hear his voice. Anything else would be gravy.

He grabbed his phone.

Jory answered almost immediately. "Hi. Everything all right?"

"Yeah. Great. Dev and Kyle have gone back to the cottage to get an early night." So they were probably shagging away like bunnies right now. If Kyle's narcolepsy hadn't cockblocked them again, poor sods. "I'm in the Sea Bell. In my room." He paused. "Lying on my bed."

"Oh. *Oh.* Is this where I ask you what you're wearing?"

"Well, it sorta depends on if you're alone right now."

"Completely. Bran's working, and Bea is . . . I have no idea what Bea's doing. But she isn't doing it where I am."

"So where are you, then?"

"In the kitchen, raiding the fridge."

"Find anything good?"

"There's parma ham. I'm trying to find something to wrap it round."

Mal laughed. "And there was me thinking we'd got off track with the phone sex."

There was a pause.

"Jory?"

"Don't take this the wrong way, but I really don't want to have phone sex with you." He paused just long enough for Mal's blood pressure to go through the bloody stratosphere, then went on, "I'd rather save that sort of thing for when we're together. At least for now. Does that make sense?"

Mal's heart clenched painfully. "Yeah," he said, and had to clear his throat. "Not like we got any good memories of actual sex, is it? What with me being such a fucking dick about it that time at the beach."

"Mal . . . I wasn't getting at you."

"I know. But you shoulda. I treated you like shit." Mal scrubbed his eyes. "Wish you were here right now."

"I could be. If you want me to."

Mal blinked. Of *course* he could be. He opened his mouth to say *Yeah, fuck, come on down*, but Jory beat him to it.

"I don't mean . . . We don't have to do anything. All I want is to be with you."

"Well, yeah, see, that's a problem, innit?" Mal said hoarsely. "Cos, you know, I just sorta melted into the duvet. Sorry."

Jory's laugh sounded a bit manic, but that was cool. It was more than cool.

"Come down here," Mal told him. "I'll make sure the back door's unlocked."

It was only half an hour from Roscarrock House to the Sea Bell if you walked it. Slowly. It should've taken Jory fuck all time in the car and probably did, but it felt like several hundred years before Mal heard a quiet, cautious tap at his bedroom door.

"Come in," he said, ninety-nine percent sure it was Jory, because Tasha? Didn't knock. She yelled.

The door opened and Jory stepped through. Mal smiled helplessly as he got up from his sprawl on the bed. "You made it, then?"

"Yes." Jory was smiling too, and he looked fucking lovely. So Mal went up to him, slung his arms around Jory's neck, and kissed him.

God, he tasted good. Although a bit on the minty side. "Did you clean your teeth? You never said you were going to do that. Now I'm worried my breath stinks." Shit. Had he cleaned them since those lunchtime pickled onions? Yes. Yes, he had. Thank God.

"Your breath's fine," Jory said, squeezing him tight. "Better than fine." He kissed Mal again which, fair enough, was a good way of showing he wasn't just saying that.

Well, either that or he was just as gone on Mal as Mal was on him.

"Missed you," Mal said, cos it was important.

"Me too. Um. I'm not actually sure what we do now."

"Uh, the kissing's good. Better than good." Mal thought about it. "We could try it sitting on the bed."

They sat down, arms still round each other, and kissed some more until somehow Mal found himself flat on his back with Jory on top of him. Which, yeah, was turning into one of his favourite positions to be in, so he was confused when Jory pulled back, screwed up his face, and said, "Sorry."

"What for?"

"I said we wouldn't—"

"Nuh-uh." Mal was sure of his ground on this one. "You said we didn't have to. Not that we weren't gonna." He thrust his hips up against Jory to make sure Jory knew which page he was on, and it was the one with the rude bits.

From the hard ridge that met his dick, yeah, Jory was on that page too.

Jory laughed softly. "I just . . . I don't want to rush you. I know you've had your doubts about us."

"I'm an idiot. You don't wanna listen to me."

"You're not an idiot."

"Yeah, I am. I hurt you, didn't I?"

Jory cupped Mal's face in his hand. "It wasn't your fault. I'd say I forgive you, but there's nothing to forgive."

And . . . that was the biggest load of bollocks Mal had ever heard, but fuck it, if karma was having an off day and dumping a lot of undeserved happiness in his lap, he wasn't gonna complain. He reached up to grab Jory and pull him down for another kiss, and another, and somehow it ended up with them both shirtless and groping at each other, and it was fucking amazing, and—

And that was the point Tasha stuck her head round the door and said, "Oi, babe, I know you're wanking this time, so just keep the noise down, will ya?"

Jory froze. Mal craned his neck round to check her eyes were closed and said, "Uh, sorry, Tash, got a bit carried away." Which, as soon as the words had left his mouth, he realised didn't sound anything like what he'd have said if she *had* caught him jerking off.

Tasha frowned and opened one eye a crack. Then she opened them both fully. And sighed. "Riiight. Hi, Jory, good to see you. Imma go shove cotton wool in my ears. And bleach my brain. Night."

She left.

They both cracked up, although Jory's face went redder than anything Mal had ever seen. "Hey," Mal said when he'd stopped laughing. "Now's my chance to check how far down that blush goes." He made a show of checking out Jory's chest, not that it took a lot of acting ability cos Jory's chest was seriously awesome. "Hm, no blush here. Think I'd better check lower down—"

"Mal?" Jory interrupted him. "*Please* lock the door first?"

"Nah, Tasha ain't gonna be back."

"Maybe not, but the thought of Jago Andrewartha bursting in on us—"

Mal was off that bed and locking the door before you could say *Fuck, no!* "Right," he said, trying to switch from freaked out to seductive without passing Go. "It's just you and me, baby."

Jory gave him a look. "I'm seven years older than you. I'm not sure you should be calling me *baby*."

"What do you want me to call you, then?" Mal grinned. "Daddy?"

"God, no. That's what Gawen calls me."

"Nah, he calls you Dad."

"Close enough to be a total turn-off."

"Total?" Mal climbed back onto the bed. Well, to be accurate, he climbed onto Jory, which was way more satisfying. "Not from where I'm sitting."

Jory bucked his hard dick up against Mal's, which, yeah, was good, but naked would be even better. Mal popped open the button of his own jeans and undid the zip, letting his stiffy spring free.

"No underwear?" Jory sounded like he approved.

"Whipped 'em off after we got off the phone." Mal grinned as he squeezed Jory's dick through his jeans. "Now, this lot has *got* to go."

He undid Jory's trousers and pouted. "Aw, kecks, no."

Jory laughed. "Sorry I didn't think to go commando."

"Nah, don't worry, we'll soon sort that out. But just saying, anytime you wanna put on them tights of yours for a booty call . . ."

"Really? The climbing tights are what do it for you?"

"Have you *seen* your arse in them?" Simply thinking about it was making him harder. Mal pulled Jory's jeans down far enough to get his hands on that arse and squeeze. "Made me wanna bend you over and fuck you halfway to America."

Jory's eyes were darker than the smugglers' tunnel at midnight. In, like, a total eclipse. "Could do it now if you want."

"Fuck me, you don't have to offer twice." Lube, Christ, he needed lube. And a condom. Like, *this instant*. Mal gave Jory's gorgeous arse a final squeeze, then scrambled off him to get to his toiletries kit by the door.

When he turned back again, Jory was naked. And God, what a sight that was. Seven leagues of taut, lean muscle, all laid out like a banquet with Mal the only guest. "You are so fucking gorgeous," he breathed.

Jory had this odd, shy look on his face, but it lightened into a smile at Mal's words. "Come back here and show me you mean that," he said, letting his legs fall apart in welcome.

Mal was on that like shite on mice. At least, he wanted to be. Jeans needed to go now. He glanced at his hands, one holding a slightly squashed box of condoms, the other a tube of lube, thought, *Fuck this*, and said, "Oi, catch," as he chucked them over to Jory. Then he whipped his jeans off like a lunchtime strippagram with half a dozen calls to make, while Jory caught the stuff like a champ.

The next bit didn't go quite so smoothly. He trod badly on his duff ankle and ended up more or less falling on top of Jory. Then again, he was having trouble seeing a downside to that. Especially as they both cracked up laughing.

"Oh my God, we should *never* shoot a sex tape. It'll end up on one of them TV outtake shows."

"No, it won't," Jory said seriously, and took hold of Mal's face to kiss him. It was deeper and more intense than Mal had been expecting. More intimate. Jory pulled back after a mo. "If we shoot a sex tape, nobody gets to watch it but us."

And that . . . that took Mal's breath clean away, cos that was *so much* how he felt about Jory and had been trying to push down, to smother. "Nobody," he heard himself agree. "Just you and me."

"How do you want me?" Jory asked then, and Mal was torn cos he wanted Jory every way he could have him—but right now, there was only one thing he wanted.

"Like this. Wanna see you. That okay?"

Instead of an answer, Jory kissed him again, and it was good, so fucking good. Mal lay on top, feeling like he'd fallen on a live rail, electricity crackling at every point their skin touched. He all but whimpered when he forced himself to pull back.

"Gotta get you ready," he said, his voice rough.

Jory hitched up those long legs of his, exposing himself, and Christ, what a sight. Mal wanted to dive straight in. He grabbed the lube with trembling hands, squeezed out way too much, and set to work with his fingers, teasing and stretching. Jory was tight around him, easing off gradually, then clenching again like he couldn't help himself. "Relax, babe, I got you," Mal murmured.

"I know," Jory said, and Mal had to stop what he was doing and kiss him for that.

His hands were too slippery to get the condom out of the packet, so Jory got it for him and rolled it on, his touch so gentle it was bloody frustrating.

At last, at *last*, they were both ready. With Jory's leg over Mal's shoulder, Mal lined up his rock-hard dick and pushed in slow.

Sliding inside Jory was like nothing Mal had ever felt before. The electricity was back, crackling and fizzing in his veins and all over his skin. "Oh fuck, that's good," he gasped.

"Yes, God, yes." Jory's face was screwed up and so beautiful Mal could cry.

"Not hurting you, babe?"

"No, no, don't stop . . . Ah!" His eyes flew open as Mal slid deeper.

"Was that a bad 'Ah' or did I find the Holy Grail?" Mal asked, worried.

"Grail. Definitely Grail." Their eyes met, and suddenly they were laughing.

"Oi, Galahad, is that King David's sword in your scabbard or are you just pleased to see me?" Mal grinned.

"Galahad was chaste," Jory said with a glint in his eye. "I'm not."

He grabbed hold of Mal's hips and pulled, and fuck, that was it, Mal was off again, sheathing himself in Jory over and over. Jory's dick was leaking on his stomach. Mal dragged his fingers through the little puddle of clear liquid and put them to his lips, wanting more of that deep-sea flavour. Then he bent awkwardly to kiss Jory, passing it over with his tongue.

Jory moaned and licked Mal's lips, and that, that was not fair because then Mal had to break the kiss and just pound into him as hard and fast as he could, Jory giving him wordless cries of encouragement all the time.

He was so bloody gorgeous. Mal couldn't believe he'd nearly let this pass him by.

"You're mine, you got that?" he gasped, teetering on the edge.

"Yours," Jory panted, and came.

White light exploded behind Mal's eyes as his own orgasm slammed through him. He felt it in his balls, in his spine, in his fucking *throat*. Jory was still painting his stomach white with his spunk, and Mal could feel every pulse resonate with the clenching of his body.

It seemed to go on forever, and even when he stopped moving, little aftershocks thrilled through him, his nerves jingling. Mal was blinking back his vision when Jory grabbed him and pulled him down for a lingering kiss.

Mal drew away long enough to ask, "You're gonna stay, right?"

"Always," Jory whispered, and kissed him again.

CHAPTER
TWENTY-NINE

Waking up with Jory in his bed was, like . . . Shit, Mal was useless at words this early in the morning, but it was good. Really, really good. He lay there, just watching Jory breathe. Was that romantic or creepy? Romantic, definitely. It was only creepy if you weren't already shagging.

He couldn't resist leaning in to plant a kiss on Jory's shoulder. Jory snuffled into the pillow but didn't wake up. It was cute as fuck, so Mal did it again, and then again for good measure, by which time Jory was starting to stir. And, well, his mum was always telling him, *Waste not, want not*, so Mal rubbed his morning stiffy against Jory's hip. Although that probably wasn't the sort of thing she'd had in mind.

"Morning," Jory said, blinking and smiling.

"Morning." Mal ground against Jory's hip, and Jory took the hint and rolled with it. Or, more precisely, he rolled with Mal, a nifty move that ended up with Jory on top and their dicks giving each other their own morning greetings.

Mal's dick thought it was fucking tremendous waking up with Jory's dick. It didn't take long before they'd made a right mess of each other.

Cos he was a gentleman, Mal felt around under the bed for the tissues and wiped them both off so they could snuggle back down together. Once he had his head on Jory's shoulder, he could feel Jory breathing, which was even better than watching him.

"I suppose we'd better get up," Jory said after a while, with a kiss to Mal's head.

"Don't wanna."

"Realistically, how long do you think we've got before Tasha bangs on the door and yells something embarrassing at us?"

"Fair point. But don't move yet." Mal reached over to the bedside table and grabbed his phone. Lucky for him, Jory was still all shagged out and dopey, so he didn't realise what was happening until Mal had snapped a picture.

Jory's eyes widened, and he did flaily hands. "Okay, no. Seriously. I'm not feeling at all photogenic right now."

"Nah, you look fucking gorgeous. Bed hair and all." Mal showed Jory the photo.

Jory made a face like he'd just seen a pic of the prime minister, naked. "Well, if you can say that with a straight face, then at least I know you're genuinely fond of me."

Mal flicked to the next, which had Jory with OMG-face.

"Oh God. Please delete them."

"Nah, I was thinking Instagram. Or Facebook. Which one are most of the people you used to work with on?"

"Give me that. Now." Jory made a grab for the phone, but Mal was quicker, holding it out of reach until Jory, the bastard, started tickling him.

"You *fucker*," Mal gasped through his laughter, as Jory wrenched the phone out of his grip. "Nah, don't delete them. I'll keep 'em to myself, I swear."

Jory sent him a deeply suspicious look, but handed the phone back. "But just for that, I'm taking one of you." He grabbed his own phone, which had been snuggled up to Mal's all night.

"Sure thing, babe." Mal lay back with his hands behind his head and pouted for the camera.

Jory laughed. "Do you have any shame?"

"Nope. None at all. Well, maybe a bit. I draw the line at dick pics. At least, not until Mr. Frisky's feeling a bit more, well, frisky again."

"'Mr. Frisky'?"

"Shut it. I *could* have called it Excalibur, you know."

"Not if you ever wanted anyone to take you seriously in bed."

"Baby, any way you take me is fine by me." Mal grinned, stretched, and sat up. "Hey, you gonna stay for breakfast? You're welcome, but

I ain't gonna be hurt if you can't face Tasha smirking at you over your cornflakes."

Jory rubbed his beard. "I'm more worried about Jago Andrewartha's reaction if he finds out I spent the night here."

"Think he's gonna go all medieval on you for sullying my virtue? Nah, he'd be cool with it. And not just cos he knows I ain't no blushing damsel. He gave me a lift up to yours yesterday, didn't he?"

"Still, I'd rather not rub his face in it." Jory cupped Mal's face with his hand, which, yeah, if he was honest, made Mal feel pretty damsel-like, but fuck it, he liked it. "Will I see you later today?"

"Yeah. Course. Uh, you're not working, are you?"

Jory shook his head. "It's Monday. The museum's closed. Fortunately, as I'd be a couple of hours late already."

"Then you should come and meet Dev. At the cottage."

"Are you sure? Maybe I should meet him somewhere more . . . neutral."

Mal frowned. "The cottage *is* neutral."

"No, I mean . . . he might prefer somewhere he can walk away from."

"He ain't gonna walk away from you."

"He might. After all, what claim do I really have on him? I'm just the brother of the woman who rejected him."

"No, you ain't. Well, you are, but the main thing is, you're my bloke. So he ain't gonna walk away." He paused. Jory was smiling at him in a way that made his insides do weird somersaults. "What?"

"I'm not sure who's luckier, here—you, for having a friend like Dev, or me, for having met you."

Mal rolled his eyes, cos it was that or blub like a little girl. "Well, *duh*. It's me, innit? Cos I got you too."

CHAPTER THIRTY

Jory's euphoric haze lasted all the way from the Sea Bell, right up to when he got out of the car at Roscarrock House. That was when he got a text from Mal saying he'd spoken to Dev and arranged for them to go to the cottage at two.

Then the nerves set in.

The trouble was, Jory wasn't only preparing to meet his long-lost nephew who had no reason to feel kindly towards anyone from his birth family. He was also about to meet one of the most important people in Mal's life. And despite what Mal had said, Jory didn't want Dev just to tolerate him for his friend's sake.

It was probably partly hunger that was making him feel queasy, he told himself, so after a quick shower, he rustled up a hearty brunch of bacon and beans on toast.

Bran wandered into the kitchen as Jory sat down at the table to eat. "You were out last night."

"Yes." There didn't seem to be a lot else to say.

Bran paused. "With . . . the boyfriend."

"Mal. Yes." Jory wished Bran would get to the point and let him enjoy his bacon in peace.

"You don't have to move out," Bran said abruptly.

Jory put down his fork. He wasn't quite sure how to take that. As an olive branch? That was most likely how Bran meant it. "Thanks. But would you be happy for me to have my boyfriend over for the night?"

Bran's jaw tightened. He didn't say anything.

"Then I do have to move out," Jory said gently. Not that it was the only reason, but it was the easiest one to make Bran understand without it coming to a shouting match. Then, because he genuinely wanted to know, "Is it because he's male? Or because I'm technically still married to Kirsty? Both?"

Bran looked away. "I'll draw up a list of properties that will be convenient for the school," he said, and walked briskly out of the room.

Christ, he was so bloody frustrating sometimes. Jory jabbed angrily at his bacon, then took a deep breath.

If Bran needed to feel like he was doing something for him, well, maybe Jory should learn to live with it. He didn't have to take any of the places his brother found. And . . . it was nice that Bran was trying to help, in his own way.

Two o'clock seemed to take an age to arrive—until all at once Jory was panicking he'd be late. He hurried out of the house, only now questioning whether he should be taking a gift of some kind. Why the hell hadn't he done some baking?

He'd arranged to meet Mal outside the Zelley cottage, and when he half jogged down the cliff path, he saw a familiar lean figure already there. Mal was standing outside the little cottage garden, his phone in his hands. He lifted his head as Jory approached, and smiled. "Hey, I was just texting you."

"Sorry I'm late."

"Nah, you're good. I was early." Mal shoved his phone in his back pocket. "Didn't wanna go in without you, though. So it's lucky Kyle and Dev ain't looked out the window."

They walked up to the house, which bore a slate plaque proclaiming it to be *Mother Ivey's Boudoir*, and around to the front door. Jory had always thought it a rather saucy name for what was presumably merely a typical, well-kept Cornish cottage. Then again, he'd never been inside it before. Maybe it was all tarted up in red velvet like a Victorian brothel?

"You nervous?" Mal asked.

Jory gave him a twisted smile. "What do you think?"

"Yeah, me too."

Oh. He hadn't thought of that, but of course Mal would be nervous. Dev was his best friend. If this went badly . . . Jory made up his mind firmly that it *wouldn't* go badly, and tried to be unobtrusive about wiping his palms on his jeans.

Had the jeans been a step too far? Would Dev take them as they were intended, an attempt to be informal and relaxed, or would he think Jory was taking the piss?

Oh God.

The door opened. The slightly ethnic-looking young man Jory remembered from Mal's photos stood there, his eyes narrowed—until they saw Mal. "Mal! My man." They clasped hands and hugged, clearly at ease with showing physical affection for one another.

"Dev? This is Jory. My bloke. Well, and your uncle."

"Yeah, kinda gathered that. Good to meet you."

Dev held out his hand, and Jory shook it cautiously, both relieved and disappointed when he wasn't pulled into a hug.

"It's good to meet you too, Dev. Finally."

Dev nodded. "Yeah. But, oi, you don't wanna stand on the doorstep all day. Come on in and say hi to Kyle."

They followed him through the disappointingly un-brothel-like cottage to where a tall, dark-haired man stood looking out of the window at a breathtaking view of the sea. When he turned, Jory recognised him immediately, and blurted out, "*You're* the one I met last summer. Bran got it wrong." One more thing to add to the list.

Kyle's expression, if Jory was any judge, was that of someone reminding himself firmly Bran was Jory's brother and, therefore, any comments along the lines of *Quelle surprise* might not be appreciated. "Yes," he said in the end. "We didn't really speak. Jory? Good to meet you properly."

"And you. Um. I'm sorry—I don't suppose I was very welcoming."

"Not to worry. No doubt you'd already been warned about my drinking problem."

"Which don't exist, case you were wondering," Dev put in forcefully. "Kyle's got narcolepsy."

"I'm sorry to hear that," Jory said, because what else could you say? From what he'd heard, it was pretty horrible. It was probably all kinds of wrong to be proud of his nephew for not letting Kyle's condition put him off. But Jory was finding it a struggle not to be.

"If it helps," Kyle was saying, "I took *you* for the sort who'd chuck me off the cliff if I caused any trouble."

Mal winced. "Uh, mate, you might wanna hold off on jokes about cliffs and stuff till you've heard about the family history."

"This something to do with all them pirates in the family tree?" Dev asked, looking interested.

"Bit more recent than that." Mal turned away, but not so far that Jory couldn't see him mouthing, *Shut up about it.*

"My father. Your grandfather. But it was a long time ago. Um. Best not to mention it to Bran or Bea . . ." Jory trailed off awkwardly.

"Yeah, well, shouldn't worry about that too much." Dev seemed grimly amused.

"She's not so bad," Jory found himself saying in a rush. "I mean, I know what she did to you was—"

"'S okay. She's your sister. Don't worry. I ain't gonna slag her off to you." Dev cocked his head. "What's she think about you meeting up with me? Or don't she know?"

"She knows." Jory hesitated. "I don't think it's going to change anything for her. I'm sorry."

"It's okay. I got used to it now."

Looking at the tense line of Dev's jaw, Jory wasn't sure how true that was.

"I'll put the kettle on," Kyle said. Dev seemed to take it as a timely reminder they'd leap-frogged all the social niceties and invited them to sit down, put their feet up, and call the dog a bastard.

Jory hadn't even *noticed* the dog, until she trotted out of the room at Kyle's heels. She was a chocolate Labrador and seemed a lot less excitable than most dogs of Jory's acquaintance. Was she a service dog? He didn't like to ask.

Dev cleared his throat. "So, uh, Mal said you work at the museum?"

"Oh. Yes. But it's only temporary—after the summer, I'll be teaching English at a local secondary school."

Mal leaned forward. "Yeah, Jory used to teach at university. But he packed it in cos he wanted to be near his kid."

It was nice of Mal to speak up for him, but . . . "I should have done it a long time ago," Jory admitted.

Dev's sharp gaze flickered over to Mal, then back again. Jory had the impression he'd been about to speak but decided against it.

"And you're a mechanic?" Jory asked, desperate to break the awkward silence.

"Yeah. Never was academic." Dev's gaze was challenging.

Jory almost laughed. "You mean, you prefer to do something that's actually useful. One thing I shan't miss about my former career is the intellectual snobbery." He hoped it came across as sincerely as he had meant it. He'd hate Dev to think Jory was patronising him.

It seemed to have gone okay, as Dev leaned back in his chair just as Kyle arrived back with their tea. "So go on," he said, taking a mug with a smile that betrayed his affection, "what have you two been up to around here? Got any tips for a couple of tourists?"

And somehow the conversation seemed to flow, after that. Mal had a gift for retelling their misadventures in a manner that made them seem far more comical than they had been at the time. Jory's attempts to keep him on the straight and narrow of factual accuracy were, apparently, even funnier.

Jory realised, after the dregs of their tea had long since gone cold, that he was enjoying himself here. There was so much obvious love in the room—between Kyle and Dev, and Dev and Mal, in particular. If the former relationship hadn't clearly been so strong, Jory might have been jealous of the latter, but as it was, Mal seemed to be going out of his way to make him feel secure.

Jory had thought he was just gaining a boyfriend. Apparently he was getting a whole lot more. And he genuinely liked Dev. There was a wary air about him, certainly, but once he relaxed, he was a good man to be around.

He couldn't help wishing Bea and Bran knew what they were missing out on. But then, perhaps they did and didn't care.

Jory wasn't sure he'd ever understand his family.

Dev's boyfriend was, in some ways, the easier of the two to get to know, although there was another unfortunate moment right at the start. Jory had been trying to bring him into the conversation. "Mal tells me you're an artist—you work in ceramics?"

Kyle had looked pleased. "Yes. You might even have seen some of my work on sale, if you've been to the pottery—although they're stretching the definition of 'local artist' to the breaking point there. But this place seems to inspire people. I saw some very good driftwood sculptures by a local woman last time I was here. Kirsty Fisher—have you heard of her?"

Jory was horribly aware of Mal stiffening by his side. "Ah. Yes."

"She's Jory's ex," Mal said, all in a rush.

Dev had raised his eyebrows—then whistled a few bars of a song Jory recognised but couldn't quite identify.

Mal clearly had no such problem, as he broke into a smile and called Dev a wanker.

"What did I miss?" Jory asked.

Kyle made a sympathetic face. "It's a song by The Saturdays. Called 'Issues.' Sorry to bring up an uncomfortable subject. Again."

"No, it's . . ." Jory gave Mal a rueful look. "It's a little awkward right now, but we're going to get over it. She's the mother of my son, Gawen."

"He's a great kid," Mal put in. He nudged Jory. "Show 'em a pic. I know you got like zillions on your phone."

Jory had dutifully got out his phone—and, of course, the first photo to come up was the one of Mal pouting in bed. Everyone laughed, Mal threatened to show his pictures of Jory, and after that, the conversation had flowed far more smoothly.

It was good. More than good.

Later, Jory and Mal walked down to the Sea Bell together, because Mal was determined to prove that Jory and Jago would get along fine over a pint. Jory still had his doubts about that, but since the meeting with Dev had gone so well, he was prepared to give it a go.

The skies were still cloudy, but there was a lighter feel to the air as they looked out to sea. "Think we've had the last of the rain?" Jory asked idly.

"God, I hope so. Had enough the other night to last me a lifetime. Hey, that thing with the seaweed, does that actually work?"

"Thing with the seaweed?"

"You know. You hang it up outside your window, and it tells you the weather."

"What, if it's wet it must be raining?"

Mal stuck up a finger. "Git. But it must've been well dodgy being a fisherman in the old days if that's all you had to rely on when you put out to sea."

"Oh, that reminds me: I found out something about Mary Roscarrock for you. Or rather, Bea did, and she told me. Although I'm not sure it's what you wanted to know. She didn't really concentrate on the piracy side. More the, er, family side."

"Yeah?" Mal's tone was cautious. Maybe Jory should have left Bea out of the story, but . . . she was still his sister. That wasn't going to change.

Jory recounted what Bea had told him of Lady Mary's tale. Leaving out Bea's reaction to her discovery because, well. It didn't exactly show her in a good light and he didn't think she'd thank him for sharing it.

Mal grinned. "Hey, so you're not the first queer in the family."

"I'd be amazed if I was." To be honest, there had been times he'd wondered about Bran. "But anyway, we could try and dig a bit deeper, building on what we know so far. See if there are court records that mention her, that sort of thing. Although if she changed her name, perhaps took a male name, it might be difficult."

"Yeah, if you want." Mal didn't sound all that bothered.

"I thought *you* wanted to."

"Nah, it's just . . . Okay, don't laugh, but it was just this idea I had, you know? I wanted to find a Roscarrock Dev could, like, relate to or be proud of. Whatever."

"And you chose a pirate? Is there something I should know about Dev? Latent criminal tendencies? A fetish for tricorn hats?"

"See, I knew you'd laugh. But you know what I mean. Someone who didn't just do what was expected of 'em. Took their own path and sod the head of the family. Uh. Not literally."

"I'd hope not. But yes, of course we can still do that."

"Nah, don't need to anymore, do we? He's met you."

Jory's heart flipped over at the warmth in Mal's eyes. "Me? I'm not exactly a role model of rebellion. I've spent my life doing what my family wanted."

"Yeah, and now you ain't doing it no more." Mal snaked an arm around Jory's waist and pulled him close. He leered. "Now you're just doing me."

"That was awful," Jory protested, laughing as he pushed Mal away in mock disgust.

"Nah, you love me really," Mal said—then he froze, uncertainty in his eyes. "Uh . . ."

Jory pulled Mal in tight again, emotion threatening to overwhelm him. "Yes," he said, his voice hoarse. "I do."

EPILOGUE

"**J**eez, it's cold round here." Mal shivered, the thick woolly fisherman's sweater Mrs. Quick had hand-knitted him out of an actual sheep doing sod all to stop the wind slicing through.

"I told you you'd need a jacket." Jory sounded smug, but he also wrapped his arms around Mal in a big, warm hug, so Mal decided to let him live. "It's almost December, you know."

"I was fine back home." Home was Jory's cottage on the outskirts of Porthkennack. Well, it was Jory's for now. After Christmas it was going to be *theirs*, properly and officially rather than just a case of Mal generally not getting around to leaving at the end of the day. He was going to move his rats in and everything. The thought made Mal feel all warm and fuzzy inside although, sadly, not outside.

Jory was going to be coming back with Mal to his mum and dad's for Christmas. Mal hoped there'd be room in his parents' flat, what with Morgan and her husband bringing the baby over for Christmas dinner. But he couldn't wait to see his nephew again.

Even if Morgs *had* insisted on calling him Calvin and not Mordred or Tristan like he'd suggested.

Tasha was going to be looking after the rats, seeing as she had her own reasons for staying in Porthkennack for Christmas. And Dev and Kyle were coming down again for New Year, so they'd all be together then.

"It's a lot more sheltered back home," Jory was saying. "Here, there's nothing but sea between us and Newfoundland."

"No wonder King Arthur and the knights were always going on all them quests. They had to do something to keep warm. Where's a fire-breathing dragon when you need one?"

"I think they all flew south for the winter. But don't worry, you'll warm up in a minute."

Jory was probably right. They were standing on the bridge that connected the not-quite-island of Tintagel to the mainland, taking a breather after climbing down about sixty zillion steep stone steps. There were another sixty zillion they'd have to climb up on the other side to get to the castle.

Mal smiled up at it. "Can't believe I finally made it here."

It'd taken a few months, mostly because Mal's git of a brain insisted on associating trips to Tintagel with panic attacks. But, yeah, apparently not all counselling was a waste of time, and Mal got on pretty well with the bloke he was seeing now. Although they seemed to spend a lot more time talking about his relationship with his dad than Mal would have expected.

He'd decided at the end of the summer that he wasn't going back to work as a driver on the underground. Well, he was going out with a teacher, so the shift work would have been a bit of a bugger anyway, even if him and Jory were both living in London. He could've taken longer to make the final decision—his old boss had been really good about it—but it'd seemed daft not to accept the museum job when it fell vacant.

Mal still couldn't believe they were letting someone like him look after a museum, but apparently Jory's recommendation was enough, either cos he was a Roscarrock or cos he was Jory. Or both. And Mal had plans for that place—Jory's mermaid exhibition at the end of August had gone down a treat, so Mal was going to follow it up with one on women pirates. Starring, of course, a certain Mary Roscarrock, seeing as how it'd struck him that Dev wasn't the only bloke in town who could do with a relative he could relate to. In the meantime, the downturn in visitors after the summer meant Mal had plenty of time to work on his Open University arts and humanities course.

Jory had suggested he sign up for the full degree course, but Mal hadn't had a lot of time to think about it, what with registrations closing, so he'd played safe and gone for just the first-year course in case he hated it.

He'd already decided he'd be doing the next two years too. Well, he needed something to do while Jory was marking homework or hanging out with his old mate Patrick, didn't he? Or visiting Gawen at his mum's cos, yeah, that level of awkward wasn't going away overnight. Then again, they mostly saw Gawen on his own these days, so that was cool.

"I always knew you'd make it here eventually," Jory said in his ear. "Even if we had to hike all the way from Porthkennack."

"Yeah, and looking at all them steps, aren't you glad we didn't have to do that?"

Jory grinned. "Race you to the top!"

He set off at a run, the bastard, so Mal followed, behind at first but gradually catching up cos months of walking everywhere was fucking awesome for improving your general fitness. Halfway up the steps, he had to tear off his sweater, now way too hot and itching like a bitch.

Old grannies in pack-a-macs and families in bright waterproofs scattered out of their path. They were probably glad of an excuse to stop climbing for a mo and watch the madmen go by.

With a final burst of speed he'd be paying for tomorrow, Mal surged ahead of Jory. When he reached the top, he turned and punched the air. "Oh, yes! The winner!" He swung his sweater around his head in a victory wave.

There was the sound of clapping, a few cheers, and even a wolf-whistle from the slow-coaches on the steps.

Mal gazed down at Jory, who smiled up at him from a few steps down, chest heaving.

He'd won a lot more than a race.

Explore more of the *Porthkennack* universe:
riptidepublishing.com/titles/universe/porthkennack

a PORTHKENNACK CONTEMPORARY

Wake Up Call
JL Merrow

Foxglove Copse
Alex Beecroft

Broke Deep
Charlie Cochrane

Junkyard Heart
Garrett Leigh

House of Cards
Garrett Leigh

Tribute Act
Joanna Chambers

a PORTHKENNACK HISTORICAL

A Gathering Storm
Joanna Chambers

Count the Shells
Charlie Cochrane

Dear Reader,

Thank you for reading JL Merrow's *One Under*!

We know your time is precious and you have many, many entertainment options, so it means a lot that you've chosen to spend your time reading. We really hope you enjoyed it.

We'd be honored if you'd consider posting a review—good or bad—on sites like **Amazon, Barnes & Noble, Kobo, Goodreads, Twitter, Facebook, Tumblr,** and your blog or website. We'd also be honored if you told your friends and family about this book. Word of mouth is a book's lifeblood!

For more information on upcoming releases, author interviews, blog tours, contests, giveaways, and more, please sign up for our weekly, spam-free newsletter and visit us around the web:

> **Newsletter:** tinyurl.com/RiptideSignup
> **Twitter:** twitter.com/RiptideBooks
> **Facebook:** facebook.com/RiptidePublishing
> **Goodreads:** tinyurl.com/RiptideOnGoodreads
> **Tumblr:** riptidepublishing.tumblr.com

Thank you so much for Reading the Rainbow!

RiptidePublishing.com

RIPTIDE
PUBLISHING

ALSO BY
JL MERROW

ABOUT THE AUTHOR

JL Merrow is that rare beast, an English person who refuses to drink tea. She read Natural Sciences at Cambridge, where she learned many things, chief amongst which was that she never wanted to see the inside of a lab ever again. Her one regret is that she never mastered the ability of punting one-handed whilst holding a glass of champagne.

She writes across genres, with a preference for contemporary gay romance and mysteries, and is frequently accused of humour. Her novel *Slam!* won the 2013 Rainbow Award for Best LGBT Romantic Comedy, and her novella *Muscling Through* and novel *Relief Valve* were both EPIC Awards finalists.

JL Merrow is a member of the Romantic Novelists' Association, International Thriller Writers, Verulam Writers and the UK GLBTQ Fiction Meet organising team.

Find JL Merrow on Twitter as @jlmerrow, and on Facebook at facebook.com/jl.merrow

For a full list of books available, see: jlmerrow.com or JL Merrow's Amazon author page: viewauthor.at/JLMerrow.

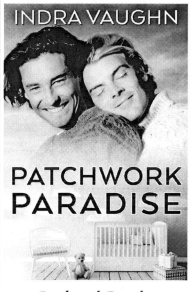
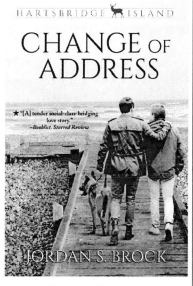